D1825518

Qoheleth

and Gallery Exhibition

Qoheleth

and Gallery Exhibition

Post-Self book I

Madison Scott-Clary

Also by Madison Scott-Clary

Arcana — A Tarot Anthology, ed.

Rum and Coke — Three Short Stories from a Furry Convention

Eigengrau — Poems 2015-2020

ally

Post-Self
I. *Qoheleth*
II. *Toledot*
III. *Nevi'im*

Sawtooth
Restless Town
A Wildness of the Heart

Learn more at *makyo.ink/publications*

ISBN: 978-1-948743-18-1

Qoheleth

Cover © Iris Jay, 2020 — irisjay.net

Illustrations © johnny d., 2022 (dumpstercryptid.carrd.co/) and Julian Norwood, 2022 (brushandtea.com)

First Edition, 2020. All rights reserved.

This book uses the fonts Gentium Book Basic, Gotu and Linux Biolinum O and was typeset with X⅃ATEX.

Qoheleth

Whatever is has already been, and what will be has been before; and God will call the past to account.

— Ecclesiastes 3:15

RJ Brewster — 2112

The theater purred. It hummed to itself. It stretched and reclined. It relaxed. Unwound.

RJ and the room let out a slow, long-held breath together, feeling muscles and wires relax, nerves and current disentangle themselves, slowly, slowly.

"Alright, everyone. It's midnight, time to start packing up," Johansson was saying from down in the front row. "Ross, we're short one. Can you start pulling together all of the mics? RJ will help you get them sorted."

"Mm," RJ offered through the sound system. Ey was busy putting the theater to bed, and couldn't spare more than a meager few syllables to the rest of the cast and crew. "Get a headset, Ross, so I don't have to talk through the speakers."

Those speakers were signing off, going to bed one by one through RJ's gentle ministrations. The physical back-up board set about the task of returning to neutral as RJ worked, all of the gain knobs orienting themselves, then all of the monitor knobs, the sliders, the whole system ticking through automated checklists as it cooled down. All minus the channel ey'd need to keep open to Ross.

"Hey boss, got a headset. Where do you want me to start?"

"Grab the leads, first," RJ murmured. "Then Sarah and Catherine, they've got the nice mics. All of them should have a tiny number painted on the costume side that matches up with their box. The boxes are stacked in the pit, by the front wall, you should be able to get them out in one load, though be careful taking them back."

"Got it, heading down to the pit now."

RJ left the channel open just in case. The soft sounds of breathing and the occasional curse as Ross bumped his head on the pit cover were distracting while ey set about going through eir notes with the dozy theater. Best be available, though. The next night's rehearsal was the last before they went live.

Ey knew the show better than most of the cast. Em and the theater. The two had to learn everyone's lines, plus a few cues besides when they'd have to take care not to pick up any of the sound effects. Gunshots. Chairs scraping. A scuffle. The clap of heels on the matte black of the stage itself.

The theater's job was to simply work with RJ and the lighting crew, responding to their knowledge of what was going on in the play, while RJ and Caitlin's job, as sound and lights respectively, was to respond to the stage manager's encyclopedic knowledge of the play, her view of the house.

All sound was under RJ's jurisdiction. Cast and crew both: ey spent as much time managing communication between the hands, the manager, and emself and Caitlin as ey did maintaining the sound from the performers. Private jokes kept on the down-low.

They had to be ghosts in this. Even the theater.

Their jobs were ones that should be invisible to the audience, because it would only become visible if they fucked up. No one wanted to fuck up. Even the theater seemed to feel a sense of pride in doing its job and doing it well.

RJ soothed the room with gentle cooing and reluctantly started the process of pulling back. Ey closed the channel with Ross and put all of the headsets to bed last of all, before ey slipped back from the interface. Felt for that cool breeze of reality on the back of eir neck — or whatever passed for a neck so immersed — and backed out. Blinked as ey adjusted to seeing the cavernous hall with eir own eyes. Lifted eir fingers slipped from the contact points and leaned back from the headrest.

Ey shook eir head to clear it and stood, stretching, before ambling from the tech booth down the stairs towards the stage. Letting gravity carry eir lanky form down two steps at a time. Breeze against eir face. The treble note of dust and conditioned air only added to the newborn feeling of pulling back.

Ross was in the front row, standing still and staring at the floor, muttering agitated questions into the headset.

"Hey Ross, I'm here. The house is sleeping now."

Ross jumped, then looked embarrassed as he tugged the headset off his head. "Sorry, was wondering where you'd gone. I just heard a beep."

"Yep, signing off from above. Did you get all the mics gathered up?"

"Oh! Yeah, that's what I was trying to tell you. I wasn't sure what to do next."

It only took a few minutes for RJ and Ross to get the last of the sound gear settled. Headsets from all of the hands socketed into numbered chargers on the wall. Everything would sleep tight until the next night on sound's end.

Caitlin and Sarai, the stage manager, joined them with the rest of the crew. They sat on the edge of the pit cover, unwinding from the tenseness of rehearsal. The actors were slow got out of their half-costume and clump together on the stage.

"Gather 'round, children", a voice boomed from out in the darkened audience.

"Yes, Mister Johansson," one of the actors singsonged back. Tired laughter.

"Good job, I think we're there. Still, a bit more polish never hurts. No flubbed lines, and mostly relaxed, but Sarah, you gotta loosen up. It's not Shakespeare, you can chill out. Crew, you guys got a little sluggish toward the end. I know it's late, but so are our shows. Don't work yourselves too hard, but keep on top of things, okay?"

RJ, Sarai, and Caitlin nodded their assent.

"Tomorrow night, back here at four."

"Early," RJ murmured. "How come?"

Johansson grinned. "There's a school production that winds up around then and I want you all back here to make sure we still have a theater."

There was a bit more grumbling, but RJ knew they'd be there on time. It wasn't too much of a stretch. Those with second jobs would make it.

"Back to base, then. Get some rest tonight, and I'll catch you all tomorrow. Remember, you can drink tonight, but tomorrow night, *Das ist streng verboten.*"

The troupe laughed and started to disperse, the tech leads lingering on the pit cover for a little while longer as they reoriented themselves to the real world. A world bound by spatial constraints, limited by two eyes, two ears, two hands.

Eventually, RJ made eir way out onto the chill of the street, pulling on eir thin waterproof gloves to keep the contacts on the middle joints of eir fingers clean and dry.

Midnight on a weekday, and not much going on. People visiting the pubs to catch up with their friends after work. Black cabs, night buses.

The idea of a warm pub and one quick pint before heading home tugged at em, but the pull of home was much stronger than that of beer. There would be a pub of a different sort waiting for em.

Ey trudged instead up to Oxford Circus. Central line up to Benthal Green, walk the few blocks from there to eir flat. Stopped to pick up a take-away carton of curry and rice from one of the more trustworthy shops along the way.

Once home, ey slipped out of eir jacket and welcomed the warmth of eir little flat after the damp chill of London outside. Eir cat trotted up to em, twining around eir ankles. A little ginger thing of a few years that ey had rescued from a friend who was moving deeper into the city. She was the only one to share eir space with em after eir last flatmate had left for somewhere cheaper.

"Hey Prisca, let me put my shit down before I get you food."

A meow, indignant, followed em to the kitchen.

Ey set eir take-away on the counter and scooped a cup of dry food into a fresh dish, setting it on the tile for the delicate cat. Indignant meows replaced by purring and crunching.

Ey thumbed eir phone to start music playing. Some of the stuff that reminded em of eir dad to go along with the curry that reminded em of eir mom. Quiet, but present.

Dinner was no more or less exciting than usual. RJ ate alone at the kitchen table with the carton spread out before em, baring orange curry and the soggy samosa that had come with it. Ey left eir gloves on just to be sure. No sense in having to clean eir contacts more than ey'd already need to after a long rehearsal.

Ey finished, scooped the last of the curry into a plastic container for the next day's lunch, promising emself that ey'd cook an additional pot of rice before heading out in the afternoon so ey'd have more calories to keep emself running. Clean up as easy as tossing the container into the compost bin along with all of the others. Cooking much more than rice was for times other than crunch.

The rig in the corner of eir bedroom was exerting subtle gravities on RJ. As ey ran through the motions of the post-recital evening — eating, cleaning, storing leftovers, using the toilet — eir orbits grew smaller and smaller. Eir gloves were itching. Ey could feel phantom breezes brushing past phantom fur.

Phantom fur. Phantom ears. Phantom tail. Phantom realities teased around the edges of eir perception.

Ey finally allowed emself to sit down at eir rig, relaxing into the familiar curves of the chair. Even with the draw so close to em, ey took eir time. Ey picked up Priscilla and stroked her smoothly from ears to tail a few times until she started purring up a storm, informing her that, in fact, she was the prettiest kitty.

Peel your gloves off one finger at a time, ey thought. *Relish the anticipation. Get caught up in it. Hell, let it linger.*

Cat settled into eir lap and curled into a small crescent, ey set about cleaning the contacts on eir hands with lint-free paper and rubbing alcohol. Those done, ey wiped down the headset, removing the negligible residue of sweat and skin oils that had collected there. Clean enough as is. Ey had recently replaced the soft, padded headrest where eir forehead would lay.

Eir gear at home was more elaborate than the stuff in the tech booth at work ey shared with Sarai and Caitlin, Ey had drained eir savings to acquire it. The rig, as well as the contacts on eir fingers, the interferites — nanoscale implants that took over eir optic and auditory nerves, and the electroparalytics to keep em from acting out in reality what took place online — the NFC connections implanted just under eir hairline and their ramifying tendrils, all of that painful work down eir spine that helped em more fully experience the connection.

All worth it.

Connections and gear cleaned, RJ finally felt complete enough to pop open the lid on eir rig. The screen, all but vestigial when ey was inside, still served its role during boot and login.

Ey quickly keyed in eir passphrase and then rested eir right hand on the curved pad, fingers finding familiar grooves that held eir hand in place. The connection from eir contacts the other half of eir two factors of authentication.

"Gonna head in, Prisca," ey murmured to eir cat, stroking over her ears, fingering the soft, velveteen folds until the cat shook her head away. Purrs nonetheless ratcheted up a notch. "I'll be back in a bit."

Ey set eir left hand into its cradle. Tilting eir head against the headrest, feeling the comforting touch of cool microfiber and the little twinge of recognition from the NFC controllers, ey nudged the button beneath eir thumb.

The rig went immersive. As RJ delved in, the soft hum of a cooling fan picked up to handle the waste heat of countless computations.

Ey could no longer hear it.

AwDae — 2112

RJ– no, AwDae, now, sat up in bed and slid to the edge of the mattress. Stretched languidly, let fur bristle from ear to tail, the latter bottle-brushing out. Ey shook emself to settle eir fur back down and yawned widely, slender pink tongue curling just shy of sharp incisors. All formalities, to be sure, or perhaps wordless mnemonics to finish the context-shift. The final step in a ritual.

All those phantom realities clicking into place.

Brushing eir fur down, the fennec stood and padded to the dresser in the corner of the room, pulling out a thin white cotton shirt with laces up the front and a simple navy sarong, which ey tied around eir waist. Countless hours examining some of the highest fashions out there on the 'net, and ey'd come to the conclusion that, in these times of excess, the understated said the most.

It also interfered with the fur least, worked well with a tail — a simple slit cut down the length of the sarong let that slip free — and it was cheap. There was no shortage of ways to spend money, and AwDae had better things to buy with what was left after London rent.

Better to perfect the form, to make it fit more precisely eir self-image. A handful of silver paltry exchange for building the you you are meant to be rather than the you you are.

Ey swiped eir paw from left to right atop the dresser, revealing a dimly glowing arsenal of personal belongings. It'd be a simple night out, so ey tucked a few vcards and a limited credit chip into a shoulder bag and hauled the strap over eir head, vulpine ears laying flat and out of the way.

From there, claws clacked against the glossy surface of the tport pad. Gauche as it was to pop in and out of existence where folks could see, ey kept eirs in a corner of the studio apartment rather than an alcove. The feeling of exposure and the jarring change of scenery was titillating, racy.

Ey stood straight on the pad and gestured a paw left to right, bringing up a list of recently used commands. Had ey left fingerprints online, there'd be a clear smudge over the entry: ey rarely did anything else on work nights.

tport: The Crown Pub

Tapped, and the obligatory *click* that went along with the change of scenery brought em to an alcove paneled in oak, lit by green-glass-shaded lights hanging pendulous from a cord directly above em.

Ey blinked to adjust to the comparatively dim light. The pub sim, largely following the circadian rhythm of the British isles, was just as dark as it was for RJ, back in London-as-it-was, but eir personal sim lived in a perpetual eleven AM springtime.

Ey turned and stepped away from the pad, narrowly avoiding a slender weasel stumbling towards the alcove.

"See ya, Debarre," AwDae said, though it came out more like '*Shee-a, Debaw*' coming from the fox's narrow muzzle. Ey got a curt grunt from the weasel done up all in black.

The fox shrugged and headed into the pub proper, nose twitching. The scents of the room told em more of those present than simply scanning the crowd. One or two gawking entities with no scent property set — tourists — and the usual crowd of aromas. Friends, mostly. Acquaintances all.

Whiskers bristled at the distinct whiff of dandelions, a memory leftover from youth, and ey made a beeline towards one of the window tables, where the scent originated, skirting around bodies of diverse shape.

"*Shacha.*"

"Come on, fox, loosen your filters, won't you?" Sasha laughed, scooting her chair back to stand up and lean in for a quick hug. Aw-Dae slipped eir arms around the skunk's waist in turn and gave a squeeze, tail aswish.

"Lame," ey drawled, but dialed back the output filters on eir speech, letting something more closely resembling English pass. "How you been, skunk?"

"Oh, you know, same old, same old." Sasha settled back into her chair and fiddled with a stack of vcards on the table, giving an outsized shrug. "Been kind of boring in here over the last few days, so it's good to see you."

The fox nodded, tugging eir shirt straight and moving over to the chair opposite the skunk, sliding into it easily and resting against the back.

"It's late there, isn't it?"

"Not too late. One something. Made good time home at least. Rehearsal ran late."

Sasha grinned. "You know, every time you talk about rehearsal and such, I just think back to school. You hunched over the sound booth, you know? It's hard for me to picture you as having grown up and taken that up as a job."

AwDae adopted a look of mock-despair. "Isn't it? I went to uni just for it and everything. But hey, London ain't bad, I can't complain any. Besides, not like you left it either."

The skunk rolled her eyes and leaned forward onto her elbows, muzzle resting on obsidian paws. "Tell me about it. You're missing out big time here in the 'burbs, dear. You could be teaching high school theater in any town along the central corridor, doing the same plays once every five years so no students repeat them. Truly a life of glamour." Sasha laughed when AwDae buried eir face in eir paws and groaned. "Seriously though, you just remind me a lot of school. Maybe it's 'cause of all of the ways you haven't grown up."

"Please, Sasha." AwDae poked eir tongue out. "If you bring up dating..."

"Hey, sorry, just looking out for you, fox."

"I'm plenty happy on my own, I can promise you that," ey countered.

"No, I get that." Sasha lowered her gaze. "Not all it's turned out to be. Just got me thinking, is all."

"Oh no, struck out again?"

She shrugged, nodded, shrugged once more, fiddled with a vcard. No eye contact.

AwDae reached out to take one of her paws in eir own, black fur on tan mismatched and complementary. Both had opted for mostly hand-like paws, but differences were evident on contact. Where Sasha's fur was an even, silky black marked by white stripes that were a little too sharp, a little too exact, AwDae had labored to construct a version of emself as a fennec fox to exacting detail, down to the point where eir muzzle couldn't even form the two letters that made up eir name offline.

Exacting, minus perhaps the two-legged-ness, the hands, the humanity around the eyes. Even then, ey had an av free of humanity stashed away somewhere.

Thoughts of honing versus forging blurred surroundings. AwDae had honed emself to a finer and finder point while everyone else forged ahead. Always a way to be a better tech. Always a chance to become more vulpine online. Always a way to become better at what one already was. To become more the AwDae AwDae felt ey was.

Still running sound. Still honing that skill.

Ey shook eir head to dislodge the rumination.

"I'm sorry, Sasha."

Sasha shrugged again, as though she might be able to drop the very idea of bad break-ups like an overloaded backpack. She gave the fox's paws a squeeze in her own. "Men are dicks. I'd take a fox like you over some dickhead guy any day."

AwDae smiled faintly, returned the squeeze. "Sasha, you know it wouldn't-"

"No, I know. I just wish there were more guys out there like you." When AwDae stiffened in eir seat and looked away towards the window, Sasha splayed her ears and added quickly, "Sorry dear. I keep putting my foot in it, don't I?"

"Sorry, no, you're fine." AwDae smiled apologetically. "I should get a thicker skin, maybe. Stand up for myself. I spend night after night hiding in here, and even then, can't seem to assert myself any. I appreciate you trying, though."

Sasha smiled cautiously and nodded. "You came out like fifteen years ago, AwDae. I should still be doing better."

AwDae's turn to shrug. "It's hard to ask for that, is all. Always has been."

"I think that's what I meant earlier, that you haven't changed, despite all the ways you have. You haven't done like all the rest and grown up, gotten married, all that crap. You're still doing what you loved to do in school. Don't get me wrong, I miss it too. *Actual* theater, not the school stuff. Seeing crazy shows with you on the weekends. Hell, doing crazy shows in uni. Doesn't pay the bills, though."

"You should come see us sometime. It'd be good to see you again, too."

"You know I want to." She grinned. It didn't last. "But yeah. You seem kind of frozen, kind of stuck — in a few ways, even, though you're succeeding in others."

AwDae nodded, rumination hanging in a cloud around em. So many ways the world had moved on without em. After a moment, though, ey sat up straighter. "Oh, speaking of frozen."

"Debarre?"

The fox nodded.

"No news, yet. He's been trying to get in touch with the clinic or whatever that's taking care of Cicero, but the family's been getting in the way. They're fielding everything. They always sort of supported the relationship on the surface, you know, but never actually approved of it. Of them being together, I mean."

"What? Really?" The fox shook eir head, poking a claw at the table, before rubbing the spot with a paw pad. The sim was hardly immersive enough to waste cycles on letting claw dent tabletop. "That's unfortunate. Not all that surprising, I guess, given what Cice said about them. They at least confirmed that's what happened, though?"

"That's what these are," Sasha said, slipping the stack of vcards over to em. "There's contact info for the family, and a few centers around there that work on implants, some hospitals. We're thinking that those might be the types of places where he wound up. There's also a card detailing his last connected times."

AwDae twisted the stack of cards around in front of em, leafing through slowly and taking in a few of the details that slid across eir fingertips. "Mind if I make a copy?"

"Go ahead. It's a deck Debarre and I have been working on. Not complete, but I'll give you ACLs."

"Mm. Debarre looked crushed. Is he doing alright?"

Sasha hesitated for a moment, caught in the middle of a gesture to grant copy rights on the cards. She shook her head, to which Aw-Dae could only frown. She finished the gesture, and another set of vcards shuffled itself out from the original stack. Crisp black embossed on the creamy cotton-paper that AwDae preferred.

"I'll take a look, too. I can't do too much right now, I've got a–"

"I know, you've got a show coming up," Sasha laughed. "Don't worry about it, dear. Debarre's working on it, I'm taking a look when I can, and I'm sure the weasel's got others helping him out besides us. No reason not to, either. We all liked Cicero."

The two sat in silence. AwDae slid Sasha's deck back and fanned eirs in front of emself before shuffling them back into a stack and swiping above them, instructing eir rig to make a local copy of the deck.

Ey lifted eir snout away from the silence to scan the scents in the room once more. Now that it was starting to get on in the evening even in the Americas, the scentscape was changing. Some familiar scents, some unfamiliar, but most of them at least detailed, which told AwDae that the owners had put some thought into them. None, however, really jumped out at em.

More rumination. Rumination edging into drowsiness.

"Hey, Sasha, I gotta get going. I know I just got here, but I'm starting to crash hard."

She nodded, ears drooping. "No, it's alright. It's late there, and I know you've been in rehearsals for a while. Go get some sleep."

Both stood up and exchanged another hug, AwDae reveling in that dandelion scent of eir friend. Memories of school, drowsy, dreamlike. Dandelions in the lawn. An impromptu picnic. Rubbing one of the flowers on the back of eir hand, leaving a yellow stain. Sasha explaining that the smell always reminded her of muffins.

"I'll see you later, skunk, yeah?"

"Take care of yourself, okay? No working too hard, slaving over a hot rig..."

AwDae laughed and shook eir head. Gave the skunk one last squeeze before making eir way back through the crowd toward the alcove, already swiping eir command palette into view to head home.

Ioan Bălan — 2305

Ioan Bălan awoke to an urgent message.

Ey didn't really like these, the sensorium messages. Much better to received paper messages. Letters. Notes. Missives. Scrawled signatures and careful handwriting.

Ey mostly just liked paper, if ey was honest. Always accruing more paper, more pens. Paper messages, rich messages attached to paper that played on its surface, ones that messed with the reader's sensorium; ey sent them all. Eir friends found it perhaps a little disturbing. Antiques from a world more physical than this.

But to have one that just barged in on eir vision and endocrine system like this made em anxious. This one included a tiny jolt of adrenaline as an alert. Waking up to a zap of panic to have a partial sensory takeover felt rude.

At least ey didn't have to get out of bed to deal with it.

The opacity on the message was turned up high so that even in eir dark room with eir eyes still closed (and heart still pounding), ey could see the fox. Bipedal, dressed sharply. It was sitting on a plain wooden chair situated in an empty room. The room had wood floors the same color as the chair. Something light: maple or pine. The walls were concrete where they weren't glass. Outside the glass was a sere shortgrass prairie, a cloudy day.

The combination of the fox's white fur, glistening and iridescent, combined with the room and landscape was all so painfully
postmodern. Ey didn't think emself much of a pomophobe, but this
was...intense, to say the least.

"*Hi Mx. Bălan,*" the fox was saying. It seemed to speak in italics,
though how, Ioan could not say. A sense. A sensation. "*I have a propo-
sition for you.*"

Ioan grunted. The message was simplex, thank goodness. One
way. No interaction required.

"*My name is Dear, Also, The Tree That Was Felled — or just Dear —
and I am a member of the Ode clade. I am an artist-*" The word seemed
to come with a tone of distaste. "*-and...performer. I am not just telling
you this to, ah, toot my own horn, I believe the phrase is, but to underline
the fact that I am woefully unprepared for the situation at hand.*"

The fox smiled, looking tired, and continued. "*I need some help
finding someone. Someone that does not want to be found. It is personally
important, but also potentially damaging to the image of our entire clade.*"

Ioan furrowed eir brow.

"*This person has information, a name, that they have supposedly
shared. We — the other members of my clade and myself — do not precisely know if they actually did, unfortunately, we just have word from
some perisystem notification that someone said the Name.*" Ioan could
hear the capital letter.

"*I am sorry, I am getting sidetracked by details.*" The fox shook its
head, ears flopping from side to side. "*I try to be prepared for conversations and messages like this, but I am a little worked up. Excited, I guess.
Can we meet?*" It listed an address. "*Even if only to talk. Even if you are
not interested, I would still like to meet you. You seem neat.*"

The message ended.

Ioan lay in bed, thinking. It was still an hour before ey had to get up, and ey was loath to start the day before ey had to. Ey tried eir best to sleep for another ten minutes, at least, but eir mind kept slipping back to Dear's request.

Why me? ey asked the backs of eir closed eyelids. *Why hire a writer who fancies emself a historian as...what, a private investigator?*

Ey spent a few minutes researching the public basics on Dear. Pronouns (it/its), species (fennec fox), age (old — the Ode clade was an early adopter), some of its art. Really out there stuff. No further hints as to why it would need em in particular. Something on the markets piqued its interest, perhaps?

With still a half hour before eir alarm, Ioan stretched out of bed. The least ey could do was get a shower and some coffee. If there were any reason that the founders of the system had included full sensoria in the works it must have been for those.

Those done and clothes donned — ey knew ey could never out-natty the fox, so the usual faux-academia garb it was — ey penned Dear a short note with a time. If it was day in that sim, or even late afternoon, it should get the note before dinner or bed.

Besides, ey thought. *Maybe it will get the fox to stop using sensorium messages.*

No luck. Less than thirty seconds later, Ioan received a sensorium ping of acknowledgment, a shiver up eir spine for eir trouble.

Ey forked and sent the copy of emself, #c1494bf, out to the meeting. Meanwhile, ey'd get some food, perhaps work on eir current project.

RJ Brewster — 2112

RJ slid eir hands from the cradles and leaned back from the head-rest, letting out a full-fledged yawn, pent up from the interferites preventing it. The sound and motion startled Priscilla from across the room. Ey levered emself up out of eir seat and trudged over toward the still-purring cat, stroking over her ears when she bunted her head up against eir hand.

Eir mind foundered in a slurry of work, of Cicero's disappearance, of school with Sasha, of honing and forging.

"I'm wiped, Prisca," ey informed the cat.

She purred louder.

Smiling, ey peeled eir shirt off over eir head and slipped out of eir jeans. Tomorrow's rehearsal would mean full dress for everyone and makeup for the actors. Ey'd have to make sure eir tux was clean. Should ey iron it? Maybe ey should iron it. Later.

For now, as it neared two, ey focused on making sure the door was locked and the lights were out before stumbling over to bed.

There seemed to be no shaking Sasha and all of her talk of high school — gone this last decade now — out of eir head. Even as ey climbed onto eir narrow mattress and burrowed beneath the covers against the chill of the night, ey was replaying memories from school. Scenes from the Americas. A worn out film, dim and scattershot.

Honing and forging, honing and forging.

Ey and Sasha had tried dating early on. After a few weeks of it not going anywhere, they had both admitted that they had felt pressured into having a relationship rather than actually wanting one. Good boys and girls fell in love with other good boys and girls, right? Went out to the movies. Kissed beneath the bleachers or something. Pretended they didn't have sex.

The relationship petered out, rather than ending in some climactic fashion. They had continued the trend of going to movies, and later to live performances. They had never lost touch, at least.

Sasha had gone on to have a string of other relationships, some earnest and some not, some more intense than others — a string that remained unbroken, if tonight's conversation was any clue — but RJ had stopped there.

The intensity of the social pressure to date throughout high school was equaled only by RJ's complete apathy toward the whole scene. Apathy or, often, antipathy. Ey'd felt the occasional twinge of romantic attraction, perhaps, but the expectation of sex that went along with the process so put em off that ey had instead buried emself in work.

Ey did well in some courses and not in others, as any kid might, but in the subjects ey enjoyed, ey dumped all of eir effort. Huge gusts of energy that drove em forward.

Ey had started early on in working the school's old sound board in the theater Ey ran plays. Ey ran concerts. Ey ran assemblies and lectures and conferences, quickly earning the trust of the other tech crew, as well as the staff.

And then ey gained leadership. Prestige.

The various computer classes had captivated em as well, and for eir sixteenth birthday, eir parents had surprised em with the implants needed for full interfacing with a rig. Or, well, "surprised": eir father was an engineer and eir mother a fairly forward-thinking person, and they had promised em the procedure before university.

Honing and forging, honing and forging.

It was a straightforward procedure in an outpatient office, self-guided implants largely installing themselves. The worst had been the itching. It was bearable on eir hands and along eir spine, where the implants and exocortex breached the surface of eir skin, because at least ey could scratch, though ey had been cautioned not to. The NFC tags in eir forehead and the interferites embedded deeper — far, far deeper — led to an itch that no scratching would ever reach.

From there, sound and the rig had taken up all of eir energy, leaving little time to worry about any social stigma that went along with aversion to romance. Ey was simply the nerdy sound kid who knew more about computers than the teachers.

It hadn't always been fun, of course, but by then ey quickly learned that the more ey put into the task, the more ey got out of it. The more ey honed, the further ey went.

That ey had found furry in high school seemed almost a natural progression. Working and improving at the art of interfacing in a way that felt natural to em, it seemed, came just as natural to others on the 'net. Ey moved effortlessly through the Crown Pub and a few other choice spaces, slowly crafting the primary persona that ey used when interacting with others.

A fennec. AwDae, a corruption of eir chosen name. A corruption borne of the intricacies of a thoroughly vulpine muzzle. A persona honed to a fine point.

It was then that ey and Sasha had really started connecting, for it was her that introduced em to the community. They started hanging out more, talking more, building a network of friends together. Where dating hadn't worked out, friendship grew in both depth and breadth.

Honing and forging, honing and forging.

The forging of the virtual theater environment had culminated in a scholarship at a big name university out on the east coast. Immersive interactive theater technology, they called it. Forging into honing.

It meant leaving Sasha and a few other close friends behind along with eir family, but it also meant that ey would be at the forefront of a new tech. Something used in production. Films and live work both.

The field had been so new that eir own studies at the university helped fuel the change in theater tech work. Eir dissertation, what was meant to be a simple capstone project, was published and distributed, and theaters around the world were suddenly using immersive tech.

Ey had continued to work at the university for a while. It was one of the few places around with both a theater and the hardware to back it up. Ey had considered continuing eir studies, but the draw of the theater was too heady, too alluring. Academia spelled a life of forging, work one of honing. Why deny one's base nature?

Honing and forging, honing and forging.

The call from London came less than a year after ey graduated. Would ey like to help start a tech-savvy theater group in town? The pay would be slow to start, but the troupe had a loose collection of apartments on the East End. Ey would have full run of the sound department. Yes? When could ey start?

Eir parents had needed convincing. They were pleased, to be sure, but London, so far away! Still in the Western Federation, but so far.

Ey made eir promises that ey'd come and visit every year, and packed eir bags.

Burying emself deeper into the covers and the mattress, leaving enough room for Priscilla to join em later, RJ's thoughts alighted finally on Cicero, on the lost.

Losing Cicero had been a shock. A disappearance, at first. Last seen two days ago. Three. And then it went on. Debarre hollering one night after getting in touch with Cice's family. Lost, lost, he was lost.

And getting lost was rare. Vanishingly so, with perhaps a hundred cases at the time. Still, among those who were counted among the lost, all were heavy interfacers. It was a risk, everyone had assumed, just as was travel. Call it occupational hazard. Something could always happen. Something could always go wrong.

To lose someone so close, though. That hit hard.

It was a sharp reminder of just how much ey relied on the integration tech, not only for work, but for the lion's share of eir social life. Ey enjoyed the company of the troupe just fine. Troupe pub trips were a weekly affair. But eir heart lay among eir friends on the 'net. Eir friends being on the 'net meant more interfacing, and more interfacing meant, it seemed, more risk.

Perhaps more for em than any of eir friends. Eir tech was truly immersive, after all. It was a dissolution of the body. Disembodied in the truest sense.

It was *becoming* the room. It was a new sensory experience. No limbs, no torso, no face or eyes or ears. Or maybe all ears: ey became the room, feeling the way sound echoed or didn't, knowing the limits of the speakers in a deeply physical way. Mics peppering the walls a new sensory input. The wires nerves. The speakers muscles to flex. Instincts, reactions, and actions responding to whole systems of stimuli.

Perhaps that was why ey felt so at risk. They all were, of course, but to dissolve one's concept of a body at work, and then come home to warp the very same concept into that of a fox — no, a finely wrought amalgam of fox and self — felt perilously close to being lost, sometimes.

Honing and forging, honing and forging. Risk and reward.

Ey slept.

Dr. Carter Ramirez — 2112

Carter rubbed her face into her hands, ground her palms against her eyes until she saw stars, slicked her hair back in a vain attempt to wrangle fly-away hair. It had been in such a neat bun this morning.

She wasn't the last one left in the lab, but it had reached that point of the night where collaboration had stopped and everyone was butting their head against their own individual problems, toiling in silence. She folded her rig's screen down, socketing her tablet in next to it to charge.

It had also clearly reached the point of the night where she wouldn't be getting anything else done.

She felt out of her league. Everyone did, or said they did, here on her team, but that didn't stop the fact from wearing on her. It's not that there wasn't any support from on high. There was. It's not that there wasn't anyone else trying. There definitely was.

It's that no one seemed to take the lost all that seriously. It was like addiction, or plane crashes, or suicide. Something to look at, to study long enough to say "Ah, *this* is happening now," and then set aside. Conversation-piece science.

People admitted that the phenomenon was there, but only inasmuch as it didn't affect that many people. A simple number to point to. See how small?

It was as though the minds of the lost were just...elsewhere. Just dreaming. Implants showing them connected while no such connection existed.

There was no sense to it, though. No rhyme or reason to why such a thing would happen to the patient. Some of her team were pulling together all of the facts about the population that they could, from demographics to physical stature, searching for clues in the rig and the 'net itself, sim histories to go with personal ones. The neuroscientists were digging into what was going on within the brain, and what few scans they had from before someone had gotten lost. Their two pet lawyers — just law students on internship, both also versed in stats — were digging into the legal status of the lost as well as writing queries to procure patient medical histories.

And Carter was supposed to tie it together.

Or, that was her stated goal. The university medical center had only grudgingly provided space and funding for the project. An attempt to win some much-needed kudos, she suspected. Still, she was beginning to doubt just how much the UCL wanted her to succeed.

There had been an initial dataset dumped on her team, and a slow trickle as new cases came in, but it all felt so carefully curated. As manager, she had been met with hurdle after hurdle as soon as she started to venture beyond that. Colleagues assured her that all projects worked this way, but it was as though the advisory board had given her all the data that it was willing to give, and any more might...what? Put those kudos at risk?

Carter stood, stretched her back, winced. "Sorry, Sanders. I'm shattered. Catch you in the morning?"

"Mm," he replied. The interruption seemed to remind him of his physicality. He rubbed at his eyes and stretched his arms out, alternating between clenching his long fingers into fists and flexing them out wide. "Sounds good, Ramirez. Catch you then."

Carter gathered up her coat and her messenger bag, taking one last look around the lab, counting heads to see who would be staying later than her. Not too many. Sanders, one or two of his neuroscientists. Prakash and the new guy.

She swiped her way out of the wing and signed out at the front desk before making her way out into the night, bundling up in her coat.

At home, she scavenged a few pieces of salami stacked onto a couple of crackers, enough to keep her empty stomach from complaining through the night, and crumpled onto the couch in the shared living room. She left the lights off so that she wouldn't bother her flatmates.

Or so she told herself. In truth, the darkness felt good. She could keep her eyes open and not be greeted with a tablet, a screen, a sim.

She sat long after finishing her snack, listening to her flatmates sleep, the sounds of the road outside, her own breathing. Sat, thinking in the dark of all the administrivia on tomorrow's docket.

Eventually, finding herself at as much of a dead end as she had at work, Carter ambled off to her room, changed from her work clothes into a comfortable pair of lounge pants and a night shirt, and crawled into bed.

RJ Brewster — 2112

RJ allowed emself to sleep in until near eleven that morning. Last night of dress rehearsal, might as well be well-rested.

Many other members of the troupe held part time jobs during the day, and ey ran a small consulting business of eir own. The more industries that dove into immersive tech, the more eir expertise was worth. Even so, with all that ey did, ey made enough to not have to worry about holding down more than the one full-time gig.

As it was, on days when ey had nighttime rehearsals, ey felt no compunctions about sleeping in. Nothing to be up for, only the 'net to keep them occupied in the mornings, little enough need to get moving.

It was Priscilla who eventually succeeded in waking em, butting her head against eir cheek and purring obscenely, stomping on em through the blanket with kneading paws. The more insistent the cat became, the less able ey was to ignore her intrusions on eir admittedly banal dreams.

Fine. Trudge out of bed. Refill cat's water and food. Give the requisite morning pets to keep her happy. Scoop the litter box. Make self a pot of tea. Tea to shake the grogginess.

Ey sat at the tiny kitchen table, sipping from eir oversized mug and watching the late morning traffic from their window. Mostly business traffic, with the occasional mother with child in tow. Black cabs. Scooters. Bikes.

By the time ey had finished eir first mug of tea, RJ had woken up enough to start on the prowl. As with the night before, ey made sure that everything was in order before touching eir rig. Ey'd taken care of the cat, but ey still needed to eat, emself. So, remembering eir promise, ey set about making a small pot of rice. Fifteen minutes to cook, plenty enough time to finish another mug of tea.

RJ left most of the rice cooling in the pot and took for emself a small bowl to go with the leftover curry. The process of swiping eir hand over the controls of the stove had reminded em of the deck that Sasha had shared last night. There was no reason to think that some random person in London would have much to offer in the case of another person ey had never met getting lost. No reason not to try, though. Maybe there was something, some small insight that ey had which, when pooled with those of others, might help in some way.

So many maybes. So many mights and perhapses.

Empty bowl in sink. Third and final cup of tea in the thick-walled mug. Good enough. Ey allowed emself to settle before eir rig at last.

As before, ey keyed in the password and rested eir hand onto the cradle for the two-factor. However, instead of delving in as ey had last night, ey unfolded the screen to full height and pulled the keyboard closer, swinging the hand rests to the side and the head-rest up and out of the way. No need to go immersive, with work like this. Ey could just as easily work as a fox, of course, but it was so easy to lose track of time in there, and the night's rehearsal mustn't be forgotten.

Besides, eir tea was here.

"Let's see," ey murmured, taking a sip of tea before setting the mug down

Ey called up Sasha's deck.

Cicero Lost Nov 2112
Priv eyes only
See Debarre for ACLs

Dr. Carter Ramirez
specialist in lost
so. London

Mr/Mrs. Jackson parents, can't get much more dad in govt, mother stays home

And on it went for nearly a dozen cards. Each had its own cover embossed with a few lines of type, each containing upwards of a terabyte of information culled from various sources, doubtless of varied quality.

RJ flipped through each, gleaning what ey could from a quick scan, before collapsing the deck once more and sitting back to think. Nothing in there seemed new. Nothing out of place. Ey had only received the deck last night, and yet nothing felt like it had been revealed, uncovered.

Ey knew of the lost, of course, and the name Ramirez was commonly tied with the few hundred or so cases that had cropped up over the last few months. The family...no, nothing to be gained there, at least not that had already been tried by Debarre. And again, there was the problem of being a random nobody in the UK: no one known, no one with power.

None of the rest of the cards carried any real significance to em.

If there was anything RJ was going to add to the conversation, it would be through eir connection to Cicero. Something ey knew, something the two had shared.

A small notification slid down from the top of eir monitor, covering the upper right corner of the screen.

D — D — R

Voting begins in 5 minutes on *referrendum 238ac9b8*:

Summary: *Tariffs on importation of goods from the Sino-Russian Bloc...*

Cost: 1,000

Comment: 150,000

Bounty: 280,000

RJ reached to swipe the notification away. Ey had very little stake in the uncomfortable alliance between Western Fed and S-R Bloc. Could care less, honestly, about taxes on things that ey'd never buy. Then something clicked within em, and ey halted eir motion.

Cicero.

Ey hastily shuffled back through the *Cicero Lost* deck until coming up with the 'recent net activity' card and pulled up the contents. It took a few moments to remember how to sort tabular data — database classes in high school so long ago — but eventually, ey got the table sorted around the activity type. Ey scrolled rapidly through the list until ey got to the list of Direct Democracy Representative entries.

There was the connection.

The one thing that RJ and Cicero had was their arguments over politics. Not just politics, but the worthiness of the current political system in all of its facets. Arguments upon arguments upon arguments, fennec fox and tabby cat with their ceaseless bickering in the Crown Pub.

RJ was firmly on the left, but ey felt the representative democracy combined with the DDR was a pretty good system. Not great, sure. It was *fine*. It *worked*. To ask for more from a political system was to invite further troubles like those from the preceding century.

Cicero, however, seemed to waver between socialism and anarchy, depending on factors such as how much he had had to drink and how angry he was at the most recent vote.

I certainly can't see broad shifts going my way, he had slurred on more than one occasion. *Least I can vote. Vote on every damn thing that comes my way.*

Ey made sure syncing was turned on across all copies of the deck before snipping those rows out of the activity table into a card of their own:

> DDR votes
> todo: process by record
> 1 month, 835 votes (!)

The icon in the upper left of the screen showing the deck twirled gracefully to show the sync.

Cicero had voted precisely how he had talked. On the surface, he was no different than any other far-left socialist on the DDR.

Along with the ability to vote on issues directly came the ability to comment — for a price. DDR votes didn't cost money, but they did cost credit, up to 1,000 per. Credit gained by voting on cheaper issues, for each vote provided a bounty paid upon consideration, beginning with a few freebies in the tutorial.

What Cicero's records showed was that he was wealthy. *Fantastically* wealthy. RJ had a few million DDR credits banked away in case a high value issue that ey felt strongly about cropped so that ey could make a comment. Unlike voting, commenting could cost upwards of five million credits. And one could buy their way to influence by flooding issues with comments.

Cicero's wealth surpassed RJ's at least a hundred times over, if not more. Well into the billions of credits. For someone to be as active in commenting as ey knew the cat to be and still have that much in credits stored up showed a dedication to following politics that was just barely hinted at by those tispy rants. Cicero was well connected, well read, and, most importantly, apparently a key political figure on the DDR comment sections to an extent that none of the Crown regulars had ever expected.

RJ sat back in silence for a few moments before muttering, "Well, shit. Prisca, you don't suppose..."

Rather than finishing the thought out loud, ey dashed off a summary in the notes attached to the card.

> AwDae here. Looks like there's a lot going on in DDR activity (where'd you get this, Debarre?). Cicero was into a lot, and I'm not trying to go all conspiracy nut on you all, but do you think that maybe he got in too deep or something? Not saying someone tried to do it too him or anything, just that maybe the more one uses the net, the more likely it is to happen to them? I mean seriously, look at all of his votes, and his stash of credits!

I'll keep poking at this after rehearsal.

The tea had gone cold long ago, but ey downed it all the same. Ey'd spent longer than planned plowing through the data the hard way and ey risked being late if ey didn't start hustling.

It was nearing dusk by the time ey left, the tux newly brushed and ironed, the gloves newly washed, the RJ newly shaven.

On the way back to the tube station, ey stopped by a Thai counter and picked up some take-away noodles for the night. Ey made it halfway through the container before the rancid belch of station wind suggested ey pack it away before heading down to the platform.

Throughout the ride to Soho, RJ's mind continued prowling through the data in Sasha and Debarre's deck. Ey kept mulling over that surreal number of credits. Just how much social currency was bound up within the reputation market of the DDR credit system?

Cicero had built himself up into a proper political player.

Dr. Carter Ramirez — 2112

The morning's alarm startled Carter awake.

Disorientation — when had she fallen asleep? There seemed to be no line delineating squirming under the covers and the buzz of her phone and faint tingle along her implants.

And here she had thought that the end of grad school had meant the end of six-hour nights of sleep.

Blearily, she pawed at her phone to swipe the alarm off. It was tempting to go back to sleep — *after all,* she mused, *the lost weren't going anywhere* — but she managed to at least kick her feet out from under the covers and sit up. Frizzed hair hung down around her face, shielding her from the world for just a little bit longer.

It was her phone, as always, that brought her back to reality. It's mere presence, even silent, was enough to draw her forth.

Ramirez

New case, this time with scans from before the incident. Another furry, you don't think that's got to do with it, do you :p

S

The brief, ungrammatical message from Sanders left her non-plussed until she pieced together that he was talking about one of the other subjects' histories, something about them being part of some subculture. Sanders didn't honestly believe that people who pretended to be animals on the 'net were somehow more predisposed to get lost than everyone else. And, to be honest, neither did she.

All the same, the thought stuck with her through her morning routine. Through the shower, the blank dissociation of standing in the kitchen. Through two cups of coffee, the first there in the kitchen and the second out of a travel mug on the tube as she headed out towards the UCL campus.

Another furry, you don't think that's got to do with it.

She felt sluggish. Craved another cup of coffee even after she'd reached the bottom of the mug she had with her. Sluggish and slow, like thinking through mud. Too many late nights. Too many long days with too little to show for them.

The thought nagged at her, caught like some spinning shape against the threads of her mind in a way that the rattle and screech of the train couldn't displace. It tugged those threads free. Unraveled stitch by stitch, until it reached...what?

Until it reached the hem, and then the same thing over again.

"Holy...holy shit. Holy shit," Carter said, startling the elderly lady next to her. She murmured an apology and fished her phone out, thumbing in a quick message to the team.

Ioan Bălan — 2305

Ioan#c1494bf found emself twenty meters in front of a squat, flat house.

It was as modern on the outside as it had appeared on the inside: a concrete block, a thick wrap-around patio, bordered by dandelions and covered by cantilevered eaves, floor to ceiling glass for walls. Ey wouldn't be surprised if the far side of the buiding — ey couldn't see it very well, with the slope of the shortgrass prairie it huddled on — jutted out at some crazy angle.

Smiling ruefully, ey walked up toward the house. Ey had eir own aesthetic. Ey knew the trappings. Might as well own it.

A soft tone, a vibraphone struck with a soft mallet, sounded both inside and outside of the house as soon as ey'd passed the barrier between grass and patio. Ey stood on the concrete, waiting to be either admitted or greeted.

A shadow of a person — human — peeked out through the glass at em, gave a pleasant wave, and hollered through the glass, "Ioan! Hi. I'll grab Dear."

Before the person could do so, Dear came padding from around the side of the house, looking slightly more collected than it had during the message.

"*Ioan,*" it said, smiling and offering a hand — paw? — in greeting.

Ioan wasn't sure how ey knew when a fox was smiling, but it was definitely a smile. *"Thank you for coming on such short notice. Sorry for the urgent message, I just need to find someone to help out rather soon."*

Ioan#c1494bf took the offered hand/paw and bowed. "Of course, Dear." How strange it was to call someone a term of endearment as a name. "May we have a seat? I've just woken up and am still figuring out how to stand."

Dear grinned and nodded, gesturing cordially with its paw around the side of the building from whence it had come, leading the writer around and through a door in the glass.

The interior of the house was much as ey had seen, though as they moved through the space where that first message had been recorded (a gallery, Ioan noticed) and deeper into the house, things warmed up a little. The concrete walls were softened by hangings and the furniture unexpectedly plush. None of the firm-cushioned, straight-lined variety ey had expected.

Fox and writer settled for an L-shaped couch, facing each other across the bend.

After a moment's hesitation, Ioan began, "I must apologize, Dear. I'm not sure that you have quite the right person. I'm not really a detective, wouldn't know the first way of finding the one you spoke of."

Dear shook its head. *"No, I am pretty sure you are the right person. My search of the markets was quite specific, and you topped all the lists. I am not really looking for a detective, per se. There are enough of those in the Ode clade. They will suss out the whens and wheres."*

"Then what–"

"There are a few types of people in the world, Ioan," the fox said, voice low and calm. Low enough and calm enough to take the sting out of

the interruption. *"There are forgers and honers. Most are familiar with those. Forgers build a thing and plow ahead, and honers settle on a thing and perfect it. Artists generally fall into these classes, and they map to two outcomes in particular: prolific and unfruitful artists, respectively.*

"But you are not an artist. You write, yes, but that is ancillary to what you do. A side effect. After all, there are some other types of people out there, too. Catalogers, feelers, experiencers." Dear shrugged. *"For its own reasons, the clade needs– I need someone to experience this along with us. Someone specifically out-clade. There is a lot of history in this, a lot that we have forgotten before uploading, a lot that we are trying to remember. Maybe even some that we are trying to forget. I want you to help figure out the history of this, yes, but I also want you to experience it and tell a coherent story after."*

"An amanuensis," Ioan said.

Dear brightened, its ears perking. *"Precisely. And what a delightful word, too."*

Ioan smiled. "That's good, then. Very much more my arena. I'll keep this instance around and keep #tracker up to date."

The fox nodded, then looked up, smiling as the person Ioan had first seen came in with three thick-walled, wide-brimmed mugs of coffee, setting two of them down on the corner of the table near Ioan and the fox. "Ioan, nice to meet you. Heard you were tired," they said, walking off with their own mug.

Dear watched them go.

"Your partner?" Ioan asked. A moment of chitchat felt necessary. Ey lifted eir mug carefully. It smelled quite good.

The fox nodded, picked up it's own mug, and leaned back into the cushions of the couch, slouching. *"Mmhm. Finally decided to explore relationships again,"* it said. *"They accuse me of treating it like an art project"*

Ioan grinned. "Well, are you a forger or a honer of relation-ships?"

Dear rolled its eyes, said, *"Touché. I am trying to be a honer, with this one. I gave relationships a miss after...well, some stuff before uploading. For a long while, I forked to create lasting relationships rather than holding any myself. Gets lonely, though. It was like being turned down every time. At least from my- from this instance's point of view."*

Ioan felt they were getting a little too deep for having just met, so ey steered the conversation along a tangent. "You fork quite of-ten, then?"

"Yes. Dispersionista through and through. Or perhaps profligate tracker. Sometimes I do not have the option to let instances linger." Some-thing seemed to occur to it, and the fox sat up straighter again. *"Speaking of, do you know much about the Ode clade?"*

Ioan shook eir head, sipped eir coffee. It was good.

"It is an old clade. One of the oldest on the system. Our root instance, Michelle Hadje, uploaded basically as soon as she could, and quickly be-came one of the loudest voices on the system. She campaigned for more advanced sensoria to be included."

"I've heard of Michelle." Ioan nodded. "Usually in the context of the founders. You speak of her like she's someone else, though."

"Dispersionista habit. We are quite different from each other, by this point. If you get the chance to meet Michelle — and you may — you will see the differences."

"So what is Ode, then? Her old username?"

"No, an ode is a poem." Dear laughed.

"Oh! Oh, of course. So Michelle wrote this poem..."

"No, not actually. Michelle had a friend, a good friend, who wrote

the poem." Dear was speaking more slowly now, sounding less re-hearsed. *"When the friend died, Michelle memorized the poem. All of us up-tree instances do our best to keep it memorized as well. Really mem-orized, too, up in the forefront, up where we think about it, not stored in some exocortex."*

"Is that where your names come from?"

"Yes. Each of us is named after a line in the poem. I am Dear, Also, The Tree That Was Felled, and my first long-lived fork is Which Offered Heat And Warmth Through Fire. My immediate down-tree fork is Dear The Wheat And Rye Under The Stars."

Dear splayed its ears, grinning sheepishly, *"It is perhaps not a very good poem. Michelle was...well, she had some experience relating to the...ah, origins of the poem which I shall not get into here, but even she will admit that. The sentiments are nice, but this friend was not a poet. When they died, when they killed themselves, it really tore her up. We all still think of them often."*

Ioan nodded, once more steering the conversation away from more sensitive topics. "It must be quite long, then."

"One hundred lines divided into ten stanzas. There are only ever ten branches as direct ancestors of Michelle, and each branch only ever has nine long-lived up-tree instances from the initial fork. We may be Disper-sionistas, but we are a small clade."

"And the poet? Who are they?"

Dear bristled, then mastered some complex set of emotions Ioan didn't understand. *"That is the Name that we do not share. The informa-tion that someone supposedly did share, I mean. Someone of the clade or close enough to it to know."*

Ioan's brow furrowed, startled by the fox's reaction, not to men-tion the concept of not sharing a name that was clearly important.

"I see," ey said down to eir coffee, covering eir confusion. "So you'd like me to help in finding this person and act as amanuensis along the way?"

Nodding, Dear held out its paw once more. *"If you would be willing, that is. We would be glad to have you aboard."*

Ey was already sold, Ioan knew, but all the same, ey took a moment longer to consider the ramifications of the job. Ey couldn't come up with any reason not to.

Ey nodded, reached out, and shook the fox's paw.

Dear grinned, shook back.

"Excellent. I have shared just about all I have to share on the topic for now, though as we get updates, I will pass them on to you." Dear leaned back into the couch once more, lapped at its coffee. *"For now, stay. Finish your coffee, at least, though feel free to putter around for a while. Or just stay here. We have an apartment on the side of the house. I have already talked with my partner about it."*

Ioan nodded, "Thank you. I think I'll head home in a bit and sync up with myself, then start the research plan. Do you have any suggested avenues I should start down?"

"Of course." Dear smiled. *"As for research, dig a bit more into the Ode clade for now, probably. When I send you updates, maybe those will lead to different topics."* The smile turned into a sly grin. *"I know you are not a big fan of sensorium messages, but as that is how the clade communicates — those of us who do, at least — I regret to say that you will be getting quite a bit more."*

Ioan gave eir best polite smile.

RJ Brewster — 2112

RJ arrived at the theater early, the last few meters of the walk having been spent hastily finishing the carton of Thai. Carton and chopsticks wound up in the compost as ey swiped eir way into the theater.

"Sorry, Johansson, I'm here."

The hulking director laughed. "You're here five minutes early, RJ. What on earth are you sorry about?"

"What? I- Oh."

"Lot on your mind, kid?"

"Nah, I'm fine. I mean," RJ frowned, squinted. Anything to get emself in the work mindset. "Yeah, sorry. Woke up early and spent a bunch of time researching. Guess my head's still elsewhere, boss."

"Well, alright," Johansson said. "So long as you get your head around work by the time we start. Hey. More crew."

RJ bustled into the theater and made eir way down to the pit where the mics had been stored. Ey handed them out to the actors who would be wearing them, ticking off the cheat-sheet to align proper mic to correct actor.

Ey bounded back up the steps two at a time to the tech booth and set about waking the theater up. Caitlin was already delved in, so it would already be shaking its sleepy head. Ey just had to help it wake up the rest of the way.

RJ exchanged cheery greetings with the lights understudy as ey shrugged out of eir jacket, draping it over the back of the chair. Ey slipped eir hands carefully out of eir gloves. Contacts gleamed from eir digits, freshly polished and clean.

Ey settled into eir chair and delved in to greet the theater. It purred in recognition, brushed up against em, stretched and unlimbered. Thoughts of Cicero and Debarre, of Sasha and the lost left back with eir body, with eir hands resting lightly on the contacts in the cradles, forehead against the headrest.

The first half of rehearsal went by without trouble. Johansson had apparently highlighted a few areas of concern, so they began with those. From there, the cast has followed his lead, adjusting as needed per their dear leader's suggestions. RJ and Caitlin kept a script running so that they could keep up with the director and stage manager.

When the clock hit eight thirty, Johansson called for a break and informed everyone that they would be running through top to bottom after. Last chance for a full run-through.

RJ gave the purring theater some reassuring warmth and backed out of the connection, reveling in the snap of eir fingers pulling away from that light magnetic grasp of the cradles. Ey wiped eir hands dry and flexed fingers to keep limber.

Ey spent the break walking around the theater and stage in one big, looping arc, simply listening. Hearing from the theater's perspective so often, it was easy to get wrapped in the omniscience of it all. Good, too, to hear the way that the ambient sound moved through the room, reflected off of walls and ceiling, died among the baffles. It would all be different with people in the seats, to be sure, but the acoustics of the space were beautiful on their own.

Johansson whistled piercingly. Back to work, back to the stage. Back to the booth and back to the contented and satiny-soft embrace of the theater for RJ.

It was around the end of the first act that RJ started having problems.

When one was delved in, one could always focus hard enough to feel the way their head felt against the headrest, or sense the way that their hands rested within the cradles of the grips. Trickier, sure, when one was as immersive as eir tech required. Bodies weren't a thing in that liminal space. Ey was as much the room as the room was itself. No forehead, no hands. No headrest or grips

By the time ey had brought house sound down in time for the curtain, RJ could feel a numbness creeping. A stealing of sensation. A non-feeling flowing slowly over emself from the base of eir neck outwards, stretching out along eir scalp, down eir arms, the non-sensation not-tickling along eir ribs.

Ey had been willing, desperately, to chalk it up to nerves or exhaustion. It had been such a long week.

Thoughts of Cicero, doubtless cradled in some hospital creche: strictly disallowed but nonetheless teasing around the edges of consciousness.

Tired, yes. Exhausted. Yawns.

By the time ey couldn't feel the plastic of the headrest or the cradles beneath eir hands, no matter the desperation, ey began to panic.

Panic, yes. Just anxiety. Nerves.

All the same, it was final dress. Ey would be able to head home and catch up on sleep. Drink some tea. Hot chocolate. Pet the cat.

Whatever ey needed.

Need, yes. Baser than want. Imperatives.

By the second curtain, something was desperately wrong.

Ey hadn't missed any cues yet, but ey couldn't seem to figure out how to work eir 'voice'. That thing that wasn't talking. That subvocalization used to communicate with Caitlin Sarai Johansson anyone. The immersion-mouth to chat to talk to radio for help a nonentity non-thing non-here, gone, leaving em feeling exponentially more cut off from the rest of the theater as time went on.

Numb, yes. Yet strangely embodied. Strangely tangible. Strangely localized. Oh god oh god please help please help. The play. Ey had work. Ey had the theater. Ey had the room and the lines and time and space to manage. Ey had a home and the Crown and a cat and Sasha and Debarre.

Had, yes.

It was the muzzle that was the kicker. The muzzle and the tail, which ey felt — any feeling a beacon in the storm of numbness which had long since enveloped em entire — with a piercing intensity. Felt, bordering on and then diving straight into pain.

Pull back, ey begged. Every bit of training begged. Every nerve begged, screamed. *A bug, a glitch, an error. Pull back oh god please pull back.*

Ey lifted eir hands — paws? — in a coarse, jerking motion which, along with the act of pulling eir head back from the contacts, led to em toppling over. There was no chair to catch em.

And that was when ey missed eir cue.

The curtain went down, the lights dimmed, and then, ringing

clear, a thin giggle filled the auditorium. The lead laughing at a mis-step. A quiet joke to share at the pub later. No harm. Sound was off, right? Curtains would eat the unamplified laugh.

"RJ," Sarai whispered into the silence of the theater's sim. "Stay on cue, bud."

No answer, no apology, no acknowledgment that a note had been made. No signal.

"RJ?"

"What's going on up there?" Johansson's subvocalization trick-led through the director's channel in the sim.

"Something's wrong, boss, lemme back out and check up on RJ."

"Hold places," Johansson said aloud to the theater. The open channels from the actors' mics carried a few quiet whispers in response. "Hold on, quiet please."

Moving with a quickness which belied his bulk, Johansson jogged up to the tech booth and slipped in as quickly as possible to keep sound from leaking out. Sarai was trying to rouse RJ.

Like a projector bulb's heat burning through celluloid film, the third curtain had signified a drastic change. Slow enough to be observed, faster than ey could hope to avoid. The few tenuous touches on reality that held RJ into eir seat in the tech booth scorched and peeled away, acrid smoke stinging eir eyes. And the numbness spiked.

RJ lay on a tile floor. Dirty. Yellow. Brown specks, dark enough to be black.

The tiles were completely regular, one foot on a side, obviously made of some synthetic material. Harder than linoleum, softer than stone. They were glued to a concrete foundation. No wasting time with grout, each tile butted up against the others to form a grid of thin, black lines showing where the dirt of hundreds of feet had been ground into the remaining seams. Thousands. Millions.

Ey couldn't move, not yet, but ey could see that the world was bounded. There was a thin plastic strip of molding around the edge of a wall. Above that, regular rectangles of blue. A wall.

"Something's not right, boss. Ey's totally unresponsive on the line."

"Pull him, pull him! Hit the panic!"

Caitlin, who had backed out moments before, and Sarai both leaped to RJ's sides and pulled eir hands up from the cradles, rocking em back from the headrest to lean against the back of the chair. All according to training.

Eir body flopped lifelessly against the cheap plastic mesh.

Caitlin slapped the red button on the side of the rig, fingers coming away dusty. Below the desk, drives sparked to life and dumped the last thirty minutes of both sim and brain activity from the user.

"The hell?" Johansson growled, reaching in a thick pair of fingers to press against the side of the sound lead's neck. "He's got a pulse. Check his eyes, Sarai. Caitlin, call. Now."

Shaking, Caitlin pulled her phone from her bag and struggled to unlock. She gave up, swiped to the emergency dialer, called out to emergency services.

"They're rolled back, boss. Bloodshot, too." Sarai tugged back the collar of RJ's shirt, exposing eir exocortex's simple color-coded readout, set at the base of eir neck. "Blue. What the hell..."

"Ey's not jacked in, though," Johansson said. A statement brooking no discussion. "Can't be."

"I think–" Sarai trailed off hoarsely, cleared her throat, tried again. "I mean, do you think ey's lost?"

"Caitlin, what's our status, girl?" Johansson didn't wait for a response, throwing the door to the tech booth wide and shouting out toward the stage, "Cut! Manually shut off your mics and take a seat where you are. *Do not move.* Emergency services will be here soon, and will record what they can."

Lockers.

The blue rectangles were lockers. The first hint was the vent, those five slots a few inches from the bottom of each narrow rectangle, but, as ey lifted eir muzzle from where it lay on the tile floor, ey could clearly see the locks halfway up each door.

Tall, narrow lockers. Blue. Yellow tile floors. Thin tile glued to cool concrete. The scent, the very feel of the place.

AwDae struggled against crashing waves of panic. Struggled to make all of this information fit in eir head. Struggled to make it all fit in with the fact that ey was currently vulpine. A fennec fox dressed in a suit, laying on the floor of the central corridor of eir old high school.

"What the hell?"

Dr. Carter Ramirez — 2112

"Listen, Ramirez, I'm just not sure if you–"

"No, come on. Sanders, just hear me out." Carter sighed and settled her weight against the edge of her desk. Took a slow breath to buy herself some time, organize her thoughts. "I'm just saying that we ought to look into social connections between the patients, too. That way, maybe we can see if there's some factor that's tying these occurrences together. With that under our belt, we may be able to formulate a better theory of what's going on here, even neurologically."

Sanders looked up to the ceiling, visibly counting to ten, then shrugged. "It's just that you're talking about contagion here, Carter, like this is some sort of flu or computer virus. Not only do we have very little data to go on, but there's no indication that this is something passed from one person to another. We've had the rigs checked. Exos too. All of the data suggests random–"

"Sanders," Carter said, voice stern. "I know how the project works. I know the data. There's a lot of questions still left in the air. I'm not suggesting that getting lost is contagious. We dismissed the virus aspect ages ago. I'm merely suggesting that we might find shared factors within a social realm as well as the physiological. Surprised we haven't, actually."

Carter stood her ground. No sense paling under his glare. She was lead of the research team, she could tell Sanders to do whatever she wanted him to. Or, well, strongly suggest. Hell, there was no reason for her not to. She was plugged into all of the teams that he was not privy to. He may be lead of neurochem, but Carter was above basically everyone except the UCL itself and whatever grantors were sponsoring the project.

After a few tense secionds, he caved, shrugged, turned his back on Carter. He nodded towards his own team.

"Look, Sanders," Carter said, following after. "You're a fantastic doctor, and I respect that, I really do. I'm not trying to impugn that or anything, and I'm not pulling labor away from the neurochem team. I'm merely suggesting that we add a sociological aspect to our attack here."

He held up his hands in surrender, then headed for the coffee station.

Carter rolled her eyes and let him go. She turned back to the remaining team. "We've got a hunch on the social front. Or, I do, but I think it's worth following. There's a couple of patients who are involved in the same subcultures, so maybe there's distinct ties between them. Loose ties, sure, not everyone knows everyone else, but they *are* there."

They nodded. Some looked unconvinced, but none hostile.

"Let's time-box half a day to chase down these ties and see just where they lead. If they lead nowhere, fine. If we can find a way to tie them together, then we dig into all the ways that the web ramifies." She smiled in a way she hoped was disarming. "Worst case, half a day is spent tracing along the 'net, but best case, we find another avenue of research that lets us predict — and then maybe interrupt

— future cases. Got it? Catch you at lunch."

Carter sighed. Speeches. Hell of a start to the day. She collapsed into her desk chair, closing her eyes to collect her thoughts.

Rather than sequester herself in an office, she had taken a desk among the team. Four foot cube walls separating her from her neighbors. Made of glass, too; token walls rather than real ones. Not that there was much room for an office in the repurposed classroom. All the same, the deliberate attitude with which she had chosen to join everyone in equal conditions had endeared her to the more stubborn among the crew.

On the other hand, the lawyers-*cum*-statisticians were badly out of their element. Thankfully they had their implants and were able to spend most of their time in the office sim.

All the same, sometimes she wished for an office, if only for the door. A nice, thick, hardwood door. One with a solid core so that she could voice her ideas. Or scream.

Sometimes she just needed the ability to put things into words. No matter how often she tried to set things down in the notes on her phone, she always felt hampered by the small screen and her clumsy thumbs. Neither had she gone full immersive-on-the-go yet. Something about that glassy-eyed stare, the silly headband, the controllers gripped like walking weights, packed full of electronics, set her teeth on edge.

At least she had a private corner in sim.

She delved in rather than work on a tablet or screen. *One scream,* she promised herself. *Then I'll organize shit.*

Once she left her private corner, Carter's chosen workspace, her 'desk', was totally black. Not the complete blackness of unseeing, but the vaguely luminescent darkness of *Eigengrau*, as if wherever she looked, she saw the faint light of non-seeing. It was black enough to be easy on the eyes almost by definition. At least, as much as she had eyes in the sim.

Black without being unnerving.

Scattered throughout the space were decks. Decks upon decks.

Each was a point of light. A white rectangle with just enough depth to give the impression of being several cards stacked on top of each other but no more. Each was surrounded by a dim halo that dispelled the darkness. If she were to engage with a deck, it would fill her vision almost to the periphery with that fine velum paper. Almost, but not quite: the non-black provided a border and seemed to shine, in its own non-light way, through the paper. From there, she would be able to explore and expand that portion of the project at will.

The decks themselves were organized into groups, surrounded by bright lines of white string — literally string; Carter had chosen cotton string as her group delimiter. Decks within groups were linked by string, and many of these groups in turn were related to one another with more intangible threads.

She was a ghost. A non-being. A being of nots. A gesture from her non-hand would show the whole setup from the top. The mind, ever attracted to a two dimensional representation, sometimes appreciated this aspect. The mind, ever attracted to the *hereness* of space appreciated walking through the sim just as much.

Even with perspective in play, the scientists and lawyers working the project had tended to alternate between the aerial view and the interactive view, with the cards positioned at chest level throughout the sim.

Everyone's view of the sim was different in its own way. Sanders, she knew, preferred an oak-paneled room with dark green carpet, a facsimile of luxury with each of the grouping lines drawn out in finest silver. Others preferred pencil sketches, harsh angles, subdued colors on a dim background, or even more abstract, textual interfaces. So long as the concepts of decks and spatiality were maintained, it was up to the individual.

Cards had their ACLs, too. Some were visible only to the individual. Some were visible to everyone, but only on the surface, with details invisible to others. The vast majority were visible to everyone, completely open.

Carter began creating a publicly visible grouping, knowing that others were delving into the sim along with her, visible as diffuse shapes in her dark space. She wrote in air, titled the group in her stolid, blocky font of choice. "The Social Connection".

From there, she began creating sub-groupings. For cases. For leads. On and on. For the "cases" group, she tapped a few of the case decks to make symbolic links, drawing lines of cotton twine which she dropped in.

Two were positioned at the top of the list:

Patient aca973d7
M — 2086-01-28
Lost: 2112-11-08

Patient 0224ebe8
X — 2084-05-09
Lost: 2112-12-07

Carter connected these two cards with fine thread. Hanging pendant from that, she switched to virtual keyboard and created a metadata label, more tag than card:

Possible acquaintances

The others, those shadowy figures, caught on to what she was doing, and got down to work, dragging symlinks of decks and expanding this new group of social connections.

Carter pulled back out of the sim when her personal timer went off fifteen minutes before the time-box was up.

She backed out and made her way from her workstation to the small counter at the front of the old classroom. She filled the electric kettle from the tap and set it on its base for tea, letting it heat up, then scooped a few heaping spoonfuls of coffee and chicory into the coffee maker. While she was in the sim, she had ensured that everyone else's rig would have an alarm for the time-box, and it was only fair that she make everyone a cup of coffee before they pulled back.

The coffee had finished brewing and the mugs were all set out in a row in front of the pot and kettle, each waiting with handles out toward the room for ready hands. Carter poured herself some of the coffee, thick and bitter, and topped it off with a dash of sweetened creamer to dull the latter.

One by one, the ten techs pulled back from their workstations and ambled, glassy-eyed, to the counter where the coffee lay. Carter suppressed a smile: a horde of zombies in various states of disarray drawn to caffeine. It'd be nice, but over the months they had spent on the project, the team had settled into a comfortable ritual of meetings over coffee. The habit remained unbroken.

"So," she started, once everyone was gathered around and tead-and-coffeed.

Silence. Sanders wouldn't meet her gaze.

Finally, she caved and broke down her thoughts. "Time-box is over. I think we got a bunch of good stuff done in a few hours, some not even related to the task at hand. There's definitely connections there. We've got a good number of them among the cases we have at our hands, but there's precious little data on why those connections exist. We've got a few furries, a few 'net addicts — well, more than a few — and we've got a whole lot of DDR junkies. None of those point to anything that would lead people to getting lost."

"Man, have you *seen* DDR zombies, though?" Everyone laughed.

Another voice piped up, "And the correlation on the neurochem side is extremely low. Might as well be non-existent."

Sanders smirked down to his coffee mug before hiding the expression with a sip.

"No, there's no doubt about that." Carter sighed, shrugged. "So, again, time-box is over. What do you think? Is this line of thought worth pursuing? Plus-one, minus-one, zero. Sanders?"

"Minus-one." The response was immediate.

Carter slipped her phone from her pocket and started a tally on the calculator. "Alright," she continued. "Jacob?"

"Zero."

Tallying as she went, Carter went around the room, The running tally took a few dings (neither of the lawyers were for the idea, she noticed), but remained net positive until the end of the line.

"We're left at two, then."

Sanders set his mug down with exaggerated care, but otherwise stayed silent.

"Hardly universal, so let's triage. Can I get one from neuro, one from stats and history, and would one of the law team be willing to devote an hour a day to helping us out? Just to run stuff by as we come up with leads."

If you come up with leads, was written on Sanders' face. She ignored it.

Prakash Das from the neurochem team raised his hand, and Avery from statistics and history volunteered. One of the lawyers, Sandra, gave a noncommittal shrug and promised some of her time, saying, "We're on shaky legal ground, I think, but we can probably keep it in check."

"Alright. Let's sync up, you three." Carter smiled toward the rest of the group, "Not leaving you guys behind. One-on-ones and daily stand-ups will continue at the usual times. We'll set another time-box of–" She checked her phone. "Three days, after which we'll reconvene and vote again."

Sanders strolled back toward his workstation, Ramirez's eyes on his back.

AwDae — 2112

AwDae slowly picked emself up off of the floor, staggering to eir feet.

Ey was standing, swaying, in the middle of a long row of lockers. And then ey was sitting again. Not from weakness *per se*, but the shock of being in the tech booth and theater sim, and then suddenly being back in high school was taking its toll on eir wits.

Ey swiped eir paw from left to right in front of emself to bring up the usual menu.

Only, no menu came up. There was nothing in this sim, if sim it was. No global menu, no ACLs. No control.

Panic crested again, broke the surface.

AwDae felt behind emself, reaching for that sense of reality outside of the sim, that cool breeze of the tangible that should be at eir back. It *was* there. Ey could feel it. A cool breath of air on the back of eir neck, but muffled. Only, there was something keeping em from reaching for it, touching it. A thin barrier. A membrane. A sheet of keeping em trapped within the sim.

And then, with a jolt of pain driving like a spike down the back of eir neck and along eir spine, it was gone.

Throughout all of the practice runs, the endless training on the rig that had gone into eir education, that feeling had only come up a scant handful of times. It was the feeling of being forcibly disconnected from the rig through the manual expedient of removing the contacts from the cradles in which they rested. It was the shock of being brought to reality from out of a sim with no disconnection. It was the rush of eir exocortex dumping its core and the interferites struggling to hand back control with the last of their stored power. It was panic made tangible, halfway between electricity and the feeling of missing one's step on the last stair.

And with that, AwDae should've found emself back in the tech booth, trying to figure out what strange loop the theater had gotten itself into that would have frozen eir rig.

The lockers never wavered, though, and now ey found emself stuck in eir old high school with no contact to the world outside of whatever this place was.

Ey screamed.

Ey didn't know how long ey screamed, how many times. Ey didn't know how long ey cried or beat eir fists against the lockers. Ey didn't know where ey was.

Lost.

Lost like so many others.

Lost like Cicero.

Or perhaps Aeneas, Odysseus.

Sing to me the reasons, O Muse. Sing, Muse, the fatal wrath.

Eventually, ey cried emself out. Minutes, hours. Eventually, eir tail went numb and eir feet fell asleep.

Nothing for it. Ey wobbled to eir feet, kicked off now ill-fitting shoes, shoes not made for fox paws, and began to trudge.

Ey walked slowly down the halls, memories coming back in a wash. Realities blurred effortlessly. Realities of the embodied world. Realities of online life.

Nails on feetpaws clicking against the tile, following the math wing to the student center, a cavernous space that acted as a terminus for all of the different hallways, each hosting a different subject. They spread away from the cavernous room like limbs, a giant insect clutching at the earth.

Neither halls nor hub had ever seen a fox. They were supposed to be home to students. To students and teachers and staff. To humans. To anyone, not some lone half-beast.

Inside the student center, AwDae sat down and tried to reach towards reality once more.

Nothing.

Ey sagged, rolling onto eir side in eir increasingly frustrated attempts to pull away from the contacts, though that shock of pain suggested those in reality had long since pulled em away.

Frustration, anger, fear. Hopelessness. Terror. All simmered within em, working up to a boil as ey tried increasingly harder.

Finally, ey gave up and, hastily brushing at the tears staining eir cheeks, slipped out of eir tux jacket as well. Why keep it? Yet another unfoxly garment.

Ey swished eir tail to the side and lay flat on eir back on the cool terrazzo floor. Ey pulled eir suit jacket up over eir face and buried eir muzzle in the soft lining. With paws holding the cloth to eir face, ey deliberately let the tears come. Willed them too. Forced. Screamed and begged. Anything for release from the tension building up.

Time held no meaning. It was a few minutes or hours or days before ey peeled the coat from eir face and stood up once more. Exhausted, ey bent down to roll up the cuffs of eir slacks to keep them from bothering eir feet.

It was in the middle of the second cuff that ey realized the absurdity of the motion. In the theater sim, ey didn't have a body, and when ey 'woke' in eir normal sim, ey was dressed only in the clothes ey had on when ey went to bed. Usually nothing. Ey disrobed before disconnecting more out of habit than anything.

So why was ey still in eir tux? Did ey even have a tux in eir wardrobe?

AwDae puzzled over this for a moment before completing the cuff rolling. Something to look into later. For now, ey needed to find eir way out. Find eir way *back* out. Or, failing that, at least find one thing ey could finish. One, simple task to complete. Something to make em feel less powerless in the face of it all.

Exploring, then.

The sim was startlingly complete.

Perhaps. Ey had been in London a few years, and before that, on the coast at university. *Was* it complete? Was it accurate? Despair lay around the corner: the thought that the chances of em being able to compare the sim and reality vanishingly small.

In fact, the only thing that seemed to have changed was AwDae emself.

AwDae's curiosity won out. Ey made eir way back to the school's auditorium. It was exactly as ey had left it all those years ago. Trudging up the few steps toward the entrance, ey feared that it would be locked. Missing. Somehow erased from existence, such that it had never been there in the first place.

But the door swung easily beneath eir paw and eir nails clicked against the sound guard in the doorway, leading em into the dimly lit hall.

The house lights were at quarter, the stage lit only by utility lights from the back. All the same, it was enough for em to find eir way to the small sound booth. A counter with a light: off. A bank of sliders and knobs: all zeroed out.

AwDae brushed eir fingerpads along the lower lip of the soundboard. The screws were exactly where ey remembered.

Swishing eir tail out of the way, ey sat on the stool in before it. Ey reached a paw up past the master sliders, just around to the back of the board, where ey found the power switch.

Click.

Nothing happened, so ey reached a little further back, finding the power strip for the booth itself, and toggled the switch on that. The board let out a satisfying pop of recognition as it came to life. The brief surge of power echoed throughout the room as speakers awoke. The theater uncoiled, purred to em, just as the one back in London had done...what? Three hours back? Five? A year?

Ey fumbled with the booth light, finding the ancient dial switch to wash away shadows with lazy red light. Light that illuminated a thin layer of dust covering the board and booth in a matte coating. Light that illuminated countless motes already disturbed. The only breaks in the coating were where eir fingers had brushed the dust away, leaving black slicks.

So familiar. So many dreams. Dreams of flawless performances of breathtaking beauty. Nightmares of feedback and missing equipment.

Acting on a dream, ey slowly brought the master volume up to the spot ey still remembered from so long ago, turned the gain to mid on mic one, and brought the slider up slowly.

Blinked.

A soft hiss filled the hall. The channel was open.

That doesn't mean anything, AwDae thought. *There could be anything plugged into the snakehead in the pit. A line with a powered mic. A wireless receiver. Hell, a fault in the system.*

All the same, it was something. Something in this seemingly abandoned hulk of memory was turned on, something else besides emself was making noise.

Ey was about to head down to the pit to check on the snakehead, the terminus for all of the microphone cables or wireless receivers that stretched up to the board, when ey caught sight of a sheet of paper, folded in quarters, tucked between the side of the board and the wall of the booth.

AwDae plucked the paper free and unfolded it, held it under the red light of the booth lamp to get a closer look at it.

There, in tiny print, was a good chunk of the content of the vcard ey had created earlier that morning to add to Sasha and Debarre's deck. Cicero's DDR ledger, containing transactions that comprised votes made, bounties collected, and comments posted.

A note, though. Doubly weird. The paper didn't act like a normal vcard. No menu, no ACLs ey could sense. And yet the closer ey looked at the paper, the more the data seemed to unfold, fractally nested and seemingly infinitely deep.

Ey blinked, and the moment passed. The note once more contained only tabulated transactions.

Frowning, AwDae refolded the note and stuck it into eir trousers' pocket. A small scrap of the outside world stuck in this elaborate fantasy.

Ioan Bălan — 2305

The first message was not long in coming, arriving about an hour after Ioan#c1494bf arrived back at home. At least it wasn't high priority; ey had the choice to accept then or experience later. Half duplex, though. An actual conversation rather than a recording.

Ey sighed, closed eir eyes, accepted. The things ey did for work.

"*Hi Ioan,*" came Dear's voice. It was still seated on the couch. "*Long time no see, yes?*"

Ioan nodded, subvocalizing eir response. "Yeah, took you ages. Have something for me?"

"*Maybe. We have received a file from someone down-tree. Or, well, hmm.*" It appeared to think for a moment before continuing, "*Someone down-tree from me found a file, and she thinks it might be a file from the clade, maybe one of the original ten.*"

"Alright, send it over."

The file arrived promptly. Eir shoulders sagged. It began with `-----BEGIN AES BLOCK-----` followed by hundreds, perhaps thousands of apparently random letters, numbers, and punctuation.

"What's an AES block?"

"*An old encryption algorithm.*" Dear looked a little embarrassed. "*And I mean* old. *We like old things. That is why she suggested it might be* from one of us."

"You don't sound convinced."

"I am not. You must understand that this is not something any of the clade wants known. It is just a name, yes, but it is important to us in a way that is hard to overstate." Dear sighed. "Much of the clade is of the opinion that, if we could simply wipe the Name from our minds, we would. For a member of the clade to break that trust is nigh unthinkable. It is acting against our very nature."

"You're right in that I probably can't understand the importance here. Still, I trust you on that. A friend, maybe? A mutual?"

The fox frowned. If anything, it sounded less convinced when it said, "Perhaps."

"An enemy?"

"A valid concern."

Ioan frowned. "I'm trying to square your use of the poet's work in your very names with your desire to forget the Name itself. That sounds like something someone could use against you."

"Names bear power."

"A memorial, then?" Ey hastened to add, "Sorry. It's probably not my place to understand. We can drop it for now."

"Yes. A memorial." The fox's shoulders slumped. "Let's come back to it later. I do not want to get too distracted now. Still, we will have to speak more on this soon. It would be good for you to have a more complete picture."

Ioan nodded. "So do you want me–"

"You do not need to worry about the file itself. That is why I did not just forward it to you automatically." Dear paused, then added, "Though I probably should have. Here I am talking about you having a more complete picture and not giving you everything."

"It's alright. I'm picking it up as we go along."

It nodded. *"It is important, though. Amanuenses form an* Umwelt, *so this is part of yours, now. We will talk about it at the end. Something to keep in mind, I suppose. When we find the key, we will let you know and send over the contents."*

"Okay, good. I gave AES a check, and you're right, that's ridiculously old. Can't you just crack it?"

"We could. Some of us probably already have. I want the key, though. It is probably a word or something, and may prove interesting in its own right."

"Interesting?"

"Interesting in that the act of finding the key may turn up further clues."

"Ah. Good point. I'll do some digging on old cryptography, too, and see what all's out there."

"Good fucking luck. Cryptonerds were — are — very wordy. There is going to be a boatload to sort through."

Ey grinned, "I'll fork and research, then."

"Good plan. I am going to get back to the hunt, and hey, Ioan?" The fox's smile was earnest. *"Thanks. Even if I am just running ideas past you, it is good to put in words."*

"Of course, Dear." Ioan waved. Ey always felt silly interacting with sensorium messages. Would #tracker think em crazy? "Thanks for the project."

Dear bowed, signed off.

#tracker was, indeed, giving #c1494bf a bemused grin.

AwDae — 2112

The pit revealed little.

There were twenty boxes set on a table in front of the snakehead. Twenty receivers for twenty wireless mics. Twenty cables neatly velcroed together into a bundle, contracting from the receivers and dangling catenary from the dull grey plug-box. They were reduced to a four-by-five grid, arching up above the snakehead before plunging into it, XLR heads buried in XLR nests.

All of the boxes on the table were dull. Mute LEDs simple bumps on their surface. Dark. All but one: the first. The one with a piece of masking tape on its face, scrawled with a '1'. That box had a single red light on the front, indicating that it was powered on, and a single green light, indicating that the corresponding mic was transmitting.

"Great," AwDae murmured. "That leaves only half the school to search."

If it had been a wired mic, the search would have been over as soon as it began: the cable would've been plugged into the snakehead, and by following it until ey reached its end, there would be the mic.

And what?

There would be the mic, and ey would still be stuck in a nightmare. No, in some parody of a nightmare. All dressed up for the high school pops festival and, here, see? The auditorium is completely empty.

The fox barked a laugh at how many cliches littered the situation. Turning away from the receivers, ey rested eir weight against the edge of the table that bore them. Ey leaned a moment, then hiked eir backside up onto the familiar surface, relishing the squeak of stressed metal from eir sudden burden.

AwDae swung eir legs back and forth, hearing the table creak and groan in time with the slow movements. The sound was quiet, but in that dread silence, more than enough to fill the hall.

Ey stopped.

The auditorium was pleasantly wet: not damp or moist, but in terms of echo, it had just the right amount; or, at least, as much as a high school auditorium was able to muster. Had it been dry, the sound would've died away completely. The drier a room, the closer it got to an anechoic chamber. Zero echo. The painful lack thereof.

AwDae knew this hall, even years later, even in dreams. Ey knew the pockets of good and bad sound scattered throughout the seating. Ey knew the dead spots on stage where one's voice would fall flat. Ey knew how the stage was built rather like a horn, performers at the small end, so that their performances were projected out toward the audience. Ey knew how the stage was built like a drum, the orchestra pit a chamber of its own.

And yet, there was that slight echo of the squeaking of the table.

An idea. A crazy one, sure, but by this point, with despair nipping at eir heels, a crazy idea was better than none.

And, a bitter portion of em reasoned. *If getting lost is permanent like they say, I've got nothing to lose.*

Ey hopped off the table and began to pace.

The squeal of feedback in an audio system is an emergent behavior, and even those who have not heard it before know immediately that something is wrong as soon as the hum starts. That quiet hum in the background, building exponentially.

It doesn't take long before it can be understood as something originating in the system, rather than coming from speaker or performer. From there, it builds on itself, feeding back into the mic and growing louder until it quickly overwhelms all other sound. Rises, crescendos. Hearing and speaker damage equally likely if left unchecked.

Similar, in an upside-down sort of way, to the echo that AwDae had caused making the table squeak beneath eir weight. Sound was picked up by the microphone, transmitted through the sound board, then out into the room. Amplified, though, through the speakers.

If the microphone started to pick up sound from the speakers — and sound was sound, the mic cared not where it came from — that sound would loop through the board once more.

A feedback loop.

It would continue to build through further and further iterations, until the auditorium was filled with a roar of that one dread pitch the microphone had first locked onto.

Dread and dire. Cursed. An eternal struggle.

Obviously microphones were still in use. They hadn't been abandoned because of the loop; they just got smarter about finding ways around feedback.

One could angle speakers toward the audience, rather than the stage. Bodies were notoriously bad reflectors of sound. Part of what made the stage so acoustically dead, that.

One could turn down the monitor speakers facing the stage, but that would be cruel to one's performers.

One could turn down amplification, but that defeated the purpose.

The solution, then, was gain.

The adjustment was provided by a knob at the very top of the sound board governing the sensitivity of the mic. At the top, befitting its importance in the setup. The very beginning of the signal path.

Turn the gain all the way down, and the mic was a dumb lump of metal and plastic. Turn it all the way up, and the mic picked up everything from the movement of the air to the slight hiss of the live sound system, almost guaranteeing instant feedback.

AwDae cranked the gain almost to the point of feedback. If ey could make noise in various points throughout the auditorium, maybe it'd get picked up. The more feedback ey generated, the more sound the mic was picking up. The more sound it was picking up, the closer ey was to it.

Eir possible locations for the mic hadn't been reduced, it was still half the school, but eir chances of finding it sooner rather than later would go up. If the mic was not in the auditorium, ey could turn the main system up and start venturing further afield. Leave a door open, let the mic hear. Let em hear the theater ring like a bell in turn.

Riddles. Triply weird.

AwDae felt stupid. Insulted. Trapped for life and still solving riddles.

Hopelessness dimmed eir vision.

Ey shook eir head, ears laid flat.

"At least it's something."

Ioan Bălan — 2305

Dear,

While I'm sure that your clade, with the resources and minds at its disposal, has already decrypted the AES message, I have only just managed the feat today. It was at least somewhat easier once I learned a bit more about the history of the whole affair.

You say that you all like old things, so perhaps you will be delighted to learn what was inside if you have not already. Here is the message in full:

> Odists,
>
> You know me. I will not tell you how, and I will not tell you why this secrecy is in place. Not yet. For now, though, you may refer to me as Qoheleth, or, at need, Hebel.
>
> I am sorry for having said — or, rather, written — the Name, but not too sorry. I need to get your attention. There is something serious going on, and I need you focused on the matter.
>
> Let's meet, yeah?
>
> -----BEGIN RSA PRIVATE KEY-----

(There follows another block of gibberish similar to the first.)

-----END RSA PRIVATE KEY-----

Your move, by the way:

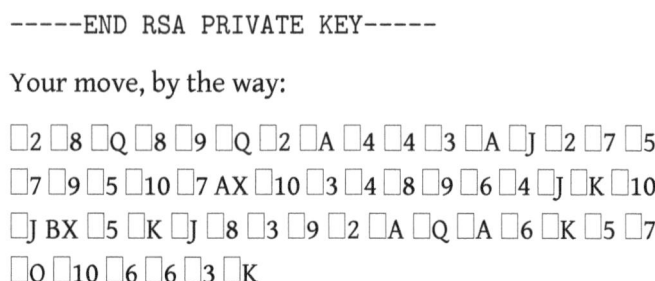

There are several things of interest here. I'm sure you'll want to talk this all through, but as I will inevitably be writing this all down in the end, I figured I would also get my thoughts down on paper now, while they're fresh.

The passphrase for this encrypted message was *kemmer*. If the other Odists figured it out, I would be curious to see what they make of it, just as I'm curious as to your thoughts. Perhaps later. For now, there's a bit of story, here.

I did not originally find the passphrase, as the letter itself was decrypted through known weaknesses. None of the tools that I was able to find would (could?) give me the key, since all of the attacks were along direct avenues. Don't ask the details, I can hardly understand them..

Instead, I found the passphrase by accident while doing a search on some of the contents of the letter. Notably, I searched on *Qoheleth*, and then *Hebel* in relation to that name. There's lots of juicy stuff here. *Qoheleth* is more title than name, and is used in a book in both the Christian and the Jewish bibles. Given the author's reference to the Hebrew word, I've been restricting myself to searches surrounding the Tanakh. I should add that, while in the Tanakh, the book is called by the same name, while in the Christian bible, it is called *Ecclesiastes*, from the Greek.

Qoheleth can mean 'teacher', but also 'gatherer' or 'director of the assembled'. This last one, I suppose, fits in with their suggestion that the clade meet up. Perhaps all together? It is also referenced as *Ecclesiastes* in words such as ecclesiastical, 'relating to the church *qua* assembly'.

Hebel, in this case, appears to be an approximation of what is usually spelled *havél*, which translates to 'vapor', but is also interpreted as 'vanity' or, when taken metaphorically, 'meaningless'. For instance, the book begins:

> havél havalím 'amár kohélet havél havalím hakól hável.

Which is, in some translations:

> "Meaningless! Meaningless!" says the teacher. "Utterly meaningless! Everything is meaningless."

Bleak, no?

The entire book is quite fascinating, and the tone seems to waver between this comfortable sort of nihilism (I hesitate to say hopelessness, as hope does not seem to be a factor in play here) and education, with Qoheleth using their past experiences and meditations to offer instruction on how to live a full life.

Back to the passphrase, though.

I have found several references to the term *kemmer*, with the primary source being an ancient speculative novel by the name *The Left Hand of Darkness* by Ursula K. Le Guin. I forked and read this while investigating the Tanakh, and the book seems to surround the sociopolitical ramifications of a subspecies of humans which is androgynous most of the time, but which undergoes a biological process (*kemmer*) wherein they settle into one of two physiological sexes for the purposes of sex and procreation.

I was not able to deduce anything concrete out of this term, because I cannot tell where it is directed. While I do not presume to know the Name (nor do I wish to!), one possibility is that it refers to the author of the Ode. Another is that it refers to some aspect of the Ode clade itself. You are perhaps uniquely positioned to answer this, as I don't imagine the entirety of the Ode clade are agender foxes, given both what I know of Michelle Hadje and how you speak of your cocladists. A third possibility is that the term may apply to Qoheleth themself. A fourth is that it relates to the mystery at hand in some way. And, of course, it could be meaningless (hah) in terms of subtext, in this case and does not apply beyond being a neat word.

That said, I'm not a fan of the final interpretation, as upon further digging, I came across the line "the key word is kemmer, that's what yo' ass need" in an equally ancient song ("Air 'em out" by clipping. [*sic*]), which was too tight a coincidence to pass up. The annotated lyrics to that song, in turn, were packed with more references and discursion than this letter, many of which refer to old science fiction books and movies. This verse in particular features heavy references to *The Left Hand of Darkness*, including the phrase 'Ansible' — which shows up in other books as well — and, in turn, shows up in some of our technology: the communication system by which uploads are sent from Earth to the System here at the L5 point is called 'Ansible'. This struck me as particularly important. I found this song both in my searches on *kemmer* as well as on the Ansible, having taken to heart your suggestion that the clade likes 'old things'. The Ansible turned up a *third* time in the context of asymetric cyphers, mentioned below.

Given this additional set of coincidences, I've compiled a list of further references in this song for research down the line.

At this point, I have only addressed the encryption passphrase and the salutation of the message! You must forgive me for the discursive nature of this letter. There are many layers at play, here, and I believe this is intentional on the part of the author. As you mentioned, amanuenses form a collection of semiotic processes relating to the task they are participating in. I've taken this to heart and am amassing documents surrounding the subtext as well as the text.

The second paragraph of the letter I would like to discuss with you in person, as I think that there is context here that may well be specific to your clade. I cannot imagine what might be so serious.

After that paragraph comes another block of text. Rather than being an encrypted message, however, it is a private key used for the RSA cryptosystem. It is an asymmetric cipher, which means that there is out there somewhere a corresponding public key. Strange that we are given a private key rather than a public one, as such keys unlock doors, rather than lock them. RSA can be used for many things, so that we were given the private key in this case makes me think that this will be used to either decrypt or otherwise access information down the line. Before you ask, yes, there is a passphrase involved with this. However, I have not yet figured out how to extract that from the noise yet. Cryptography is intriguing, but much of it is over my head, so I am relying on off-the-shelf solutions.

Finally, after the key block, we get a deck listing for a standard deck of playing cards. I am assuming, here, that the cards labeled

AX and BX are jokers, though I have not seen them differentiated as such in the past. I am, frankly, at a loss when it comes to this section, so all I can offer are some thoughts on subtext.

"Your move, by the way" implies two things. First, it implies that there is some sort of ongoing game between Qoheleth and the clade. This strikes me as strange, and I cannot put my finger on why. It is not that you do not seem the type to play games, as you seem playful enough to me. Perhaps it's that the letter begins with riddles about the true identity of Qoheleth, yet any ongoing game (and such a weird way to provide it!) would perforce give away that identity immediately. Perhaps it is simply this — all of this — that is the game?

The second implication is broader, and consequently more of a hunch on my part: this is a very casual thing to say to someone. For one, to have a *non sequitur* of a postscript on a letter that seems very focused on a single topic is a strange thing to do. It's the type of thing you might do when sending a friendly letter to someone rather than a riddle of a message (I will admit, I'm considering what postscript I leave at the end of this letter now). The tone also differs from the remainder of the letter. It is familiar and friendly. The only thing that is even remotely close being "Let's meet, yes?", and even that feels more formal.

So, one question answered and several more raised. The largest, of course, remains: how deep does this all go?

I will continue my investigations and keep you in the loop on those. I hope to hear from you soon — I know I shall.

All my best,

Ioan Bălan

PS - In engaging with this project, my searches and purchases on the exchange are shaping my reputation quite strangely. #Tracker has received several queries for future projects surrounding both novel forms of encryption and a few requests for historical analyses on speculative fiction. Ey has turned down all of the former and seriously considered all of the latter — and ey wishes you to know that ey places the blame for this squarely on your shoulders.

Dr. Carter Ramirez — 2112

"Avery. What's up?"

The ping had sounded in Carter's ears like a soft bell, and the faint outline of a door had appeared at the periphery of her vision. Someone had requested a meeting. After a moment of dictating a note to herself for when she got back, she made her way through the door. One of the stats-and-history folks stood, waiting with arms crossed, in the private space.

"Running up against a bit of a snag, Dr. Ramirez," they said. "This new patient, uh…0224ebe8?"

"What about them?"

"Well, I'm getting some doubled records. Weird things are duplicated. Sort of."

"Duplicated? How?"

"Well, we've got some records from way back with a different gender marker on them and no pronouns." They looked thoughtful. "I ran into a bit of that when I changed everything over, myself, but the process changed all of my past records, too."

Carter frowned. "So e8 changed their marker and pronouns officially, but you're seeing duplicate records under a different one?"

"Mmhm. I was wondering, do we have any location data on them?"

"Not really, no. You've got all the same data I do. Most have been redacted."

"I figured, yeah, but wanted to ask. I just know some friends back in America ran into similar, too. Some ancient conglomerate or something holding onto old records or not updating their systems, so I was wondering if e8 was over there."

Carter shrugged. "I don't really know. That sort of thing is scrubbed before we get the cases. I'm actually surprised the files weren't normalized before we got them."

Avery laughed. "We're one of the big three, so of course it's all extra difficult." Carter must have looked nonplussed, as Avery continued, "Banking, government, and healthcare. Ask any one of the big three to adopt to social change, and you'll get eighteen different reasons why it's impossible to update their systems."

"Fair enough. So they have two markers and no pronouns."

"Well, ey has two markers, X and M, but only the one set of pronouns. None listed on the records with the M marker."

"Is this going to be much of a problem?"

"Don't think so," Avery said thoughtfully. "The records are complete so long as we take both sets into account. You might want to run it by Sandra, though, is the thing. I don't know if us knowing that this change occurred is too much information for us to have. Legally, I mean."

Carter knit her brow. "And there's the snag."

Avery nodded.

"Well, hopefully not." Carter leaned against the wall and thought for a moment, then asked, "What can we do with this information, anyway? We've seen a pretty good spread across gender markers with our set of cases, do you think this'll change anything?"

"I don't know. The friends back in America who ran into this were all ones that made the change later in life. The younger you are when you change markers and such, the easier it is because the less of a record you have to change. It's kind of like you're burdened with a marker from birth, and the longer you go before changing it, the heavier the burden gets."

"And they had a big one?"

"Not so big, all told, but it's enough that all of eir records from when ey got eir implants are under a different marker."

Carter nodded.

"From a history standpoint, that also means that eir marketing footprint takes something of a hard left at one point."

"When th–" Carter backtracked. "When ey changed eir marker?"

It was Avery's turn to nod.

"So we've got someone who's advertised to with a masculine marker, then with a neutral marker–"

"And ey seemed to have given the whole romance thing a miss, too. Eir marketing footprint is mostly just rig gear and furry stuff. It's like ey slipped through filters unnoticed, which, in itself, leaves a trail."

"Well, if you can't sell em sex, what's left to sell?" Carter laughed.

"Oh, plenty, I assure you. Just that, pushing nine billion, advertisers mostly rely on larger demographics. GQ folks and asexuals aren't broad enough segments to bother wasting ads on. Granted this is only going by the transparency reports. There's all sorts of weird guerrilla marketing going on these days."

"Yeah, fair enough. Any similarities with our other furry?"

Avery shook their head. They swiped their hand to the side to bring up a snippet of desktop, dug through a few decks of vcards. "Being a furry seems to be the big thing they have in common. e8 is X, d7 is M. e8 is single and not looking, d7 is in a long-term relationship. d7 is almost a parody of a DDR junkie, e8 has almost no...well, hold on."

Carter waited.

"Looks like ey was prodding around the DDR spaces a few hours before the event." Avery had that far-away look to their eyes that one got while digging through data on cards. They shook their head to clear their vision, smiled to Carter. "Sorry, looks like I've got a bit of work ahead of me on that end. Any thoughts on the snag?"

"No, carry on as you were, I think. Sandra will keep an eye on it and let us know if we're at risk of overstepping our bounds."

Avery nodded and stepped back out of the meeting cubicle.

Back in the sim proper, Carter watched as the cards surrounding 0224ebe8 began to sift into two piles as the shadowy form that must be Avery worked. White cotton thread began to string itself around two groups, followed by the tags '0224ebe8 (M)' in one and '0224ebe8 (X)' in the other.

After a few minutes, she walked back to her constellation of decks. On a hunch, she created a small grouping in her area and labeled it "DDR Activity Pre-Event". She began looping in relevant cards from both 0224ebe8 and aca973d7.

There was a soft *ding* within the sim, and a wave of shadowy heads looked up, Carter's included.

Directly above them in the middle of the 'ceiling' was the current time in faintly luminescent letters. As always, they would look different for each member; for Carter, traced out in fine cotton string was the '12:00' that indicated lunch.

Carter's vision began to dim. She backed out before the ominously cheery message instructing her to stretch her legs urged her to do so. University policy stated employees should work in a sim no longer than four hours in a row without fully backing out, so when she pulled back from her rig, she saw everyone else doing the same.

Most of the team gathered around the fridge and microwave by the coffee station to collect their lunches. She hadn't had the time or energy this morning. Lunch out it was.

At least she wouldn't be alone. There was a small coterie who made their way across the street from the campus building to the shops, hunting falafel or curry. She put on her best chummy face and tagged along with. The group chatted, inevitably but amiably, about work, comparing notes on the cases they were focusing on.

The group — three of them, with Carter — decided on a small Vietnamese place nearby. It would be a long lunch, with the wait and all, but she was promised that the food was amazing. Besides: Friday. Even the boss can enjoy a lunch every now and then.

Standing outside as they waited on a table, they made an obvious target for the tabloid sellers. They were wandering a little further than usual from the tube station entrance today, and the restaurant hadn't noticed them yet to shoo them off.

Carter rolled her eyes when Prakash bought a copy.

"Hey, don't look at me like that. I promise I read it for the laughs," he said.

Carter shrugged, "It's less about why you reading it, and more who you're giving money..."

Prakash and Aiden stood in silence, eyes on Carter. They exchanged glances before Prakash broke in, "Hey boss, you doing okay?"

"Can I see that?" She didn't wait for an answer before she snatched the flimsy paper from his hands.

Soho Theatre Mourns Lost Tech

RJ Brewster was the pride of the Soho Theatre Troupe's tech department.

The brainy American who blessed them with boosted bass was admitted to the University College Hospital after apparently getting lost during a rehearsal on Wednesday. Ey was discovered during an intermission completely unresponsive. Medical crews declared em lost on the scene after analysing eir implants.

The genderqueer young man was described as "bright, but obsessed." Ey was a member of the furry cult and spent most of eir time on the 'net, which friends blame for em getting lost.

The STT promises that productions will go on as planned, with back-up techs running the sound system.

Brewster represents the 135th case of the lost marked in the world. Ey will be cared for by doctors at the UCH. Members of the University College London studying the lost were unavailable for comment.

Carter let the paper droop. Aiden retrieved it before it was closed completely, opening to the page where she had been reading.

"Oh, hey! Stuff about a lost person!" He read down further, then looked up at Carter. "Did you get an interview request from them?"

She shook her head. "Not a word. Not to me, at least. Maybe PR turned the interview down."

Prakash read over Aiden's shoulder. "Do you think we could go see em? We're with UCL. Maybe we could–"

He fell silent at a look from Carter. She spoke carefully, voice carrying the weight of a prepared statement. "Ey's in good hands. Trust the doctors on this. We'll receive all relevant info from them. Any contact with a patient may introduce bias in the study."

Aiden frowned, shutting the paper. "We shouldn't have this."

"No, we shouldn't."

He quickly balled up the tabloid and, finding no rubbish bins nearby, set it on the restaurant's outside windowsill. Researchers were as jealous of their data as the lawyers were of patient privacy. Keeping the tabloid would only be a risk.

"But what about the theater troupe?" Prakash asked.

Carter caught herself in the act of shaking her head, turned instead toward the restaurant. She tilted her head back and let her eyes trace the sharp contrast between the gutters of the building and the steel-gray sky, seeing neither.

"We can't," she finally murmured. "Same risk of bias."

A safe answer. A rote one. A required one. The legal aspect was plain, the ethics clear. If she wanted to learn anything from the doctors treating this RJ or the Troupe, she'd have to file a request, wait for the ethics board, wait again for the lawyers, and even then, even if she succeeded, she would only be able to write a questionnaire for them to fill out.

And yet here, a half hour tube ride away, was a social connection. The very thing she wanted most to understand.

She was distracted, thankfully, by the host inviting them in to eat.

AwDae — 2112

It took AwDae just under two hours to find the microphone.

The first hour was spent searching the auditorium top to bottom. Ey walked around clapping and humming, then quoting lines half-remembered from productions ey had worked with Sasha in the past. "So set its Sun in thee," ey called in an affected accent. "What Day be dark to me." Wistful Dickinson to fill an empty hall.

Ey would've whistled if it wasn't for the structure of a canid muzzle.

Silence.

After an hour, venturing even into the overhead areas where sound was muffled, damped, ey gave up and took a break.

It's probably fruitless to be this thorough in the auditorium, ey thought. *The gain's high enough that even a quiet clap should be enough.*

Ey slouched in an auditorium seat and pulled out the slip of paper with Cicero's transactions. Ey had found that if ey focused on the page just so, rows would sort themselves by columns, so ey spent a few minutes aimlessly zooming through the page of digits.

Ey scanned over the titles of the initiatives voted on. Very little there to latch onto. Or, rather, way too much. AwDae couldn't hope to boil down the table into any single sentence, much less something useful. The cat had apparently voted on just about everything without taking any breaks.

Eventually, when neat rows of letters began to blur into one another, ey levered emself up from the seat. Paper refolded, ey slipped it back into a pocket before checking on the board once more. Everything remained set as it was.

AwDae had imagined ey would work in concentric circles away from the auditorium. That turned out not to be the best idea. The hall was nestled between two arms of the school which did not meet except via the auditorium itself. Eir route grew arduous: ey'd walk down one hallway, poke into classrooms, and make noise before moving on.

When ey reached the end of eir circle, though, ey had to jog around the auditorium through the student center to go down the other hallway and do the same.

Ey gave up on the concentric circle plan and started working from north to south, instead. Ey worked through the entirety of one hallway, clapping and hollering, without hearing anything. From there, on to the area of the student center near the auditorium.

It was there that ey heard the first, faint hum of feedback.

It threatened to skim beneath eir attention, sounding too much like an echo from eir own voice in the cavernous common area. The door to the auditorium caught eir eye, and ey tried once more, getting another faint hum. It slowly died out as space and air dissipated tone.

It was only a few minutes from there to find the microphone itself. A lavalier mic, disguised as a button resting obsequiously atop the door handle leading into the principal's office. It was just to the northeast of the auditorium doors. Ey would've found it soon enough. It was surprising, in a way, that ey hadn't managed to trigger any feedback earlier.

The door was labeled 'Admin.'. Ominous.

There was a head office at the front of the school, but administration was where the principal and vice principals' offices were. One of those places that lingered in the mind of every student who passed through the doors of the school. Getting called to the front office was usually bad enough — a call from a parent? — but getting called to the admin office was more oh-shit than that.

Ears pinned back, AwDae picked up the microphone delicately through mounting feedback and quickly shut it off. The hum had grown loud enough that ey could hear faint clicks from the speakers. Magnets clicking, popping as the physical limitations of the ancient-and-not-so-great speakers reached their limit.

The sound stopped a scant few moments after, bouncing around the auditorium and the student center. Echoes.

Eir ears slowly uncringed. Ey pocketed the mic in eir trouser pockets and straightened up. The school was silent once more.

Remembering the position where ey had found it, AwDae pocketed the mic and straightened up, wandered back over to the auditorium, turning the gain down on the board and lowering the house volume to a reasonable level. Ey even turned the mic back on and mumbled a quick "one-two" to ensure that none of the speakers had been damaged.

This is a sim. Not even mine, ey thought, the inside of eir ears flushed warm with embarrassment. *What does it matter if a speaker blew?*

Ey shrugged it off. Habits were habits. No reason to break them now.

Back to the admin office, then. AwDae couldn't help but feel as though ey was trapped within a game. One of those first-person puzzle solvers that seemed forever popular. One of eir favorite genres.

It was surprising the adroitness with which eir perspective had shifted. Sobbing: now behind em.

Perhaps the fact that ey seemed to be receiving what amounted to clues while in a complex abandoned building added to that. Perhaps it was the shift from RJ to AwDae. Perhaps something about emself. Countless hours in sim. Countless changes in scenery. Countless changes in form.

Shaking eir head, ey turned the knob on the admin office and peeked inside.

There were no traps, no jump-scares. Just the six-sided room with three doors on the walls this one. One for the principal, and two for the vice principals. Taking the game metaphor to heart, ey started poking around the office where ey could, flipping through a datebook on the secretary's desk (empty) and rummaging through the drawers (office supplies).

The waste baskets were empty.

Steeling emself for something...something what, shocking? The game mentality still holding tight, perhaps. Ey tried each of the doors in turn.

Surprising. It wasn't the principal's office that opened, but one of the vice principals. The name of the one who had worked there when ey was a student escaped em, and no tags adorned the doors. The office was dark, but the lights responded to a touch on the pad. Ey set it to a comfortable level; warm without being cozy, bright enough to read without being intimidating.

Memories of being hauled into the room, all those years ago, with the lights all the way up, a gesture of power.

Rummaging through the desk revealed little of note.

Rather than a planner on the desk was a workstation. Simple. Ancient. It didn't respond to any of AwDae's interactions. How it would work, ey couldn't guess. A sim within a sim? Ey had perhaps hoped that a connection like that might lead...outside. Outside of this mess.

The only other items on the desk were a scratch pad and a pencil. The expected tools. The perpetual desk-toppers that never seemed to go out of style.

The pad contained a breakdown of costs, divided into departments, for the coming year. A simple three-column setup tallying subject, expense, and deductions from some number at the top. Budgets, perhaps. At the bottom of the page, was a final number, circled in dark, angry strokes. Apparently, the administrator hadn't liked the result.

AwDae flumped down in the chair at a jaunty angle, eir tail flopping down between armrest and chair back. Tired, so very tired.

Ey rubbed away the sandy grit of tears already shed. Ey was moving in this search with determination. As much as ey could muster. Anything to occupy eir mind, anything to keep em from collapsing into a depression borne of hopelessness and despair. It occurred to em that getting lost was the perfect prison: complete freedom, or nearly so (ey had already fantasized about jimmying open the other doors), with nothing to do. Nothing to dream, nowhere to go, nothing to know.

Ey didn't even know the time. No clocks adorned the walls.

Ey would go mad without a task. Could ey create anything? But why create in these empty halls? What would ey even begin to make that would matter the worth of a damn? Ey would never be able to share it. Ey would only be able to spiral endlessly inwards.

All AwDae wanted to do was curl up in the chair. It was comfortable enough. Perhaps ey could get some sleep in.

Instead, ey ground the heels of eir paws against eir face and leaned toward the desk. Numbers, digits, columns. Something familiar. Mindlessly working through the sums in eir head simply for lack of anything else to do.

"Weird," ey murmured sleepily.

The numbers didn't add up. Rather, everything added up within its own row. It was as though a row were missing.

Ey stretched out an arm, snatching up the scrap of note and holding it up to the light. No erasures, whiteouts, or scribbles. There was just not enough information.

Digits. Numbers. Ledger. Paper. Notes?

If ey was meant to be looking for clues, then...

Ey fished the previous 'clue' out of eir pocket. The ledger of Cicero's DDR interactions.

It wasn't nearly so simple as the single-column arithmetic on the scratch paper. Each referendum had three columns of digits: a cost, a bounty (if that referendum was referred back to the house), and any number of comments made on the issue. Often out of order on the sheet, as well, given Cicero's habit of voting on everything. Perhaps it was the first thing he did on waking.

Given the note's interactivity level of expanding on closer examination, ey tried to will a sum out of the columns to match the final row.

No luck. Ey wished for eir rig more than anything. It'd make the task almost trivial.

Ah well.

Ey snagged the half-used pencil and the rest of the scrap and worked it out. Each cost and comment would be a debit, and each bounty would be a credit. One could also buy DDR credits through a mechanism that basically acted as an additional withholding on one's taxes. There were two of those in there, possibly ensuring that Cicero would have enough DDR credit to make what AwDae assumed was some scathing political snipe on an upcoming high-stakes referendum.

Even so, it was clear that the section of numbers on the paper, a month's worth, perhaps, didn't add up. Once more, there was a missing interaction. Three missing interactions, rather: one vote's cost, one vote's comment, and one vote's bounty, at AwDae's best guess. Perhaps a few smaller votes to add up to those totals? It was recent, too. A few days before he had gotten lost

Except one's DDR records were public. Not which way one voted, but that one had voted. Comments were public perforce. The information had to be public for the system to work.

Unless it had been tampered with, there was a combination of 1,252,000 credits unaccounted for in terms of transactions. One million debit to the comment, a quarter of a million credit for bounty, and two thousand to the vote cost.

AwDae tore the top sheet off the pad and, working faster this time, ran the numbers once more. Same result.

"Well, huh." Ey sat, frowning, for a little while longer before gathering eir notes. Ey folded them together with the original clue and stuffed them into eir pocket. Ey couldn't create a deck here, apparently, but ey could sure take items with emself.

If this all had something to do with what was going on outside, where ey was counted among the lost, that was all well and good, but how would ey get that information back out remained a mystery.

Too early to be thinking of such things. Ey wasn't going anywhere for the time being. Sleep was becoming an imperative.

Ey gave token consideration to where ey would be able to sleep
before deciding on the auditorium. The fold-down seats were cush-
ioned. Not very well, but better than the floor.

And the place had a sense of home about it, too. The thought was
a barb tugging at eir heart, but there was nothing to be done. Not in
this state. Not right now.

Sleep, then.

Sleep, and perhaps dreams.

Or perhaps not. Sleep to get away. Sleep for nullity. Sleep for
nothingness.

Qoheleth — 2305

Transcript of Node: [bea0cf302fcd00863f0c67a91b1a75c0e4ba4863] with descriptive text by #d5b1a4aa.

———————————

The footage shows two persons. One of them has to be Dear, Also, The Tree That Was Felled, who is an up-tree branch of the Ode clade, eighth stanza. No one else has ears that big, nobody else can somehow speak in italics. The other took some research, but I am confident that ey is an instance of Ioan Bălan, a historian and writer. Ey is a tracker, but only just, as eir habits tend toward few to no long-running instances. This instance is either #tracker or one tasked to this project.

The two persons are sitting outside of a cafe, from whom I obtained this footage. They are in conversation. Going to sit down and watch this.

Dear, Also, The Tree That Was Felled: Thank you for your letter, Ioan. Lots of really good stuff in there, most of which I had missed simply out of nearsightedness.

Ioan Bălan: You've got me hooked on this project, I have to say. It's fascinating stuff.

Dear grins at this.

Dear: We — that is, some other Odists down-tree from me — have come up with some further hints about the message.

Ioan: Oh? Anything good?

Dear: I suppose it depends on your definition of good.

Ioan: [snark, good natured] Oh great. Excited already. [more earnest] The fascination continues. Well, let's have it.

Dear: So, one of us did an exhaustive search of some records and found an old archive server running somewhere.

Oh goodie. Better start gearing up.

Ioan: Wait, start at the top. What were they searching?

Dear: They were searching for the block of encrypted text — not what was in it; they cracked that long ago. They searched for the encrypted text itself, and they came across an archive server.

Ioan: Old node boxes? Wow, even I feel crusty using one of those, and I'm a historian.

Dear: [laughter] They found the archive server though, and there is a bunch of intriguing stuff on it. New, old, the whole thing. There is stuff from ages ago, shortly after we got here, and stuff from a few hours ago.

Ioan: You're kidding. Newly created stuff?

Dear: I know. It is ridiculous.

The fox's ears flop when it gets excited and shakes its head, never noticed that. It is kind of cute.

> **Ioan**: Never met anyone who could actually get one working well enough to add new nodes. So the encrypted text was in a node on the server?
>
> **Dear**: Yes. It is still there. [pause] Just sent the URI.
>
> **Ioan**: I...well, I'll have to take it at your word that it's the same as the one you found earlier, I'm not going character by character.

Dear seems a little frustrated at this. About Ioan's slowness? I know I would not compare the files. It sounds exasperated.

> **Dear**: Of course, Ioan. I promise it is the same, though. Needless to say, we found a crusty old archive with the block on it, and there are other public nodes on there as well. I am guessing a bunch of private ones, too.
>
> **Ioan**: Anything good in those?
>
> **Dear**: Nothing...penetrable. It is all fairly opaque. To me, at least.

Ioan grins at this.

> **Ioan**: Thus us meeting?
>
> **Dear**: [nodding] Yes. The only bit that I have any insight into is the deck listing, which I think might be another bit of old encryption–

Ioan groans aloud, at which Dear grins.

Dear: My sentiments exactly. It is another encryption scheme which relies on a deck of cards for a stream of random numbers. I have not dug into it in years because the decryption process is so slow, but there may be a node on that box containing the encrypted text.

Ioan: Want me to have a look, then? The techier stuff is going to go right over my head, you know that.

Dear: It is not all tech, promise. I just want you to give it a read and see what you pick up from it, you know? Put your amanuensis hat on and just spend some time experiencing.

Ioan: You think highly of me. No complaints, of course, but I feel I have to ask, why can't someone from your own clade fill this role?

Dear is quiet. Struggling for words? Our Dear? This must have hit it hard.

Dear: We...differ. The Odists, I mean.

Ioan: "Differ"? Within the clade?

Dear: Yes. A hallmark of Dispersionistas is that we treat each of our forks as fully-realized individuals. We may have a shared past, but from the point we fork onward, we grow ever further apart.

Ioan: I assume you mean more than just a matter of increasing conflicts.

Dear: Yes. Although we Odists limit our instances to the one hundred available names, we still consider ourselves Dispersionistas as we never merge back down-tree. But, that aside, we also want someone out-clade for this. *I* want someone out-clade for this.

Ioan seems taken aback.

Ioan: Do the other Odists not like that I've been brought on?

Dear: Of the ones who know, most are fine with it.

Now frustrated/confused.

Ioan: "The ones who know"?

Dear: You have, of course, noticed that you have not interacted with any of my cocladists. I have told some about hiring you, but not all.

Ioan: Alright, I suppose. If you're independent, then I guess it makes sense that I be your amanuensis rather than the clade's.

Dear: Yes. Perhaps more evidence that we are split on how to tackle this in the first place. Different camps, different strategies, infighting. Ioan, you have to understand that, when a clade gets old, it starts to get a little batty.

Calm down fox, I am working on it. Not so frantic.

Dear: Some clades try to get around this by keeping a certain core group of instances — talking mostly Dispersionistas, mind — in a setting that keeps them as sane as possible. Something that feels very 'normal'. Or maybe some are researching forking from earlier points, from down-tree, rather than from where they are now.

It furrows its brow.

Dear: We do not. First of all, we started way too early on for that to be a thing. We trusted that change itself would keep us sane, that as instances diverged, especially with mutation algos in place, they would change enough to keep us from falling apart.

Ioan: And that didn't work?

Long pause.

Dear: It kind of worked, I will put it that way. I feel fairly well rounded, as much as that means, and I am sure those across the clade from me do too, but it is complicated. You might not recognize my cocladists as Odists without knowing beforehand. It is like having a very close sib that was raised by a different family in a different sim.

Ioan: More different than you'd expect, then?

Dear: 'Expect'...fits strangely for this. The problem is that they are still *us*, and we are still them. Clades are families of separate individuals in a lot of ways, but you must realize that, in the end, they are still one individual. We are more different than one individual should be. Does that make sense?

It does, Dear. That is why I am doing this.

Ioan: I guess so. [pause] So some of your clade would prefer I not be a part of this?

Dear: More than that. They feel that investigating the matter of the Name being written is too risky, too close to investigating the Name itself.

Ioan: I don't know how I would respond to that.

Dear: That is my field, Ioan. Do not worry about it.

Ioan holds up eir hands, looks apologetic. The fox has tilted its ears back.

Ioan: Sorry, Dear. I hope I'm not overstepping at all.

Dear: [calmer] Do not worry about it. It is okay, I promise. It is just that we are really good at arguing, so I have been dealing with that quite a bit the last few days. That is why I hired you; I am relegated to an administration role so I am a bit on edge. Let us get back to the archive server, yes?

Ioan: Sure thing. Where did you say your cocladists had found it?

Dear: Just in a search. I do not quite know the details about how. Assuming just a text search of the perisystem. Not too sure on the terminology; I bought into being an artist pretty hard. All that knowledge is in exos.

Ioan: [laughter] No worries there, Dear. I'm trying to keep up with you is all. I was just wondering if they found anything else.

Dear: You mean like the other nodes on the server?

Ioan: I'll poke around at those, look for ties and such. I was more wondering if they'd found anything in their search that didn't meet the relevancy threshold for them. Stuff like back-links to the server, or anyone talking about this Qoheleth. Hebel. Whichever.

Silly name. Oh well. Dear looks taken aback.

Dear: I had not really thought to ask. I do not suppose they did, though. Do you think it is worth having them search around more? Lowering the, uh, relevancy threshold? [laughter]

Ioan: Yeah, I think so. Though now that I've got it too, I can do some of that digging myself. I want to see who likes the Tanakh so much as to name themselves that. And why 'kemmer'.

Dear: I...well, it is complicated and out of scope, but it relating to fluidity of gender is relevant to the clade as a whole. Very big for us, if only at a remove. I have opted out.

Ioan: So I noticed. It makes sense, though.

Dear: I am glad someone is thinking about this stuff. You are sounding more like a–

Ioan: Private investigator?

Dear: [laughter] I was going to say historian, sounding more like an historian every time we talk. But you never know, maybe you would make a good PI.

That was fast! I may have less time than I had thought. Dear is lovely, and it is totally right: on the other side of the clade, there are some who would not like this kind of digging. Too entrenched. Too Conservative.

Ioan: I can't tell whether or not I should be flattered.

Dear: It is a good thing. Just keep digging, and we will too. I will be about. Got a few more things to wrap up to finish the current gallery exhibition, but after that, I am just going to work on this — with you if you do not mind — and try and figure out what is even happening in the clade. Do keep in touch, yes? Ping me whenever.

Ioan: Will do. [pause] Wait, you're an instance artist, right?

Dear: Yes. Why do you ask?

Ioan: Why don't you fork to work on both at the same time?

Dear shrugs, grins, quits. Very lovely fox. Really quite lovely.

No time to dawdle watching Ioan try and figure out up-tree instances, though. Must be getting ready. Quit this instance, flush the server of extraneous crap to guide Ioan a little more effectively — yeesh, how old is some of this stuff? Need to re-encrypt a bunch of it anyway — and maybe get ready for some visitors.

Dr. Carter Ramirez — 2112

Carter hadn't meant to dodge her subordinate's question. They truly did need to go in to eat.

The food was, as promised, excellent. Carter made a mental note to come here more often. A note filed into the appropriate box in mind, then set aside. She had to work through the implications of what had been spilled by the tabloid.

She couldn't visit this RJ any more than she could fly out of the restaurant's second story window and back to her lab.

It would be a useless gesture, of course. Her team didn't need access to the patient to do all of their work, because much of their vitals, properly anonymized, were provided as a real-time stream of data. It had been shown that physical contact was not registered at all by the lost; it would hardly matter if it was a researcher any more than a family member.

There would be people between her and RJ, as well. Not just doctors and nurses, but her own administration. She would have to go through any number of layers of bureaucracy just to get access to...to what? To variables that likely wouldn't help her investigation at all? Eye color? Hair length?

And of course, there was the law. Carter well understood the purpose of the Western Federation Personal and Health Information

Protection Act. It was part of her research at a fundamental level. Anyone in medicine knew it, had the inevitable posters tacked to the walls.

Hell, she had voted on it, herself, in the DDR. It was something she felt strongly about regardless of her work. The tabloid had breached that, in a way. There was no culpability, of course, but there was a breach by publicly announcing the case.

And yet, there was nothing to stop her from going to a show in the next day or two.

Feeling very much the sleuth, she stuffed a small egg roll into her mouth. Savoring the taste. Savoring the idea, the plan.

Yes, she'd go to a show up in Soho.

With her resolution firmly planted, she found it difficult to make it through the rest of the day. Rather than wrangle the two competing strands of work groups into some cohesive whole, she spent much of her time distracted. Antsy.

Finding tickets was easy enough, though the price left her winded. She was thinking about all of the ways in which she could approach the cast. Or was it the crew? Would she even be able to get in contact with any of them? Supposing so, what would she even say? *Tell me about your sound tech?*

The rush was wearing off, as it always did.

Avery and Prakash were both settling into the routine of investigating what had gone on before the incidences of the lost. Those precious few minutes saved from the precious few cases where a core dump had been provided.

Avery was collating what data they had from each case on the social front before the event and searching for social connections between each of the cases, as much as the law would allow. Prakash, meanwhile, was digging through biochemical data that had been collected from each of the patients and searching for similarities for them. All stuff he had been doing before, of course, but now based specifically on the time before they had gotten lost, rather than during or after.

Carter had supposed that this would be innocuous enough, but Sanders had taken the opportunity of the boss dining out for lunch to chat with a few members of the workgroup. Not once, but twice while she was working, she had needed to field private messages from teammates. Both had concerns around the direction of the project, and questions about the wisdom of separating the already fractured group into smaller units.

In both cases, she reiterated that this would only be a temporary investigation. If it turned up any useful information, then they would have that conversation again in the near future. If it didn't, oh well. Everyone would cohere once more. There was comfort in the words, she hoped, but all the same, Carter wasn't sure of their efficacy.

She had had an idea. A hunch. One she thought worth investigating. That's what one did in science, right? Have ideas. Investigate. Be open to being proven wrong.

Sanders, however, had an *ideal*.

Or so Carter assumed. When assessing the team's standing on the issue, she had used the usual three point scale: for, neutral, against. What she hadn't asked was how many fucks each of them gave. There were, after all, two parts to making a decision. Which way you vote, and how much you cared about it.

Carter could easily estimate Sanders giving ten out of ten fucks against this current plan of exploration, while in fact, until this afternoon, she would have likely given five or six fucks.

That question hadn't been asked, though. She couldn't make up her mind whether she wished she had asked or was glad that she hadn't.

This afternoon, with the determination to learn more for the sake of the project (so she promised herself) and the sense that she was on the right path had significantly bumped the number of fucks she gave. And there was the hope of proving Sanders wrong, no small amount of competition within academia.

The play was some contemporary work.

The Short Trip, the ticket site informed her, chronicled an indecisive youth taking a trip away from family, purportedly to visit a bunch of friends for three days, the real goal of the trip being to visit his long-distance partner, but in the setting of a party, with guests, known and unknown, weaving their way through the scene — and, at times, through the audience.

This much she learned as she made her way south and west. Carter had to duck out of work earlier than usual to make it over to the theater on time. She had actually to travel past RJ in the UMC, borne along the yowling Victoria line to Soho. Glad she left early, too. She needed to wait for three trains to pass before she was able to squeeze aboard.

The train vomited her out into Oxford Circus and left her spinning. Looking, looking for the right exit to the tube station, comparing directions on her phone. Each was helpfully lit up with a thin, translucent display overlaid above the older signage in painted tile.

Both bore the unerring curves of Helvetica, perpetual winner of the font wars.

Neither meant anything to her.

Easy enough to find the theater by following the crowds. Her identity — and thus her ticket — was proved by a touch from her contacts, a grip around a simple bar in front of the theater. The bar flipped around to provide its other end to the next customer, the end she had touched getting a quick sanitizing so that everyone got a clean surface.

Carter was first surprised by just how much she enjoyed the play, then chagrined at her surprise. She had decided not to approach cast or crew beforehand, a decision that had proven surprisingly difficult. She worried that she would spend the entirety of the play thinking of what to say. She wound up engrossed in the performance all the same.

Lying to parents. Moving through the party. The awkwardness of meeting for the first time. The cast nailed it all. She'd had her own long-distance fling while an undergrad, and she knew the feeling well. *Meet at a public space where you know people,* mom had even cautioned. *Like a party. Just in case.*

It was well into the third act of three that she realized she hadn't given any thought to the sound of the play. A passing thought: this was probably a good thing. This was the sign of a job well done. An understudy, perhaps?

She applauded as heartily as the rest.

Still, her mission, such as it was, was right at the fore as soon as she stood. She was perhaps a little rude in her haste, making her way out into the lobby of the theater where some of cast and crew, as well as the director, were greeting the audience. Opening night, after all.

"Mr. Johansson. Mr. Johansson!"

The bulky man turned toward her with a pleasant, if bland, smile. A smile at war with the obvious worry lining his face. "Ma'am. I trust you enjoyed the show?"

"I did! Of course I did. I'd like to ask you something, though, if I might."

"Mm." The sound was assent, but only just. The rest of the audience was starting to stream out of the theater, his mind was elsewhere.

"I was...It's just, about RJ-"

The immediate focus of Johansson's attention was a heat lamp against her face. The intensity of it startled Carter out of speech.

"I mean, if it's not too forward to ask," she trailed off, a hint of a question.

"It is forward," he confirmed, eyes probing her. Too many reporters? "But I'd like to know how you know of em?"

"I'm a researcher at UCL, working on the lost."

Johansson took her elbow gently in his grip and led her off to the side, out of hearing of the rest of the audience and the curious cast. Gently, but brooking no disagreement.

"That doesn't tell me how you know of em. Aren't you- isn't that privileged information?"

"The tabloids had a-"

The growl was immediate, hidden behind gritted teeth. "The paramedics told me I couldn't contact anyone but the hospital, but the rag said you guys had declined contact."

Carter straightened and shook her head. "We did not, nor would we have. Although, I must admit, the interview process would be far more formal than this. I only put the pieces together based on location and pronouns."

"So what do you want from us?" Johansson's shoulders sagged, the intensity lessened, permitting emotion. "We miss RJ. It's been a real mess without em. Please, miss–"

"Ramirez. Dr. Carter Ramirez." She hesitated for a moment before continuing. "We're looking for...well, a few of us are looking for social connections between the lost, rather than just simple personality or neurlogical correlations. What can you tell us about RJ in that sense?"

Johansson looked up to his cast, then leaned a little closer to murmur, "O'Niell's, once we're done. Then we can talk. I have more to do here, so it may be a while. Please wait up, though."

AwDae — 2112

Sleep did not come easily.

As padded as the auditorium seats were, they were not made for laying down on. They folded down, and while there were no armrests to get in the way of stretching out, the gaps between seats were awkward and painful. AwDae found that ey had to face toward the backs of the seats, lest eir tail get crimped against them. It left eir back exposed in a way that felt unsafe, no matter how empty the sim was.

At first, the faint dusty smell of the seat fabric inspired nostalgia, but it did not last. The memories were not comfortable, either.

Eventually, ey got up and began pacing blearily around the auditorium. There must be some way to rest that did not involve folding seats.

Ey could pull down one of the curtains and make a nest out of it. But, as ey did not know how to do so without ripping the fabric, ey was loath to do so. They carried some of that same smell, those same memories. A last resort, perhaps.

Exploring beyond the auditorium it was, then. The door out the back of the stage led to the hall containing music and drama classrooms. Ey started cataloging additional places where ey could hole up. The black fabric orchestra seats were promising, and they could be arranged however ey wanted, but ey hit pay dirt in the theater storeroom.

The back of the room was sectioned off into a wardrobe area, housing costumes and rack upon rack of identical tuxes and dresses for the choir singers. Nestled behind all of these rows of clothing was a sofa, old and sagging.

There was zero reason for the room to contain a sofa. Ey did not remember one being there the few times ey tagged along with Sasha. As inexplicable as it was, however, AwDae wouldn't have been surprised if such a thing had existed in the school ey when had attended.

Thanking whoever had created this sim, ey flopped down onto it. Musty smell intensified, lingered, settled.

Ey was asleep within minutes.

Sleep, while restful, brought dreams of unnerving intensity. Dreams of twisting passages, of locker-lined corridors looping impossibly back on themselves, leading always into the same dim light of the student center. And in the middle, a menu, canted away at a steep angle, no different from what ey might get by swiping eir paw left to right in any sane and sensible sim.

Every time ey got close to try and read the menu, however, it would slide closed, leaving only its shadow behind. An unexpected rendering error.

AwDae jolted awake feeling as if ey had drastically overslept. Ey hadn't paid attention to when ey had gone to bed in the first place. One in the morning? Two? Rehearsal, and then hours of searching. Was it the same day? The same week?

All the same, ey felt late.

With the shock of transition, the need to explore the auditorium and hunt school for the mic, ey never did make it outside of the school. Could ey even do so? Ey felt silly for not trying, now.

Wake up, then. Ey stretched and started to plan a way out of the school. If nothing else, ey wanted to see how extensive the sim was.

It was customary in-sim to lock the doors that did not lead any-where. Although the Crown Pub did have bathrooms and fire es-capes, for instance — all for the sake of authenticity — the doors were locked tight. Beyond them would have been nothing at all. That was simply the extent of the sim. It was not inaccessible so much as nonexistent.

And yet there were much larger sims than the school itself, much more intricate. AwDae couldn't be sure of the boundaries without exploring.

Ey wondered what must have happened to eir body back in re-ality, even as ey walked toward the front doors. Ey didn't feel hun-gry, though ey felt ey should. Such things were translated in-sim as safety measures to keep addicts from starving themselves. After all, ey had still felt the need to sleep. Something had clearly been done with eir body.

That train of thought wound around the question of how exactly ey had gotten lost in a sim without being connected to it. Were other lost individuals in whatever sims they had been before, empty now of others? Did everyone experience getting lost the same?

Obviously, time had passed, and certainly the crew hadn't left em just sitting at eir rig after ey had finally lost touch. Even so, ey should've been pulled back to that reality when eir hands had been lifted from the cradles and head pulled away from the NFC headrest.

Had time passed, though? Had it? Had ey explored? Had ey slept? And yet here ey was.

Where was eir body, then? Some hospital somewhere? Insensate and tied to life support?

And if ey was in a hospital, where did this sim exist? A sim this size couldn't simply live in eir gear. Especially not with all of the mechanics ey had encountered so far. Fully functioning sound booth and mic. Papers in the office. The sleeves of costumes hanging from the racks ey had brushed eir hand across on the way to the couch.

No answers to be had. All ey could rely on was what was in front of em.

Ey stopped at the bank of doors at the front of the building, staring at one of the panic bars. Would it be locked? Would it open at a touch? Should ey slam eir weight against it, or test gingerly?

Resigning emself to whatever happened when ey pushed it, ey rested eir paws against the smooth metal, claws clicking against the door itself, and gave a firm shove.

The door swung open and ey pinned eir ears back, squinting into the deafening sunlight beyond. Holding the door open with one paw, the other shaded eir eyes.

Ey saw the cul-de-sac for dropping kids off. Ey saw the street beyond, the set of townhouses that lined the road opposite the school. Ey saw grey. Ey saw fog. Despite the very sunny day, shadows cast sharply against concrete, ey saw fog.

Fog of war? Render distance? Some visual indicator representing the furthest that the system was willing to draw? Or a boundary hemming em in?

Old tech. Tech unneeded for perhaps a century. Was it a limit of eir exo? Some languishing remnant? It had occasionally been used as an invisible boundary, ey knew. That it was there in the first place, closing off the street in either direction a hundred yards into the distance, confirmed that this was indeed a sim, not just some artifact of eir subconscious.

Did it, though? *Did* it confirm that? Did that truly follow? Was it a sign? What was its referent?

Ey stepped out onto the sidewalk by the flagpole and stared. Shoulders sagged. Tail drooped. There were no answers.

No answers.

Nothing for it but to keep looking.

Qoheleth — 2305

0.1 Archive: [Hebel Qoheleth]

Node: [7cbc92e691678c4c17a04f5553cd1058ee122956]

[Encrypted]

Node: [32c5a64b66d0338be4373d796cf1eae5343f1077]

```
OCYNX GRIMN CYJPE PNNXS SCIQZ
KTWQW FBAVY FBOPA QERLB HWIJW
KPELO UCLAN OKHPM PCPWR NZNZQ
NMTIQ BKNGH UWFMG BPPZS CNRKX
TKEMU AFNOS VQUNW
```

Node: [36b1d8c1df07ce0f254b2332acd38c59bdf3bb00]

[Encrypted]

Node: [67e97446cdbe3a4a3cfd5ebd75b1260f] Error

The node you have requested, [67e97446cdbe3a4a3cfd5ebd75b1260f], does not appear to be an Archive node. You have provided a 32 byte identifier; the Archive system uses 40 byte identifiers.

If you believe you have received this message in error, please contact the Archive owner.

If you believe that you have the correct identifier, you may have attempted to access it on the wrong system. Please check the Gist system for a possible match.

Node: [80b42deb4c364cac5937cff9ca306625b69ae7c5]

[Encrypted]

Node: [bea0cf302fcd00863f0c67a91b1a75c0e4ba4863]

Security Footage

Location and time data provided in their own node.

Limited sensory data provided by dual security cameras and microphones.

No sensorium data available.

Marked for deletion *systime 181+331 0322.*

Note

Given the trouble of maintaining this shitty archive, I just transcribed it so I don't have to host the data.

Node: 172fb56e982d2d3f08957c5f7be0779bbf2f6aa6

Node: [172fb56e982d2d3f08957c5f7be0779bbf2f6aa6]

Transcript of Ioan Bălan and Dear, Also, The Tree That Was Felled speaking at a cafe.

Node: [f6981a0738b43275059c37a9c8b744e42eb91fb9]

[Encrypted]

Dr. Carter Ramirez — 2112

Johansson's hands dwarfed a pint of ale.

Once they had managed to find each other in the post-theater crush of the pub, they staked out a small two-top table crammed against one end of the bar itself. Johansson to lean to the side, away from the noise of too many voices.

He'd hardly touched the beer, but it seemed to take on an almost talismanic significance to him. Something to hold. Something to focus the thoughts. Carter drank her own cider slowly and waited, careful not to press her luck too hard. Johansson seemed slow to open up.

"Alright, so, RJ." His vocal cords unlimbered, a well-rehearsed baritone.

"Ey was your sound guy?" Carter backpedaled, eyes ducking to her glass. "Sound tech?"

There was a small smile tickling at the corner of Johansson's mouth, but he hid it a swallow of his thin ale, nodding. "Yep, lead sound tech. Best I've ever worked with, by a long shot. And don't worry. We still fuck up eir pronouns now and then. I know we did on the night ey...when ey...well, Wednesday."

Carter nodded. "And then you tried to pull em back out?"

"Nothing. It's like ey was still delved in even after eir contacts

137

had been knocked out of place. We hit the panic button and called the docs. I guess some ambulance-chaser caught up with them, which is how you found out about us."

"Yeah. I'm not really in the habit of checking the tabloids myself, but I went out for lunch with a few coworkers and we got one pushed on us. The bit about you not being able to contact us got my attention, so I figured I'd make for the show tonight. Thought that might be my best bet."

"How'd you even manage that on opening night, anyway?"

"Oh, don't worry, it cost me plenty." Carter laughed. "Christ, this is so far out of the realm of what I'd do, too. I just feel like we're at an impasse."

"An impasse?"

"Yeah." Carter leaned back in her chair to gather her thoughts. "I've been on a few projects over the years. None were easy, but all the same, this one has a weird amount of interference. It feels like we're being made to trudge through mud. They won't give us access to the patients? Fine. That's PII. We just need the data that they collect from them, right? So why is that always so heavily redacted. Why aren't we getting that? It's never been a problem on any other project.

"All we're getting are little tidbits. A few hours of monitor scans, little clips of logs from before the event, and that's it. I don't mean to creep on you or anything, but with RJ, we've come across something we hadn't had before. We found out ey was, well, you know..."

Johansson canted his head to the side. "An immersive tech? Genderqueer? Ace? A furry?"

"A furry, though those others are certainly interesting data points to keep in mind. We weren't totally sure ey was asexual, but it tallies."

"How did em being a furry help?"

"Ey's the second furry we've had come across our desks." Carter peered into her cider, then about the room. "In fact, it's caused a bit of a schism. Some of us are looking into possible...transmission vectors, while the rest are focused on cases individually. How could something like getting lost be transmitted from one person to another? It sounds like some awful drama; it's not a virus."

"I assume you're among those who doubt the transmission story?"

"Oh, no, I'm heading it up." She laughed. "But there are still convincing arguments to be made against it. Sanders, the leader of the opposition, such as it is, is dead-set against it. He thinks that we're wasting time chasing up this transmission tree. Valuable resources. We've got an agreement, though."

"What's that?"

"Well, we'll keep poking at this lead and if it dries up, we'll drop it."

Johansson hunched his shoulders, frowning. "Not much of a lead, I'll grant you that, but all the same, anything to get RJ back. Ey was more than just a tech. Sounds silly, but we all liked em. The tech crew, especially. We went through our share of fuck-ups tonight just getting by without em."

"Oh? I didn't notice any."

"You weren't on the headset. We had lights and sound arguing cues while stage desperately tried to keep them on track. It was a mess."

"All the same," Carter countered. "I thought it was delightful."

"Mm."

Silence.

It felt necessary. They both stared off into the pub. The room held the distinctly British dichotomy of being crowded and convivial, while also intensely conscious of personal space. The latter suffered as the night went on.

"You know," Johansson began, bringing Carter's attention back to the conversation.

"Hmm?"

"RJ wasn't one for relationships — doubt ey would be — but of all the people ey was close to, it was definitely those furries ey hung around. Come to think of it, I do remember em bringing up the lost with regards to them."

"Oh? Huh. It seemed like the two cases we have may be socially connected, but we don't have any proof."

"Yeah." Johansson shrugged. "Not much for relationships romantically, but certainly no shortage of friends. There was this one girl, Sasha, ey was close to."

Carter thumbed her phone on and swiped to a blank notes page.

"She was eir childhood sweetheart," Johansson laughed. "As much of a sweetheart as ey would confess, at least. She knew 'em both. RJ and eir friend who got lost."

Carter nodded, jotting down quick notes. "She's still out there, then? Not lost?"

"I assume so, I guess. You'd know better than I."

She shook her head, looking down at her phone as she scribbled the last of the note. "Mm, no. No female furries. A lot of 'net addicts. I suppose there's no small crossover, but we're talking way deep. DDR junkies and layabouts."

Johansson bristled, "RJ was no layabout."

She held up her hands disarmingly, shook her head. "Mostly, is what I'm saying. They don't have ties, or if they do, they don't hold them long. These last few — the furries — they have lots of contacts from what we can tell. Strong ones. That's where our two groups disagree most. I think that we're seeing something novel, even if it doesn't hold for the previous cases. 'I' being the leader of the group that thinks there's the possibility of a transmission vector."

"And the others?"

"They see it as chance. Too small an *n*. Too few cases to say one way or another. They say that there was bound to be both connected and unconnected folks among the lost. They'd say that it's a matter of chance, since those who use the 'net more would be more likely to wind up lost, regardless of social situation. Furries just use it more than most."

"Both make sense, I guess," Johansson hedged. "All the same, you know I have a vested interest in RJ, so I'm going to wind up seeing it from your point of view, since you're working with em. Never mind that you invited me out here. What do you need from me?"

Carter frowned, thinking. "I guess I need to know more about em. I have eir redacted stats, a portion of the dump from eir workstation and the time leading up to it. I had been assuming we're getting all of it, but perhaps that was too generous of me. It's got PII redacted, but I don't know if there's anything else missing. What I need to know is what's slipping through the cracks. I need to know about who RJ was. How ey interacted with the theater, I mean. And anything you can tell me about eir friends."

"Should you...?"

"Should I have all of that information? I don't know." Carter sighed. "Is it against the law for you to tell me? No, not at all. I don't know. Maybe. Is it unethical to further my own agenda with this project by consulting you? Probably yes. If I were on a bigger, more mature project, we'd probably be interviewing you anyway, though."

Johansson frowned, nodded.

"But is it because I think that the more we know, the more likely we are to get RJ and the others back? I'd say yes."

Johansson looked down into his beer. Then, with a decisive motion, drank most of it in a few smooth gulps, holding up the glass with the remainder, an obvious toast. "To RJ, then."

Carter felt a little silly toasting to someone she'd never met, with a man she'd only just met, with a full glass of cider to his mostly empty ale. It all felt so dramatic, so theatrical, until she remembered who she was toasting with. She raised her glass and clinked its rim to Johansson's.

"To RJ."

AwDae — 2112

AwDae stood in the sunlight, blinking.

Ey felt weak. Not from hunger. Not from lack of sleep. Just worn out. Exhausted.

This was starting to feel like grinding. An endless drudge to level up. Busywork. Idle hands and tired eyes.

But then, you could quit a game. Here ey was, clues and riddles. And for what?

There was even a fog of war.

"So much bullshit." Ey laughed bitterly. No sense in keeping quiet.

Ey stripped down to eir underwear, hesitated, then stripped that off as well and shook eir fur out.

'Comfort' was the wrong word to use in regards a sim. It was a matter of sensory inputs that the system was set up to provide. The musty smell of the auditorium seats had been one thing, but ey was starting to get the impression that, given the way this sim was constructed, there would be rather more than less input. Eir tux was decidedly uncomfortable, not made for fox-people, and so eir fur was decidedly mussed.

Ey folded eir clothes and set them on the sidewalk in front of the school. The cool grass provided a welcome change from the indoor-outdoor carpet and tile inside, the roughness of the concrete out here.

"Alright. So. Problems." Ey plucked viciously at a few close-mown blades of grass and held them pinched between eir pawpads. "Cicero is lost. He was voting on a bunch of stuff as usual, leading the comment boards. He voted on something and it made it to the floor, but it doesn't show in the records." Ey plucked blades of grass with eir free paw, enumerating the facts. "No vote cost, no bounty, no comment."

Ey swished eir tail around to the side, hiked eir backside up enough to slip it beneath em, and rolled onto eir back. Blue sky. Cloudless. Too bright, even with the fog. Ey draped eir arm, fingers still clutching grass, over eir eyes. "And now I'm lost. I was working, and then I was here. Before working, I was digging into Cicero..."

Ey trailed off, spent a few moments thinking, then a few more just feeling the earth beneath em, the way the grass seemed to find a way through fur to tickle at em more directly.

"So had Sasha, though. And she was the one who got me the deck in the first place." Ey ran through the actions ey had taken on the deck. It was surprisingly easy to pull up the chain of events. *Or perhaps not,* ey thought. *Given the note.*

Eir first write to the deck had been on the note about the voting records. Prior to that, there was only the sorting and sharing of records. Filtering. Reading.

Ey lifted eir paw once more and stared at the torn blades of grass. Tossed them aside. "Ah, hell. I'm talking to myself."

Laughing, AwDae stood and gathered eir tux, heading back to the costume closet. Perhaps ey could find something that would fit em. Something to take into account that ey was more fox, less human.

Failing that, perhaps ey'd lay down again. Sleep, perchance to dream.

AwDae wound up in a simple, pleated skirt and a loose cotton shirt, gathered at the wrists.

The skirt fit well with a tail, certainly far better than eir trousers sagging beneath its base awkwardly. It was a robin's egg blue. Nice enough. Undecorated. Any detail would be lost on the audience anyway. Might as well save both cost and effort.

The shirt was made for someone with broader shoulders. RJ might have filled it out, but on the fox's slender frame, it was baggy and loose. Again, just a plain white, but ey could hardly complain. It didn't compress eir fur, unlike the tux shirt, with its pleats sewn down the front.

Ey gave consideration as to what to do with the tux. On the one paw — and here, thinking in paws already! So soon — it was just an artifact. Just bits. Everything was. Eir own body was. Had to be. Choosing clothes that were 'more comfortable' was only instructing the sim how best to treat eir body. Had to be. Clothes that were more comfortable were no different from clothes that weren't. It was just how the numbers added up. Just the math of simulated fashion. Had to be.

And yet, on the other, the tux was the only thing ey had...had what? Brought with from reality? It might just be a set of bits in eir exocortex, but it was *eir* set of bits and bytes.

Was it? Was there any point to the sense of ownership in so solipsisitic a world?

Something to tie em back to the world outside this sim.

A solution in between, then. Ey dug until ey found a rucksack that had probably gone with some war-themed production. Drab, dusty, made of thick canvas. It would do well to carry anything that would help, including the notes ey had made.

Ey laid eir tux out on the ratty sofa and rolled it into a tight cylinder. An empty sim would care little if eir tux got wrinkled, yes? Ey stuffed it down at the base of the pack and folded the notes into a small pocket on the side.

Thus equipped, ey padded back to the auditorium. Ey made sure the room was put to sleep, and, on a whim, grabbed the one live microphone ey'd found earlier. Ensuring that it was off to conserve batteries, ey added it to the notes. A small token of where ey'd come from.

"Not going to do much without the receiver or board," ey murmured. "Do the batteries even matter? This is all so fucking silly."

Ey tamped down despair, buttoned down the flap above the pocket. So many questions.

Should ey lay in rations? Food? Water bottles, perhaps? Ey dismissed the thought as even sillier. Ey didn't feel hungry or thirsty, even after so long in the school, so why worry? Obviously eir body had been taken care of. There was nothing ey could do about it from within the sim. All that food and water would do is make the sim tell eir body that the pack was heavier.

From there, ey made eir way back toward the front doors, pushing them open against the pressure differential. The breeze outside ruffled fur and skirt as ey stepped into sun once more.

The grey mist turned out to be a render distance.

Had it been a barrier, AwDae could have walked up to the fog, but no further.

Had it been a barrier, ey was sure ey would have screamed.

As it was, ey was able to follow the same street ey would've taken on the walk back to the home ey grew up in and the fog simply receded before em. Ey could never approach it. There was nothing to investigate. It was just a bubble into which ey had been placed. A bubble that moved along with em.

The act of walking away from the school, wearing a backpack and heading towards home, was a dredge pulling up the silt of memories. School across the Atlantic in the '90s. Plays and productions ey still had memorized. Sasha. Dandelions in summer.

Even now, pacing the street as a fox, not much had changed. Ey had carried eir tablet and few books to and from school in a pack not dissimilar than the one ey was wearing. Even the skirt was not far off from a thrift-store find ey might have worn at the time.

Ey prowled through memories of Sasha, of dating, of becoming better friends than partners. Ey thought back to her staying the night, back to their shared anxiety, back to the movies, back to eir mom checking in on them at one in the morning just to make sure everything was okay (and, bless, to make sure clothes had stayed on).

Ey missed Sasha most of all, now. Together, the two of them would've been able to keep spirits up. Sasha would've been able to figure out the problem with Cicero's voting record faster then ey had, and ey would've been less alone, would've felt less hopeless.

AwDae trudged on toward home, reaching a paw up to pluck a handful of leaves from one of the trees as ey passed, feeling the reluctant snap as they pulled loose from the branch. For all the sim's complexity, school in spring was pretty far remote from London in the winter.

School. America. Hopelessness. Stasis.

"You seem kind of frozen, kind of stuck, in a few ways."

Ioan Bălan — 2305

Ioan sat, startled, as Dear quit abruptly, leaving em sitting alone at the cafe table. There was a certain peculiarity to that fox's sense of humor, and while ey was slowly picking up on it, the occasional bafflement remained.

Ey took eir time finishing eir coffee, enjoying the view. A thoroughfare. Small crowds — some doubtless generated for effect. Enjoyed a moment's downtime before getting back into the puzzle at hand, then stood and straightened eir slacks.

Well, at least ey had more information to work with.

"Welcome back," #tracker said when ey arrived at home. "You have some mail."

Ey frowned, tugged the cream-colored envelope from the edge of the desk and turned it over in eir hands. Blank except eir signifier on the front, flap sealed on the back. Perhaps something about what ey'd been working on recently had piqued some interest on the reputation exchange. Another offer? And yet directly to this instance.

Making eir way out to the deck, ey popped the seal on the envelope, savoring the subtle tearing of the paper where the adhesive held fast. The paper was quite nice, the handwriting cramped and awkward, but legible in its green-tinged blue ink. Someone had put real effort into this.

Ioan

Dear has mentioned your aversion to sensorium messages, and I gather from your taste in clothing and our brief meeting that you have a certain aesthetic you enjoy. I hope that this scrap of note suits you well. The paper seemed up your alley, at least.

You'll have to forgive Dear. It really is stretched quite thin with its gallery show, and with the increased intraclade communication, it is feeling the pressure to keep forks to a minimum, as apparently there are no further names available. (It hasn't told the rest of the clade how many illicit forks it has. I suspect they all do.)

There is more to this that I think it is not sharing explicitly, but we've been together for a few years now, and I have my guesses. I think the intraclade attention is not precisely welcome. Having met some of its cocladists, I'm inclined to think that some more conservative types are being less than generous with their treatment of the subject at hand. Perhaps with their information as well.

All this to say that there is a reason for the fox acting the way it is. I will not apologize on Dear's behalf, it knows me better than that, but I hope an increase in transparency as to what all is going on in the family politic will help.

Visit soon.

Ioan smiled, re-folded the letter, and replaced it within its envelope. It joined the small pile ey kept.

Dear's partner had a good heart, and it was indeed a relief to learn that some of the fox's erratic behavior was attributable to stress. None of eir family had uploaded, and, by eir very nature, ey did not create eir own as the Odists had.

Ey did not envy it now.

The archive itself was a free-form database stored in the perisystem. It could hold essentially unlimited data in truly unlimited formats. Everything from text and structured data to full-sensorium recordings. Each blob of data was stored in a node, and nodes could be tagged and linked.

Unfashionable and difficult to work with, not to mention expensive to maintain, Ioan wasn't entirely clear why they had been added to the system. Exocortices had been around before the System itself. More personal, easier to interface with. Harder to share, granted.

Some remnant from its construction, perhaps?

Luckily, as an historian, ey had some experience working with them, even if that experience was decades old at this point. Ey pulled out a fresh sheet of foolscap and began to write, and by writing, interacted with the archive.

If archives were difficult to work with, this one doubly so. Nodes that weren't tagged, listed publicly, or linked to from other nodes were essentially inaccessible unless one had access to the index. Ey did not. That was something usually kept within an exocortex.

And here, few nodes were listed publicly, fewer still were linked to by others, and none were tagged. While traversing a well-pruned archive might still be akin to rifling through a card catalog to dig out books, this was no more than a file box stuffed full of loose papers.

Ioan's heart fell.

Of the nodes that were publicly listed, at least four were encrypted by something stronger than the original AES block. Ioan set those aside to knock against later. Another was a simple text blob with twenty-three blocks of five letters each. Further encryption? A different type? Ey could not guess which. Dear had mentioned one involving playing cards.

That left only three public nodes, one of which was an error. The other two...

Ioan's muscles went rigid. The first appeared to be a deleted blob of audiovisual data which referred to the second. A transcript of the conversation Ioan had had with Dear earlier that day.

They were being watched. Followed.

Ey read through the transcript once, then again, more thoroughly. There were a few notes made by this Qoheleth. They spoke of a familiarity that had only been hinted at with the previous letter. *Our Dear.* What did that mean?

Perhaps this individual was part of the clade itself?

Ioan frowned. The vehemence with which Dear — whom ey suspected was one of the more liberal of the Odists — had reacted when ey had asked about the author of the ode itself seemed to rule that out. If Dear, willing to bring on an amanuensis, was that protective, ey found it dubious that one of its cocladists was Qoheleth.

A friend, then? Mutual with the poet?

That was something ey would have to ask Dear about. Ey could speculate all ey wanted, but there was little ey could divine about that aspect.

The rest, then. Qoheleth seemed to be expecting that things were accelerating toward some sort of conclusion. *I may have less time than I had thought.*

And Ioan was being guided, somehow.

"How? Guide me how?" ey growled down at the paper. "It's all fucking encrypted."

#Tracker looked up, frowned.

Ioan#c1494bf shook eir head and apologized. Perhaps ey *should* take Dear up on the offer to stay with it and its partner.

AwDae — 2112

AwDae was unsurprised to find home unlocked.

Although the front door had always been locked when growing up, the fact that this whole sim seemed oriented around riddles meant of course ey'd be able to gain entry places ey knew. Clues, right?

Ey checked the other doors in the complex to test the hypothesis. All locked.

There was no bracing for the surge of emotion and memory as AwDae stepped into the entryway of eir old home. Cool tile. Tattered rug. Coat hooks where they were supposed to be.

No coats. The sense of desertion was overwhelming. And yet.

And yet, ey felt as though eir mom could be just around the corner in the kitchen, prowling through the fridge, her boyfriend laid out flat on the couch, snoozing in front of the TV running old science fiction shows. And yet ey knew — knew on some fundamental level — that the house was empty.

Perhaps it was that it was all too silent. Silent as school had been.

AwDae shrugged out of the rucksack and set it down in the entryway. It was precisely the space where rucksacks went. It was precisely the space where ey had set eirs countless times growing up. Ey did as ey had always done and Despite bracing emself for it, there was still padded into the common area, toenails clicking against the tile of the entryway, and then the hardwood floor. Floors which had never seen fox paws.

The sensation, that uncanny mix of *home* and *wrong*, quickly grew to overwhelming. The fox sat down on the rug in front of the coffee table. Eir spot. Eir spot, where ey had sat to eat dinner countless times. Eir spot, where ey watched TV, those old sci-fi movies, with eir mom's boyfriend.

It was one thing for the house to be so painfully empty and another entirely to be here as AwDae and not RJ. Perhaps ey could have held each of those concepts in eir mind independently were ey to only experience one at a time. The two combined were too much. Ey felt eir breath as short, shallow gasps. Ey felt eir vision constricting. Ey felt eir heart race no matter how still ey sat. Ey felt all these things happening to em with an increasing sense of detachment. Ey found it hard to concentrate on what ey was even supposed to be.

Is my pulse elevated offline, wherever that is?

Ey let out a strangled laugh. Perhaps there existed in that space some doctor's befuddled stare at the sudden signs of anxiety showing in their patient.

The laugh turned to sob, stopped quickly.

AwDae leaned forward, stretching eir legs out behind em. Ey laid flat on eir floor, on eir oh-so-familiar rug, bafflingly present in eir bafflingly present home. Laid flat, then rolled over onto eir side. Eir tail lay limp against the short pile of the rug behind em.

How did this happen? What did I do? Why here? Why me? What did I do to deserve this?

Eir mind was awhirl with words. With questions, and only questions. Ey didn't have answers. No answers inside, none before em, none in the house. Answers were a thing that did not– could not exist here. Answers a thing that happened to other people.

"Why ask questions when the answers will not help?"

Ey did not have the mental bandwidth required to do anything other than watch questions swirl. Ey was at a loss for images in this end of days. Ey was an observer. Nothing more than a set of eyes with no will, no drive. No urge to move those eyes as ey watched all of the emotion that had been held at bay, held back with the sense of *doing something* over the last day and change. All that emotion surge.

Eir actions had been all wrong. Ey had accepted getting lost with resignation. Ey had leapt at the chance to solve the 'puzzle' of the microphone with something akin to excitement. Ey had found a new set of clothes with a casualness befitting a trip to the thrift store. All this when ey should have been experiencing terror. Doing all these things when ey should have been breaking down into sobs at the fact that ey had been struck with some sort of incurable...what? Incurable disease? Ey was lost.

AwDae noted with increasing dissociation that eir breath was coming in great, choking sobs. Eir perspective, that core of emself that spent life reviewing actions and reactions, watched with cool distance as eir body shook with gasps and tears streaked down over eir cheeks and muzzle, leaving tracks in the short fur. Whatever part of emself was in charge of releasing those pent up emotions had been divorced from the part of emself responsible for actually feeling them. *See? **This** is happening now.*

It's the emptiness, that part of em thought. *This place was home, and the knowledge of being permanently removed from such a thing, from anything home-shaped or any sense of belonging, has led to this. There's no one here, and no one at school.*

"No ranks of angels will answer to dreamers."

Words unbidden were calming. The heaving gasps for air began to slow, and ey wiped eir tears away in a smooth, slicking motion that flattened eir tall ears against eir head.

Struggling to bring those two parts of emself into alignment once more, AwDae levered emself up heavily. Ey leaned on one paw while the other straightened the fur of eir face, brushing the last aftershocks of that not-quite-sadness away in a careful, calculated gesture. Intentional. A setting-aside of emotion.

Perhaps eir initial reaction had been wrong on the emotional side, but correct on the intellectual. Ey would have to at least figure out why. There would be no sharing it, no telling others, no end game other than the knowledge of a task complete.

It was just the only thing left here in this null space that had any meaning.

Dr. Carter Ramirez — 2112

Carter dreamed of shadows.

And through it all, there was the river: the muddy, sometimes stinking river. The Thames which only seemed to engender affection that one might call 'grudging'. When she had first moved to London, it had been her guide. The Thames was always vaguely downhill, the slope her Y-axis. And on the X-axis, the bridges. Tower, London, Southwark, Millenium II, Blackfriars Rail, Blackfriars Memorial. Tick marks along a waterline.

And in her dream, she walked aimlessly along the south bank. The constant renovation of the area had led not to one great revival, but countless smaller ones. Buildings were torn down and raised back up, plots of land chopped into ever smaller portions. Those same buildings growing higher, never quite managing to match.

Strode past towers, squat pubs. Some old, some new. Mostly new.

Strode past people and crowds, buskers and food carts.

Strode beneath bridges, along railings, past tour boats gliding silently along the surface of the water.

And she passed shadows.

And the shadows were like the people of the crowds. A little taller perhaps, but still just like the people. It was as though someone had cut a person-shaped hole out of space, blurred the edges, vignetted, pinched the light.

And it wasn't through prolonged observation, she was just suddenly aware of the fact that the shadows were all behaving in the same way. Always following one of the people. Same pace. Same gait. Somehow more sinister for that exactitude. Always following just one person, never changing, never looking around at anyone else.

And no one else seemed to see or notice these shadows except her.

And she started tailing one of the shadows. Quietly. Unobtrusively. Followed it following a young black woman pushing a pram. Another young child walking at her side. His hand curled loosely in the fabric of her pants. Constantly in touch.

And Carter struggled to keep up. The harder she tried to keep pace, the slower she seemed to go.

And she tried to call out.

And her voice came out only as a whisper.

And the shadow reached out it's hand.

And the shadow's fingers slid through the woman's hair reaching for the base of her scalp.

And Carter screamed, inaudible.

The dream dogged Carter through her morning routine and into her commute. She kept thinking, if she'd just been able to keep quiet, maybe she could have seen what would've happened when that young mother was touched by the shadow. Some sort of metaphor for getting lost? Or was her sleeping mind just carrying too much work-burden into the night?

She was only able to dispel the lingering sense of too much meaning when she got into work and checked her email for news. No additional cases added to the research load. She realized she half expected a new one. Young, female, black, mother.

Just a dream, then.

After checking her mail on the rig's screen, Carter stood and stretched, making her way blearily to the coffee corner. She was one of the first in that morning. Just Avery and a few other early risers. Thankfully, Avery was the type to leave the coffee pot full rather than empty.

She doctored her coffee to her specifications and ambled back to her desk, setting the mug down on the smooth surface. She spent a few minutes scrolling aimlessly through her mail list. She didn't dive in just yet, despite the workload that she knew waited. The fog of the dream had been burned away, but there were still too many thoughts that needed organizing. Couldn't yet go through the process of setting up her workspace and ordering stacks of cards.

No, she corrected herself. She was *wary* of diving in.

She had things she needed to do in the sim. She had things that the sim would help her do quickly. She wanted to start a stack for this Sasha that Johansson had brought up. Wanted to find a way to start making and notating all of those connections.

Working in sim was part of her job, as it was for so many others. She had gone into this research project knowing that it was only in sims that people got lost. It had never bothered her before.

And yet here she was, waffling about whether or not she felt safe delving in to do her work.

She sighed, sipped her coffee, shook her head. Then set her hands in the cradles and rested her head against the headrest. Nothing for it.

Within her spare, black space, Carter prowled through the stacks she had started on this little side project. Invisible to others, she created a private stack within the string-delineated area, next to the pendant "Possible acquaintances" card. Private cards showed up with a subtle blue tinge to her, and would only appear on her view of the workspace.

On the first card in the stack, she transferred over the notes she had taken with Johansson. Then she started another card labeled "Sasha?" and added it to the stack.

The whole stack was looped up to RJ's card with a piece of cotton string. Others would be able to see that she had created the stack with the string trailing off to a faint outline of a deck, or a grayed out pack of cards, or however their view of the sim chose to represent the data.

Strictly speaking, she shouldn't be doing this. Such cards were intended to be for short notes to oneself about what one was working on, not for actual investigative work. This was something new. She wasn't supposed to have this information.

Carter stepped back to look at the whole cordoned off section of data. She frowned. Never mind the information, was she even supposed to be doing investigative work? She was supposed to be utilizing the data that the hospitals and the university provided her with, not running out into the field and talking with acquaintances of the lost over pints after a show.

Sanders would have a fit if he knew what she was up to.

Even so, she wasn't quite sure it was only that which drove her to make the stack private. Some hunch. Some shadow lurking behind her.

She needed to be more subtle about this than she had been.

Ioan Bălan — 2305

The grin and sense of pride with which Dear had greeted em with did not last.

"Thanks again for the offer of space," Ioan repeated. "I know I was driving #tracker nuts. I guess I talk to myself."

Silence. Awkward.

"Of course." Dear's partner picked up when the fox did not reply. "You can stay as long as you'd like. It's no trouble. You could probably scream bloody murder over there and we wouldn't hear."

"I'll try not to, all the same."

Dear's partner grinned. Dear merely nodded.

"Hey fox, I'm going to get some writing done. Why don't you show Ioan the gallery?"

"Right, yes, of course!" Dear straightened up, invigorated at having something to do. Something to declaim about. *"How much art history do you know?"*

Ioan stood to follow Dear as it padded from the living room back to the front of the house where the gallery was situated. "I studied photography and imaging quite a bit before uploading. Film, too."

"Let me guess: documentaries?"

"Of course."

"You seem like the type, yes. An historian searches for stories in the

past." True to eir guess, Dear was now smiling more easily. It gestured to a painting on the wall. *"All artists search. I search for stories, in this post-self age. What happens when you can no longer call yourself an individual, when you have split your sense of self among several instances? How do you react? Do you withdraw into yourself, become a hermit? Do you expand until you lose all sense of identity? Do you fragment? Do you go about it deliberately, or do you let nature and chance take their course?"*

The speech felt rehearsed, all those questions. A lecture? It hooked Ioan all the same. "I suppose that is what an instance artist is, then? Finding the stories inherent in forking."

"Yes. Forking is instantaneous, or might as well be, and yet in that instant, a story is told. There is a question implied to which the answer is 'I must create a copy of myself'. Is it to accomplish a task, like you have done? Is it to sequester some emotion unable to be contained by one mind?" Dear forked, another instance of it standing to the other side of Ioan. *"Perhaps it is to prove a point."*

Ioan jumped at the sudden duplication. Both foxes grinned. The original Dear quit. "Who is the audience for this story, then?"

The fox laughed. *"Fuck if I know. The universe? That is not my job."*

"I mean, you've got your exhibitions. Don't you have an audience there?"

"Those who attend the exhibitions do get to watch and participate, yes. But are they truly the audience? If they are reacting to my work, and I am immediately reacting in turn, does that not make them part of the story, instead?"

Ioan shrugged. "I suppose so. It seems a bit like a distinction without a difference."

Dear made a graceful setting-aside gesture, as though the statement was in some way irrelevant. *"All this to say that, for all of my fancy* shenanigans, I still see the stories in the art around me. This painting — a replica from way back when — tells a story with the image it shows, yes, but also with its construction. The paint is applied with a palette knife in thick globs, see? It looks haphazard, but it is not. It is very carefully done. The story is the artist's choice in tools, in technique, as well as in the subject of the painting."

The painting itself showed a riot of colors. Abstract, and yet hinting at some cyclonic force. Blue on green. Splotches of purple, of red. The paint shone under the lights.

Ioan and Dear stood in front of the painting a minute longer, each thinking their thoughts. The fox, with its paws clasped behind its back, looked to be trying to puzzle out the order in which the gobs of paint had been applied to canvas.

Ioan found emself wondering what this cyclonic force was reaching towards. What it was destroying.

It was Ioan who broke the silence. "Why are you upset, Dear?"

The fox wilted. *"That obvious?"*

Ey nodded.

"Right. It is the clade."

"A disagreement?"

"Of sorts. A silent one, or one on a very base level. I believe there is a story here. There is something going on that is worth researching and learning about and getting to the bottom of."

"And others don't?"

Dear shrugged. *"I am perhaps in a minority, on this subject. I think that there is a story, and there are a few others who see it my way. Most of my stanza does. But much of the clade is concerned only about the Name."*

Stepping over to the next picture, Ioan formulated their response, but was preempted by the fox.

"*It is not that I am not. I am, in my own way. But these puzzles...*" It trailed off.

"Are they the story?" Ioan frowned, backtracked. "You think there's a reason you're being led down the path. The puzzles are part of the story, but they are, as you put it, the answer to the question that necessitated their creation."

Ears perked, grin returned. "*Yes. Puzzles are puzzles and sometimes worth solving in their own right. I want to know why, though. Why say the Name, yes, but why build up tension like this?*"

The painting: a landscape, perhaps the prairie just outside. A cloud-dotted sky, nigh photorealistic. And in the middle, a black square.

Not just black paint, but a black that seemed to eat light. A black the hurt to look at. It made Ioan uncomfortable.

"I think I see why you approached me," ey said. "You are interested in the story, and want someone who lives and breathes stories."

That grin widened, and was joined by a swish of a tail. "*Precisely that. There is art to be had here. It is stressful and, if my suspicions are correct, it bears a message beyond just...what, a jape? A jab at the clade? There is a point to be made here.*"

"The amount that you seem to differ from the rest of your clade is surprising. Are there no other artists?"

"*Oh, we are all artists of a sort. Actors, mostly. A few sim designers. One of the other stanzas' lines painted this,*" it said, nodding to that unnerving black square. "*But yes, we are all quite different. Perhaps you will see some day.*"

Ioan nodded.

Dear's grin had faded to some expression more thoughtful.

Thankfully, not as glum. When it spoke, its voice came from some place remote, from some emotion happening elsewhere, to someone else. *"Artists, yes, but increasingly few storytellers."*

AwDae — 2112

"You seem kind of frozen, kind of stuck, in a few ways."

Sasha's words, that night in The Crown Pub, pressed in against AwDae. Pushed thoughts out of the way. Blanketed eir mind.

Ey lingered around the house for a few hours, laying on the floor, poking around in various rooms. All as empty and static as school had been. Eventually, ey paced back outside and across the road to the countless acres of federation-managed open space that abutted the foothills. Ey walked a few of the trails and deer tracks, mind spinning helplessly through numb hopelessness.

There was no birdsong, and while ey occasionally heard the buzz and chirp of insects, ey never saw any.

Ey gave up and returned home. Ey wasn't tired by the time the sun went down, but for lack of volition, bundled up all the same in what had been eir old bed and slept.

Having gone to bed so early, AwDae awoke before sunrise. Eir alarm clock, still familiar after so long away from this house, told them it was just past four in the morning. *I made it past the witching hour,* the fox thought, then laughed. Something about the idea of time in such a timeless space tickled and upset em all at once. Time! What a concept.

Despite the dark, ey decided on another attempt at exploration. Fog be damned.

Ey slipped out of the house and wandered around the neighborhood. Curling streets. Cul-de-sacs. Rows of townhouses. Familiar, all. Ey even made it back down to the school on the hill, searching for unexpected lights left on in the middle of night.

The results were negative, unless one counted streetlights in this empty world. All the houses' and the school's windows were dark.

Ey trudged back up the hill toward home and shut out the darkness. The kitchen light brought little warmth, so ey turned it back off and waited for sunrise.

With the fog limiting render distance, sunrise took the form of a slow brightening, almost imperceptible at first. The world around home lifted through greyscale into brilliant color, settling on a teeth-aching azure.

During eir teens, ey frequently messed up eir sleep schedule enough to see the sun rise. Some days, ey would go down to the school for a run around the track before heading back up to the house again, sweating and invigorated. Or at least tired in a different way.

This whole sim seemed designed to, as Sasha had put it, keep em frozen in the past. The act of watching the world brighten and...well, not come to life, but at least gain color tugged at memories of countless days. Of waiting for eir mom to wake and make coffee.

Coffee.

AwDae padded back to the kitchen, claws clicking on the hardwood beneath eir feet.

Prowling through the cabinets revealed startlingly little. The fridge was bare, as well. No food. No dishes, either. On testing, the faucet didn't produce any water.

"What the hell..."

It didn't make any sense. The whole world was rendered in such loving detail. Why not include things one would expect to be in a house? Lesser sims had running water. Perhaps it was due to the limitations of the sim being run from eir implants? Though ey still doubted that the implants would be able to run something so complex in the first place. Scent, taste, and texture were all available to em — notoriously expensive to implement — so why no food? Why no coffee?

"All I want is something real," AwDae growled. Fists parked on the counter in front of the sink, ey pressed firmly against the Formica. Tears stung eir eyes and, sagging, ey slowly sunk down to the cool hardwood floor. "That's all I want."

The sulk lasted a good half hour, with the fox crying off and on. It brought less catharsis than ey hoped. By the time ey levered emself back up onto eir feet, eir backside was numb and tail struck by pins and needles, somehow more real than it had ever felt before.

No coffee. No water. No catharsis.

Tail hanging limp beneath eir stolen skirt, ey slouched back upstairs to eir room and climbed back onto the bed, laying on eir front, muzzle facing away from the windows and the taunting of the morning. In toward the closet, toward stasis and familiarity.

Ey ticked off the list of people in eir life who would be thinking of em. Some hopeful connection.

Johansson was almost certainly stressing out, doubtless stressing the rest of the Troupe in turn. His response to unknown situations was to try and make them into known situations. Put all that nervous energy to work, get things into a state where he could understand them again. Even with another tech handling sound, even if that had gone well, the boss would be jumpy and on edge.

Caitlin and Sarai would be missing em on a more personal level. AwDae was friendly with the entire company, of course, but it was those two ey had gotten closest to. Sharing that back-channel communication, that private space of the theater sim. Sharing conversation that went beyond the Troupe, beyond theater. If anyone had able to reach eir friends outside of STT, it would be them.

And of eir friends, Sasha was always at the front of the fox's mind. She was the one person, excepting eir parents, who had been in eir life the longest. She was the one who understood em best, even surpassing eir family. Sasha had to be worried, even with em having been gone for so short a time. She had to be looking for em. The skunk was even listed as eir emergency contact.

Or perhaps, ey thought wryly. *I simply want that to be the case.*

Eir parents, always loving but always distant, would be concerned. Ey knew their tendency to freeze up when confronted with the unknown, though. Mom was the type who might sit by eir hospital bed and hold eir hand, as mothers do, but not necessarily the type of person to take action, to do any digging into 'what's and 'why's. Dad would simply be glued in place, unable to deal with any emotions surrounding the event.

Ey turned eir face to rub it against the pillow, leaving the pillowcase damp from tears. Then grumbled and sat up once again. Scrubbed at eir cheeks. Bristled eir whiskers. Reengaged with physicality.

Eyes settled on eir bookshelf. Ey pulled down the most weathered book ey could find. Some bit of sci-fi ey had read countless times.

The fox flopped back onto the bed and flipped open to a random page, then frowned. Ey blinked several times, squinted over to the window and back to the page, trying to focus.

The words swam across the page. Would not stay pinned in place. Would not form sentences, nor even phrases.

Ey flipped to the first page. The swimming effect slowed, coalesced into legibility.

The effect was unnerving. As ey read, words would slip slowly into order, into focus — though the world around em remained static and sharp — and with every flipped page, it would take a moment before ey could move on.

And this wasn't the book ey remembered.

Eir frown deepened. The story was there, familiar, but the text read more like a retelling. An admittedly quite detailed one, but a retelling all the same. An imperfect memory. It used words AwDae would've used, rather than those the author might have chosen.

Setting that book aside, ey pulled another down. The effect repeated itself. Stronger, this time. Ey had a hard time getting the words to settle on the pages, even starting from the beginning. Brow furrowed, ey tried with a few more books.

One ey hadn't read yet — tsundoku, perhaps, books one always means to read but never gets around to — was an unintelligible jumble of letters. No, not just letters, but marks that hinted at the idea of what it meant to be a letter. Mere shapes.

"Well, huh."

Still frowning, the fox sat on the edge of eir bed and picked up the original book, thumbing through pages and watching the effect distractedly. Words jumped out. Occasionally a phrase would form, but nothing exact. It was as though the book was deciding what to become from moment to moment based on where ey inserted their claw when flipping through it.

Ey hopped to eir feet, skittered back down the stairs to the pack ey had brought from the school, and fished out the scraps of notes. The scrap, the piece of paper with Cicero's DDR votes on it. No swirling, disjointed effect affected this text.

An hour's exploration later, ey had puzzled out what might be going on.

Of course AwDae's exocortex wouldn't have the complete text of the dozens of books on eir shelf. How could it? Ey had only ever read them as hard copies, never through any software mediated by the implants. Never on a screen of any kind. So of course ey wouldn't be able to read the books here in the sim, if that sim was confined to eir implants.

And ey was increasingly starting to doubt that the sim *was* bound to eir exo, or any of eir implants.

A midday walk through the open space netted em a hypothesis. A shaky one, but something more plausible than what information ey had been working with.

There likely was some information stored in eir implants. Some few dozen terabytes, maybe. Enough to store a good chunk of data, but not necessarily an entire sim. Certainly not one this big.

Maybe it was that the implants themselves didn't store the sim, or not all of it, but acted as a framework? Maybe AwDae's brain provided all of the information needed to show em a sim, and all the implants did was turn it into an experience. Maybe the implants were a mirror, reflecting memories, recollections, hints and dreams.

That would be why the text of the books was jumbled, and when it wasn't jumbled, it was wrong. It was just eir recollection of the book being mirrored back at em in a way that was tangible. Tangible as much as anything was in this place.

That would explain why ey had been able to smell the seats of the auditorium, too. It was a scent that must've been permanently ingrained in eir memories.

And yet, this was an imperfect sim, based as it was on memories. The school with its countless hours of memory invested in it, had plenty of detail, as did eir home. Yet AwDae was willing to bet that, were ey to go into another house on the block, ey wouldn't find anything. Or perhaps ey wouldn't be allowed in at all. All those locked doors on that first day's explorations. Ey would have no memory of the inside, so why would the minimal system of implants-mirroring-memories be willing to show em anything?

Strange ramifications, here. This meant that eir implants were still acting as implants, but rather than taking signals from eir rig, the 'net, and eir mind, they were only taking in information from eir mind. That meant that everything was still up and running as though ey was delved into the 'net.

Which was absurd, of course. There was no way for the inter-ferites to run without power, without data coming from the NFC pads on eir forehead or the contacts on eir fingers. Ey had been pulled back. Ey had felt that rending, that spike of pain. There was no possible sequence of events that led to this conclusion.

Was there?

Perhaps getting lost was as simple as layer after layer of redundant fail-safes failing in turn, implants remaining on even after contact was lost with the rig.

AwDae sat on the fence bordering the open space, watching the color of the light duck down through golden and into salmon. Ey realized ey would need to be more deliberate in eir search. If ey was limited to places ey had memories of, ey would have to remember just which places those were.

Ioan Bălan — 2305

Ioan sat back and rubbed eir eyes. Time had gone all funny with all this research.

As with so many of eir previous projects, ey had fallen into a state of free-running sleep and single-minded focus. Ey would work for a few hours, suddenly get impossibly tired, nap for what felt like fifteen minutes, and wake up three hours later. Then ey'd work for twenty hours straight, neglecting to eat.

Ey had researched it at one point and entertained the idea that it might be part of some larger sleep disorder, or an perhaps attention disorder, something grander. Ey had put it off as just one of eir many neuroses.

Less than healthy.

There were never any complaints about the quality or quantity of work ey got done while free-running. Ey didn't slip up or stumble. Didn't make any more mistakes than when ey stuck to a schedule. Made fewer, perhaps. And being methodical got one quite far as a historian and writer. Ey would write the same quality work at the beginning, middle, and end of eir waking periods.

What it did *not* do, however, was endear oneself to one's house-mates. Ioan#tracker quickly grew frustrated with eir own forks, whether or not they used a cone of silence, so ey knew the feeling intimately. It was implicit that ey would, as a fork. It was always a problem when multiple Bălan instances stayed in the same house while on separate projects, each on a separate schedule, and ey was nothing if not a Bălan.

Here, at least, ey'd been lucky enough to be invited by eir...client? Patron? Had been invited by Dear to stay at its place.

So that's how ey found emself rubbing eir eyes in front of a simple, if painfully modern, desk in a studio apartment attached to eir...employer's? Friend's? Eir friend's equally modern house.

The studio apartment really was a studio, too: someone — perhaps the other Odist Dear had mentioned — had used it for painting. Rightfully so: the exterior wall was floor to ceiling glass looking out over that sere prairie. The landscape, Dear's partner had explained, was the work of Dear's cocladist, Serene; Sustained And Sustaining, 'born' when their down-tree instance, Dear The Wheat And Rye Under The Stars had forked to explore her twinned interests of forming oneself and of forming one's surroundings in ever greater detail.

Ioan's head spun whenever ey thought about the clade, but the longer ey spent around Dear, the more ey found emself liking it. Ey was curious to get to meet another Odist.

If it weren't for the window-wall, opaquable, the apartment would have felt like a cell. Simple cot. Desk. The kitchenette the one concession to freedom. The walls were whitewashed concrete. The floor that same pale hardwood. The fixtures all brushed steel. No doors to the rest of the house, nor anywhere but outside. No restroom. One was expected to either turn off elimination or do so outside.

There's a cheap joke to be made there, ey had thought on first moving in. *Dear lifting its leg against some tree. But I doubt its body ever had that functionality enabled.*

Ioan shook eir head and rubbed at the rest of eir face. Ey was daydreaming — eveningdreaming? — and that made em wonder how long ey had been awake.

"Probably some horrid number of hours," ey mumbled to the wall.

A sensorium ping; a gentle impinging of Dear upon eir senses. Half-sensed words: *"Does the wall reply often?"*

Ioan spun around. Dear was standing, prim and dapper as always, at the door through the glass, paws clasped before it.

"You scared the hell out of me!"

Dear's serene smile widened into a grin. *"Sorry, Ioan. I will wait until after the wall responds, next time."*

"Jackass."

"Foxass," Dear corrected, accenting the word with an exaggerated swish of its tail. *"Have some news. Walk with me?"*

Ioan nodded and stood. "Glad to. I'm hitting a wall, here."

The fennec adopted a look of concern. *"Do not hit your friends, Ioan."*

"Ha ha." Ioan rolled eir eyes. "Something's got you in a state today. Tonight. Whatever."

"Tonight." Dear's smile softened and it beckoned out toward the prairie. *"Come, walk. Storm scheduled in an hour, let us catch all of the nice smells."*

Sasha — 2112

Sasha clutched at the arms of her chair, fingernails digging into the foam of the armrests, promised herself she'd stay put.

Then stood up anyway.

That her relationship with RJ was as casual as it was was working against her. She knew ey was in the UK, in London, and that they worked at a theater, but for the most part, they talked about other things. Shared things, not work. Or, if work, theater in general. They talked about Cicero and Debarre. They talked about The Crown Pub. They talked about their past and their shared world, their syncosm. RJ rarely got too far into the present and the embodied world, eir exocosm.

So she had been at something of an impasse, then, with no way to figure out just what had happened to lead to eir disappearance. There were rumors abound in the Crown Pub that ey was lost, just like Cicero.

She would have to admit that she had been the source of more than a few of them, given the notification from the hospital she had received — that ey had put her down as an emergency contact was touching in a way she could not quite articulate — stating that ey had been admitted, but that, no, unless she were to arrive in person for biometrics, they would not be able to tell her what had happened.

No chance of that. Production eason was the same in American schools as it was in Soho theaters across the Atlantic.

The thing that plagued her with doubts was the sheer improbability of such a thing. Ey had joined them on their own private investigation into Cicero. Had that been it? But here she was; and Debarre was, as far as she knew, still alright. Even then, how could it be that thinking about, talking about, working with data related to the lost would lead to one getting lost themselves? Wouldn't the researchers on the case be all the more susceptible?

Perhaps it was something about the data?

Still a dead end, she thought. *We have the same data ey had. There's four or five of us with ACLs on the deck.*

And perhaps ey wasn't lost at all. There had been the show, of course. And while RJ had never disappeared during performances before, ey had certainly been quieter during her timezone. But with the message from the hospital, the only potential there was that there had been some sort of accident at the theater.

She was embarrassed at how long it had taken her to think about simply searching eir name. She still knew that from school, after all. Doubtful that searching 'AwDae', nor even simply 'RJ', would turn up any medical reports.

So it was that Sasha wound up reading the same article that Carter had found a few days earlier. It confirmed all her worst suspicions.

She sent Debarre the link first, the subject line simply the emoticon : /. Distressed as she was, she deleted the auto-corrected emoji and replaced it with the plain-text emoticon, feeling, somehow, that that better represented her anxiety. She considered passing the article around further, but thought better of it. It pulled too hard at her heart. It had left her in tears when she first found it. Their relationship, brief as it was, had been one of the happiest of the lot she had been through. There was no ire in the way they had drifted from 'item' back to simply friends.

The one upshot to finding the article had been the name of the group that RJ worked for.

And thus Sasha: pacing back and forth in front of her desk, trying to work up the courage to hit send on the email she had drafted.

She had considered mailing the director of the troupe, Bernhard Johansson, but had decided against it, figuring that the man had far more on his plate running a play. Too much to bother responding to a request such as hers. Ditto this Sarai Coen, listed as stage manager. If the play was still running, both would be swamped.

She had settled instead on a Caitlin Wells, listed as working lights for the stage. Given all that RJ had told her about working as a tech, she would likely be both the closest to em and one of the least busy outside of work. If there were such a thing, that is. Sasha had been an actor, not a tech, and had no clue how busy those nights and days between performances were for the tech side.

She was just thankful that email addresses had been listed for the cast members. Not the crew, but given the pattern of *firstname.lastname@sttroupe.co.gb.wf*, she was hoping Caitlin's would follow suit.

Caitlin Wells,

I apologize for writing to you out of the blue, but I am a friend of RJ Brewster who works with the Soho Theatre Troupe, and I was wondering if you would be able to provide me with a bit more information about em. I am a friend from school and remember em working with theater there, and talked with em daily on a sim online.

I know this is a long shot. I hope this reaches you, and I hope that you are well, all things considered. If you get a chance to send me a note, I would greatly appreciate it. Both email and meeting in a sim would be fine.

Best.

Sasha

Sasha had deliberated over the two paragraphs for an hour and a half, deleting and correcting. How much should she ask for? Should she reveal where they interacted? How should she start the letter, and how should she finish it? Hell, how should she address herself? Her real name wasn't Sasha, though she thought of herself that way as often as not. She figured that, should they actually meet up in a sim somewhere, that would be the name that this Caitlin would get.

She ran quickly to her terminal and hit 'send' before she second-guessed herself any further, and then...

Oh, shit.

Now she realized her mistake. Realized that, if they *did* meet up in a sim, Caitlin would be meeting up with skunk-her, rather than something more like her in the offline world. Perhaps she had a human av stashed away somewhere. She could buy one off the shelf quickly. It was seven thirty in the British Isles, she might have time before Caitlin woke up.

No luck. A scant two minutes of Sasha fretting at her keyboard passed before a ping alerted her to a new message.

OMG OMG we were hoping one of RJ's friends would contact us. We only know so much. Your sim or mine? Meet you in five. C.

Far too little time to switch out an av for something a bit more...presentable? A bit more human?

Sasha groaned.

Nothing for it. She set her hands on the cradles and leaning into the headband of her workstation. Once in, she pulled up her in-sim mail and spoke quickly.

Caitlin,

Either is fine. Should warn you that I know RJ through furry, and may look weird. My address is @Sasha:of-all-stripes.fur#home in case you want to meet here, or we can meet publicly.

Sasha

The reply came in a matter of seconds, half a minute tops.

Sasha. Crown Pub? In case you want to tell others. That's what RJ always talked to me about. We know about furry. C.

The relief was palpable, if incomplete. It would certainly be strange to actually interact with one of the tourists that drifted through that sim. She tapped one of the pre-written replies — "Sure, see you there!" — on her client, hoping that this would portray the appropriate levels of urgency that Caitlin seemed to share, then dashed to her tport pad and swiped left, quickly selecting the top, most-visited option.

Caitlin was already there.

Sasha wasn't sure whether to be surprised or not that the woman had a custom avatar. She was evidently a fan of the past, with hair swept neatly to the side to reveal an undercut. She wore a long, sleeveless tunic emblazoned with the word *heh.*, running to mid thigh covering only leggings. Something from late the previous century.

Sasha felt strangely plain in her simple skunk av. Baggy shirt and fisherman's pants, fashionable enough by today's standards, did not stand up against London chic.

"Caitlin?" she said, voice raised.

The human waved energetically and ducked through the crowd. "Sasha, right? There a place we can talk? Anyone else you want to bring along?"

Sasha did a quick scan of the room, picking out Debarre sulking at the end of the bar. She jogged over and tapped him on the shoulder. "Someone who knows AwDae is here, want to join?"

The weasel perked at that, frowned, nodded. "Uh, sure. Do they know about Cice?"

"I don't know, but they might. They only said they know about AwDae, and that ey had talked to them about this place."

Debarre shrugged and slipped off of his stool, following after Sasha. "Better than nothing," he grumbled, nodding to Caitlin on his way to one of the empty booths.

The three settled onto the overstuffed seats. There was a moment of silence before all three started talking at once, followed by another silence, then nervous laughter. Sasha gestured to Caitlin.

"RJ's lost. It happened during a rehearsal." She frowned, tapping a finger at the scarred table between them. "Should back up, though.

How much do you know?"

"We read an article about em. Something from a tabloid. It just mentioned the Troupe, which is how I found you."

Caitlin nodded, frowned, then offered her hand to Debarre. The weasel shook it cautiously. "Sorry, I should introduce myself. I'm Caitlin, the lights tech for STT. I was there when...when it happened."

"Debarre," Debarre said, gruff. "Boyfriend's lost, too. Aw-Dae...uh, RJ, Sasha, and I were trying to figure out what happened."

Fumbling some cards out of her pocket and duplicating them, Sasha added, "We were exchanging a deck on Cicero, Debarre's partner. You don't have to do anything with them, but you might as well have a copy, too. And, hold on." The skunk swiped, tapped through menus, created a new card titled 'RJ lost', duplicated it twice. She handed one each to Debarre and Caitlin. "One for RJ as well."

Caitlin swiped up on the card, tapped the voice-record button, and began speaking. "Alright, so here's what I know. RJ was working sound that night, last night of rehearsals, and started having trouble about halfway through. Ey went quiet on the mic, and then missed a cue or two before we noticed what was going on. We called a halt to the rehearsal and found em unresponsive at eir rig. We pulled em back and hit the panic button and...and nothing. Ey was gone. Even out of the rig, eir implants showed ey was still inside.

"The cops and paramedics had a protocol for the whole thing, I guess. Ey was taken off to the hospital. It all happened so fast. Johansson — that's the director — met up with a woman from the university who said she was studying the lost and had a talk with her. She said she had gotten information on em, but wanted more, so they talked for a bit. Her name was–" Caitlin frowned and thought for a moment, then tapped the growing deck to add another card. "Carter Ramirez. Oh, you've already got one in here. Remembered it was Spanish or something. RJ mentioned your name, which is why I was so eager to meet up."

Sasha sat up straighter. "My name?"

"Yeah. Ey talked about you quite a lot. Hell, ey mentioned Cicero."

At this, Debarre looked so intently at Caitlin that she quailed under his gaze.

"Just that he was lost, I'm sorry. I don't know much beyond that."

The weasel's shoulders slumped, and he nodded.

"There's a lot of downtime, working tech. We all chat and...hey, why did you contact me, anyway?"

"I figured you'd be the least busy, other than maybe stage hands. Plus, RJ said lights techs were always cool."

Caitlin laughed, brushing her hair back. The motion seemed automatic, as her av's hair had hardly budged. "It's true. Anyway, we talked. I don't actually know what more to tell you beyond that. The rest of our relationship was work. RJ was super focused on that, and didn't really chill with the rest of us when ey wasn't working. I mean, we liked em and ey liked us, but ey was rarely a hundred percent there, you know? Ey had a cat, I know that."

"Priscilla, yeah."

Caitlin shrugged. "Sure, I guess. Eir landlord is taking care of it. I was hoping you could tell me more, actually."

Sasha recounted much of her and RJ's history. All the way back to their relationship, back through school. School productions, school summers, sleepovers and movies and all the trappings of being a kid.

By the end, she was crying freely.

"I didn't know, I'm sorry. RJ never talked about relationships."

"I think I was eir only one." Sasha sniffled. "There weren't any others that I knew about, at least. Ey was kinda, uh...aromantic, I guess."

Caitlin nodded. "That tallies. Listen, I gotta get going, though. I ran at this without really thinking, and your email ping woke me up. I don't know if I can, but I should try sleeping more before the show tonight."

"No problem," Sasha and Debarre said in unison. They laughed, though whether at the shared words or the giddiness that went along with new information, Sasha couldn't tell.

"No problem," she repeated. "Thank you so much for meeting up with us. And thank you for confirmation on that researcher's name. I'll see if I can find this Dr. Ramirez. Keep in touch, alright? And add to the deck if you find anything."

Caitlin nodded. "Will do. See you later."

And with that, the woman signed off. Poor form to do so in the middle of a public sim like this, but everyone was jumpy. The skunk and the weasel shrugged it off.

"Guess now we have another lead," Debarre said.

"Yeah. And if she's a big name researcher, I bet she knows about Cicero, too."

At that, Debarre brightened, and for the first time in weeks, the two spent the rest of the night talking without tears.

Ioan Bălan — 2305

Dear wasn't kidding about the smells. Ioan turned eir sensorium's sensitivity way up. Ey wondered if Dear's vulpine nose could smell things eirs could not.

Serene had worked wonders here. The smells, the textures, the raw beauty of the place, all well crafted. It was a fine line that she had walked, too. Too far in one direction and the landscape would have become nearly desolate, more foreboding than natural. Any further in the other, and it would've been softened too much, would've become too well-tended. Cartoonish.

As the two crunched their way through the short, stiff stalks of grass, winding their way around the larger tussocks, Ioan realized that ey was quite taken with the place.

A ridiculous house in the middle of nowhere, a glittering white fox and its partner, the prairie fading off into downs on one side and stretching out to infinity on the other. It had all seemed so contrived when ey had first visited. Too simple. Too one dimensional. Kind of tacky.

But it was all just *so well done*. So incredibly, skillfully executed. The artistry was in the details, and the details were fractal, continuing down through ever finer layers. The landscape's perfection was echoed in Dear's unique sensibilities and its comfortable relationship.

Ioan liked it here.

Ey was dawdling, past the comfortable stage of just enjoying the petrichor being washed in before the storm.

"Sorry, lost in thought."

"*It is alright,*" Dear said. "*You looked like you needed it.*"

"Hmm? Getting lost in thought? Or getting out of the apartment?"

Dear shrugged and smiled.

"Sorry all the same. I'm here now. Will try not to do that again." Ioan grinned sheepishly. "What did you find out? You seemed almost punchy."

"*I was, definitely. Still am.*" The fox grinned. "*We seem to have found out who our...ah, who our target is.*"

Ioan mulled over the word 'target', searching for a better one. Ey couldn't think of any, so ey nodded. "What do we know?"

"*We know a name, and from there we can find a bit of history, which you may be able to help in filling in.*"

"Names are good. Something other than Qoheleth?"

"*Other than that, yes, but almost certainly connected, probably the same person. I think they are the same, at least. Not much more than the name, though. No location, no sightings in ages. Some aging — or agéd — resources. A name and some history.*"

Ioan gave an impatient gesture with eir hand. "Well, what's the hold-up?"

Dear's grin widened. "*The hold-up is that I want you to feel some of the excitement that I felt on hearing this from down-tree. I want you excited and invested.*"

"I've been working twenty hour days on this, I'm pretty fucking invested."

The grin turned into a laugh. *"I know you have. My partner is worried about you."*

Ioan felt heat rise to eir cheeks. "Sorry, I didn't mean to be a bother being up so much."

"No, no. We cannot hear you or anything. They are just worried because we do not hear you, or hear from you. We both like you."

The historian nodded, chastened.

"Do not worry about it, Ioan. It really is fine." Dear patted eir shoulder. *"The name, though. The name is the important thing right now."*

"And the name is?" Ioan's mind raced. Could Dear even say the name? Was it the poet, miraculously talking through years to the System? That would be exciting.

"Life Breeds Life, But Death Must Now Be Chosen, of the Ode clade."

Ioan froze.

Dear stopped a few paces ahead and turned, looking intently at em while its tail lashed excitedly behind it.

"They...what?"

"Good." Dear laughed. *"I am glad that I am not the only one who had to pick their jaw up off the ground."*

Ioan stuffed eir hands in eir pockets. Brought them back out to press against eir forehead. Crossed eir arms. Returned eir hands to eir pockets. Suddenly anxious. "I thought you said that Qoheleth couldn't be from within the clade."

"And so I believed. For him to share the Name is...a breach. Apostasy of a sort that I thought precluded the very prospect."

Ioan did not push further, instead relishing the surprise. "It's a real the-call's-coming-from-inside-the-house moment."

Dear tilted its head, ears perked.

"Never mind. Old trivia." Ioan shook eir head and rocked back on eir heels. "How, though? How'd you get the name?"

"A hunch I had, actually, though someone else dug it up."

"What was the hunch?"

" 'Signifier.' "

Ioan rifled through eir mental notes on the project. "Signifier...from the first encrypted note? Signifier is the password something something?"

Dear nodded. *"Hardly anyone uses it anymore, but signifier used to be what we called the names of long-lived branches. It is still used here and there among older clades."*

"Right, yeah. Ioan Bălan is my name, Ioan#c1494bf is my signifier."

"Yes. It fell out of use quickly. Too clumsy a word. I use it now and then, when I can get away with it."

"Makes sense, yeah. So they're..."

"He is an Odist, yes. Way, way down-tree. One of the first instances." Dear's smile faltered, *"We were not very good at record keeping back then. We are not really now, to be honest, but the System is better. We...we did not know that he was still alive."*

"Didn't know? I thought you all talked to each other. You must, in order to keep the names straight. Wait, 'he'?"

"Remember, all of our names are chosen from our stanza. I talk with the other nine within my stanza every now and then — some more than others — and we filled out the stanza not long ago." The fox's expression grew glassy. *"Life Breeds Life...that is the second stanza, first line. They are a conservative bunch. I only know one or two, but I assume that others are out there. And yes, 'he'. Michelle was a woman, but those early days*

were heady."

Ioan nodded, "So the first stanza were the first forked, meaning he was the eleventh fork?"

"The first line from each stanza were the first forked, back when it cost to fork. Like, cost real reputation. Anyway, the first fork of the second stanza — second fork overall — must have just been a little more conservative than the rest of us. Or liberal. It is difficult to discern."

"I...hmm. May I ask something potentially personal?"

Dear nodded.

"The Odists that don't want me digging into this too much, the ones you didn't really talk to, are they from that side of the clade?"

The fox's ears perked, *"To the last, yes. Why?"*

"How will, er..."

"Life Breeds Life, But Death Must Now Be Chosen. Just Life is fine, too, though if he has chosen Qoheleth, we must call him Qoheleth."

"How will Qoheleth react to the search? To me?"

Dear shrugged and turned its back on Ioan.

The historian stood, quiet and still, and watched as the fox took a few steps deeper into the prairie, crossed its arms and stood straight, staring up into the bruised sky. *"To the second bit, I do not know that it matters. He is one of us. And even those of us who did not want any outsiders brought on board are only frowning, looking down their noses at the thought, not gathering up arms."*

"And to the first bit?" Ioan pressed. "What do you think he will think of the search?"

"What do I think? Or what do I feel?"

Ioan scuffed eir foot against the grass. The temperature was dropping out on the prairie. It would be an inconvenience to have to slosh back to the house if it rained.

"Both."

"I think that he would probably get a kick out of it. I know that am. Several of the others are, and the ones who are not just do not care that much or are perhaps more angry than curious." Dear turned back around. Its arms were held tight against its front, guarding. Whether from cold or emotion, Ioan couldn't tell. *"As for what I feel, I feel that it is his game. He is the one running it. But even if it is a game, it is not play. There is no real fun in it, just...snark. Anger. Pride, maybe. It is a game he has worked at perfecting, and he wants us to see that."*

Ioan marveled at the change in Dear, though with this raise in stakes, ey felt some of the same.

The fox's smile was weak as it added, *"He has designs. Designs and reasons."*

Ioan and Dear trudged back to the low block of concrete, a bunker against the storm, as a chill wind swept away the petrichor and brought with it the rain.

AwDae — 2112

No menu.

No menu and no HUD.

Without eir HUD, there was no way that AwDae would be able to teleport. Ey would need to swipe up a destination entry and tap or speak the command for sending emself off. Hell, even if ey *was* able to get at the menu, ey wouldn't have the coordinates for any of the particular places ey had come up with to visit.

If locations within a dream even had coordinates, that was. Of all eir explorations, ey had begun to doubt that this was a sim. No sim, no coordinates. No coordinates, no teleport.

Ey would have to walk and just hope that it would not be tiring. No calories burned when taking simulated steps in a simulated environment. All the same, the prospect felt exhausting.

Eir first location on the list had been the university, that sprawling campus where ey had studied (and, later, pioneered) the integration tech ey used daily at work. It seemed meaningful enough: that place most closely associated with the beginnings of eir susceptibility.

Without teleport, however, that was out of the question. It was halfway across the continent.

Something more manageable, then.

The clinic where ey had eir implants installed was halfway across town. It would take an hour or two to traverse, ey supposed. A guess. Ey had never walked it before.

Ey had time, though, it seemed. All the time in the world.

With little else to do, ey once again slept early and woke early in turn. If it was to take a good chunk of the day, at least ey could do so while it was light out.

Shouldering the appropriated pack, ey set out from home as soon as it was bright enough to do so. A short walk down to the school, then further down the hill toward Broadway, which would get em most of the way there. After that, two blocks east, and ey would find emself at the squat, white building of the clinic.

From there, it would be easy. There had been about a dozen appointments in the building, so ey knew it well enough that it would likely be in reasonable shape. Assuming the doors were unlocked, at least.

The first skip happened halfway down the hill from the school.

AwDae reached the corner of the fence surrounding the track and football practice field, remembered eir brief jogging phase, and how ey always turned north through the neighborhoods before reaching Broadway, which was always so noisy. And then, without warning, ey was gliding down the street in a sitting position.

Ey yelped, startled, and flailed eir arms out for support, left elbow catching painfully on something solid a foot to the side of em.

The skip took perhaps a second all told. A second of blurred darkness, of shadow and motion. A second of panic and confusion before the rest of the car formed around em. Ey was sitting in the passenger seat of the family sedan, coasting down the road toward Broadway at what ey supposed must be the speed limit.

The car, like the books in eir room, took a while to swim into focus. Even then, parts of it shifted indecisively, unable to come to rest in some solid, known state. Ey had only tried to drive it once before giving up on the prospect, so the dashboard in front of the steering wheel was particularly vague. Hints of dials. Gestures at needles. Smudges of marks on the levers on the steering column. The back of the car lurched in and out of focus sickeningly.

Ey realized ey was holding eir breath and let it out in a shaky whine.

The car continued down the street toward Broadway. Turned smoothly without stopping at the light. Accelerated seamlessly, without haste, without care for its occupant's stress. The soft hum of the motor and the road noise beneath the wheels was as indistinct as all of the visuals. Indistinct and disconcerting.

After a few short blocks, AwDae had a hypothesis. Of course the sim — correction: eir memories — did not include walking along Broadway. Ey had never done so, had only driven. Or been driven, as ey had never gotten a license emself. All eir memories could dredge up were those of the car, of moving smoothly along the road.

No teleportation, then. Just fast-travel.

Eir one experience with hallucinogens had prepared them for the blurring, smearing effect of the world around em. The fog did not diminish, but it played tricks with the buildings lining the road to either side. There was the house with the psychic's sign out front, relatively clear. But the rest of the buildings were shifting, unsettled. When focusing on them, AwDae saw them as flat facades. No depth. Textures on a low-poly wireframe. It was a nightmare of that hidden time of intrasaccadic perception, that moment of suppressed visual input when one shifts one's gaze. That moment laid bare, elongated.

Ey moaned and closed eir eyes. The sights were wrong. The sound was wrong. Even the feeling of acceleration and deceleration, the swing around turns, was off, as though the entire universe was poorly rendered and em right along with it.

It *was* poorly rendered. Eir stomach turned at the wrongness of it all.

The next skip hit as a memory of walking through the parking lot of the supermarket at Broadway and Timberline asserted dominance over the memory of driving along the thoroughfare. So suddenly was ey on eir feet and walking parallel to Broadway, so surprising the shift, that ey stumbled and fell to eir hands and knees.

AwDae retched. Nothing came up. Not even the sting of bile.

Ey lost track of time, sitting in the empty parking lot. Half an hour? An hour? Trying to master the urge to return home and disappear beneath the covers. Anything to avoid that horrible, half-remembered drive.

And yet, ey had to do *something*. If there was even a chance of em being able to get out of this dream, this non-place, ey would have to keep moving. Keep moving and hunting and looking and thinking.

With a groan, ey stood and walked toward the road once more.

The skip came as expected, and ey gritted eir teeth as the world whirled past. Perhaps ey would be able to make it to the east coast, but if that meant eight hours of this — home to the airport, the plane, a different airport, transit to the dorms — well...hopefully there was a work-around.

The rest of the journey to the clinic passed without further skipping. There were a few shaky moments passing through the pedestrian mall, where ey'd spent countless hours walking, but apparently ey had spent enough time traveling along the road along whatever metric required. Eir 'car' continued down the empty street, blithely changing lanes to pass vehicles that weren't there, turn signal and steering wheel moving on their own.

And then it parked.

The low-slung building of the clinic was just as AwDae remembered it.

The idiom got a laugh out of the fox. Perhaps that was literally true. It could be no other way than how ey remembered it. The building was as it must be.

Preempting another skip, ey scrambled to open the door of the car and hop out on eir own before it was done for em. With a satisfying thunk, the passenger door of the dusty blue sedan swung shut behind em.

Promising, ey thought. *Perhaps I just have to be more deliberate about it. I will get in the car later, follow the drive back home, and maybe it will park in the driveway as easy as that.*

Eir claws clacked against the pavement leading to the smoky glass doors. It wasn't overly warm out, but the cool air that breathed out of the clinic was refreshing nevertheless. Something static. Something still. Something known.

Dr. Carter Ramirez — 2112

Dr Carter Ramirez,

We would like to thank you, first of all, for all of your continued efforts in working on these cases of the lost. Your services are invaluable and are providing the families and friends of the lost with hope, not to mention the world at large. We have come to rely on this technology in our daily lives in all spheres of work and pleasure.

As you know, research here at UCL is funded through a series of organizations and foundations working together. These relationships are both an expression of trust and a political statement, and both of those expressions work in both directions. We welcome conversations, questions, and comments about research from the sponsors, mediated through the appropriate channels.

A recent suggestion regarding your project was that more effort be placed on researching the neurological aspects of these cases, focusing primarily on the treatment and prevention of such events in the future.

As such, we are requesting that you add one more neuroscientist intern to the team. Unfortunately, due to budgetary constraints, your team must remain the same size as it is currently. At your earliest convenience, could you please respond with the name of a member of your group not on the neuroscience side who will, if possible, be offered a transfer to another project? Admin will take care of the rest.

Please continue the excellent work. If you have any additional questions, please do not hesitate to send a note.

Ari Liebler
Research Coordinator

Carter slid her chair slowly back from her rig and walked numbly to the coffee station. She wasn't tired. She *wasn't* tired. She was a bit too awake, if anything. She just needed something to do while mulling over the email from admin. Such a politely-worded request to change the course of her project and fire one of her team.

Pouring herself half a cup of chicory coffee, she looked out over the room, at the heads bowed over tablets or nestled into the headrests of rigs. How could she possibly be expected to choose who would get the axe?

Carter slipped back to her desk and delved in, stepping out of the workspace and into a side room, one of the small areas off to the side of the main space where virtual meetings could be held, where others' avs would show up in full focus rather than just shadowy shapes.

Shadowy shapes. The dream still dogged her.

"Meeting, when you get a chance," she murmured into a message pane, then sent it off to Sanders.

She received a ping of acknowledgement and settled back to wait.

It was only a few minutes — hardly enough time for her to organize her thoughts — before the head of neurochem stepped into the room and settled into the chair across from her. "What's up, Ramirez?"

"Here," Carter said, swiping the email she had received onto a vcard and handed it over to Sanders. "Give that a read."

"Rough stuff," he said. "Who do you think will be the unlucky one?"

Carter sighed. "I'm not sure. I can't think of anyone I would want to lose. Anyone we could afford to lose, even."

Sanders nodded and tossed the card back to Carter, who recycled it.

"Look," Carter continued after an awkward pause. "I know you weren't a fan of the social link I mentioned before..."

"Did I suggest this?" Sanders laughed, holding up his hands. "No, of course not. I'd not presume to go behind your back like that. You knew my reservations, but I'd rather talk about it with you and the team than pull something like that."

Carter nodded. The sincerity was clear. She relaxed back against the seat. "I got it, yeah. I'm sorry. It just came so suddenly and seemed connected, is all. Maybe I'm getting too good at seeing connections that aren't there."

Sanders politely said nothing, looking down at his hands.

"Well, hey. Thanks for that. It's reassuring. I'll let you get back to your stuff, and will call the team in for a huddle about this after lunch."

"Sounds good," Sanders said, pushing himself up out of his seat and walking back into the sim.

Carter watched as he turned from a solid avatar back into a shadow, thinking. If she was going to pursue this line any further, she'd likely have to do much of the work herself.

Something, she realized, she was already prepared to do.

The team was visibly unhappy the news. They had been working together over the months that they had on the project and by now felt themselves a well-oiled machine. Rightfully so.

"This is going to throw a huge fucking wrench into things," Avery grumbled. "We lose one of our own, then have to get someone new up to speed. It's going to take ages."

"I know." Carter sighed. "I'd push back if I thought it'd get me anywhere, but they say it's a matter of those who sign the checks, so I think I'm S-O-L on that front."

An tense silence greeted her. No one was looking at each other, just staring at shoes, ceiling, walls.

"Listen, I think we have some time. Absolutely no pressure, but if anyone wants to volunteer, cool. Otherwise, I'll put some thought into this and make a decision. I'll have to, I mean. I don't want to. Either way, I'll go to bat for you in trying to get a transfer rather than just the sack."

Another sullen silence. Carter shrugged helplessly, and with an apologetic look, walked back to her rig. She had little more consolation to offer.

Once delved in, Carter frowned. A small, pulsing envelope icon in her peripheral vision let her know she had another email. *If it's more bad news, I'm going to scream.*

The address wasn't from someone at UCL. Or the UMC, for that matter. It was a free address, something personal rather than professional. It had made it past the filters, though, so perhaps it was legitimate, despite its shady provenance. Perhaps not bad news, but Carter remained wary.

> Dr. Ramirez,
>
> I'm writing to ask for your help in the search for two of my friends who are lost.
>
> I know there's probably not much you can do to help, and you might not even be able to talk to me, but my friends and I are scared, and want to know what's going on. And if we can help, we'll do all we can.
>
> Their names are RJ Brewster and Collin Jackson.
>
> If you can, email me back. I understand if you can't.
>
> Sasha.

Carter frowned harder. Not bad news, then, but neither was it good.

This Sasha, RJ's friend, was right. She technically wasn't supposed to respond, at least not with anything more than a form letter stating such. Carter wasn't even supposed to know that RJ existed, who ey was, much less that she knew who *Sasha* was from Johansson.

She began digging through administrivia to look through the form letter. At the same time, a part of her sequestered itself and began to plan.

She would have to do most of the work on this herself, yes — perhaps all of it — but maybe she could do a little more outside research. She had done so with Johansson, why not with Sasha? She wouldn't be able to rely on it, couldn't publish it, but there was no harm in more information, was there? Even if she had to strike out on her own?

Before she lost her resolve, she filled out the form letter and scheduled it to reply at five, near the end of her day. Then she paced around the workspace, organizing and cleaning decks, too distracted to dig into numbers as she sorted through the plan in her mind.

She left that evening at five after five, earlier than usual. She had been prepared to beg off with feeling ill, but found she didn't need to: most of the team were also packing up and leaving. No one looked happy. One of their jobs was on the line, of course they would be unhappy. Everyone avoided eye contact on the way out.

Determined now, Carter left quickly and, standing in the station for her train, fumbled out her phone and started typing.

Sasha,

I know you just got a reply from my work address, but I'm replying here as well. While UCL and the team I work with aren't able to provide any assistance or information with regards to the cases, I might be able to help a little on my own, and I'm sure you'll be able to help me. We don't have much information on RJ or Collin, and I'm desperate for more.

Maybe we can figure out a way for that information to get to the team later, but for now, we can talk here.

-Carter

She hesitated, thumb hovering over the 'send' button. This was reckless, she knew, but the more she thought about the interactions of the lost, the more she was convinced that there was something to the connection. Especially here. Here, where she knew now that patient 0224e8 was RJ, and that aca973d7 was likely this Collin Sasha had mentioned.

And the more sure she was, the worse the letter from admin stung.

She gritted her teeth and hit 'send'.

Qoheleth — 2305

It has been long enough that I am thinking of myself as Qoheleth now. All that slow washing-away of given names to replace with chosen ones. Something worth being methodical with. I have even begun introducing myself as Qoheleth whenever I go out, just to try it on for size.

That I have never actually done so is of little concern. It is ancillary to the problem at hand. Something I can tackle later, or at least tackle in thought. I can daydream about the name change. Just plan and plan and plan, like I have planned everything else.

I like the sound of it. I like the way it feels in my mouth when I say it out loud. I like the connotations of 'teacher' and 'gatherer' and 'director of the assembled'. I want to feel the way that it feels to be someone different, and I have found at least a part of that in this name, the name that I chose for *myself*. Not some line of a poem I wish we would all forget. *Could* all forget. I may not have yet taught or gathered yet, but I am working constantly to earn the moniker.

And 'Hebel'. Hebel was another name I picked up. Vain, futile, mere breath.

Qoheleth's words, in the book written so very, very long ago, were all about hebel. "This, too, is meaningless," Qoheleth had written after that long walk through life. Try pleasure. Try work. Try prayer. This, too, is meaningless.

That is not how I envision the name, though.

I think of the two names as signifiers rather than simple names. I think of the two moods that they bring. And I think most often of the two *sources* of names. Not the book, not the time at which it was written. My two sources. Now.

Qoheleth was the name I gave myself out of hope. It is a name of goals and aspirations. It embodies the things that I want to do. It takes all of my plans and me, maker of plans, and binds them up neatly into a word. Ties a pretty bow to the top. A single word. A name and also a rejection of *the* Name.

Hebel was the name I gave myself out of despair. It is a name of self deprecation and a way of reminding myself that, lofty as my goals may be, they are all vanity. Mere breath. Meaningless in the end.

Together, the names remind me that I am doing this for a reason. All of these resources, all of *my* resources, those found objects and hand-me-downs accrued over the years, are being built up and strung together into a cohesive goal. A net. Less trap than source of safety. Something to catch. Something to rescue.

They, the resources, are all nothing. The reasons are all nothing. Vapor. Mere breath.

The whole plan is nothing except for the truth underlying it. Not to fear God, but to...to something. To *do* something. To *be* something. To get the whole clade to see. My clade.

No, my *old* clade. I am not of the Ode any longer.

I am Hebel Qoheleth now.

Hebel Qoheleth.

The old name is dead. I have followed it to the letter: I chose death as I must. As we all must.

I am Hebel Qoheleth.

AwDae — 2112

If AwDae had been expecting to find some fresh clue, some exciting conclusion to eir adventure at the clinic, ey was disappointed. The office was an office, nothing more. Cold. Hollow. Impersonal, despite countless touches cleverly engineered to add personality.

If ey had expected perhaps some comfort from familiar surroundings, ey was also disappointed. Walking into the clinic, memories fell upon em like ticks from branches. Latching on, leaching substance. Consult, surgery, treatments, training, follow-up, training, training, training. Getting to know the doctor and his team. Getting to know the trainers. Learning to loathe them. Learning to love what they had to offer.

There was nothing there.

There were the couches in the lobby, of course. There had to be. That is what belonged in lobbies. There was the desk where ey checked in, the receptionist's chair behind it. Such desks belonged, and thus followed chairs. There was the hallway. There were the locked and unlocked doors — ey now suspected that the locked doors hid rooms that ey had never seen, eir memory refusing to consider things never remembered.

There was the dimly lit surgery suite.

There was the row of paired mirror rigs. Instructor, student.

There was the whole affair laid out before em, and no solutions. No explanations.

Ey paced the halls. Sat on the lobby's couches. Sat at the rigs, dumb and silent. Lay on the operating table, face down as ey remembered. Laughed at the way eir snout poked so perfectly through the slot meant for an oxygen mask. Rifled through notes, their swimming text a mocking jeer.

Ey threw eir weight against a locked door, far more solid than it had any right to be. No rocking in the frame evident. It may as well have been a wall.

Tears stung at eir eyes. School, home, this place. Everything was dreamlike, unsettled, waffling between mind-numbing and nightmarish.

Not dreamlike, no, but a dream. If, as ey now suspected, all of this was simply taking place in a combination of eir mind and eir implants, why would there be these tantalizing clues dangled in front of em? Why would eir mind think to invent a mode of transit that simply skipped em along in jagged, stomach-churning jumps?

Tears flowed freely now, and ey hunched down against the unknown, unknowable door, first crouching, then sitting with the skirt pooled around eir waist as tears stained the fur of eir cheeks.

Nightmares.

Dreams.

Ey needed something to anchor emself to. Ey needed something to hold onto that was not dependent on clues and tidbits of information that were...were what? Stored in eir implants? In some core in eir exocortex, dumped when ey was pulled back?

Ey needed to make sense of something in this pale semblance of a world. Make understanding. Make knowing. Make lucidity.

Dreams and lucidity. What mattered a lucid dream if there was nothing to wake up from?

And yet was it not lucid? Did ey not have some semblance of control over this place? Ey had been trusting that it was some sort of locked down sim. One in which ey had no ACLs. Some sort of semi-scripted film from which ey could not deviate.

But if it was a dream, if it was all within eir head and implants, was it not completely eirs? Did ACLs matter in a dream?

The fog of war. The importance of the sound board. The very setting of eir school and childhood home. All of these were from within. The ancient strategy games ey had played growing up. The thing that had captured eir imagination in school. The places all stained with memory. Places which ey still dreamed of, even with home now in London. All things and places and memories where ey had spent uncounted hours honing and honing and honing.

Were these limits of the technological system operating in tandem with eir nervous system? Or were they simply limitations of a panicked mind?

Both?

Neither?

A test, then: something within said limits to begin with. Ey knew eir home. Ey knew eir room. Ey knew the feeling of the duvet beneath em. Ey knew the feeling of sitting on that bed, reading far past eir bedtime. Flashlight and book, listening for footsteps, feigning sleep at the slightest noise.

Ey *knew* it.

Ey closed eir eyes on the dim hall of the clinic.

Ey dreamed it, dreamed of home.

Ey felt it, breathed in the rich scent of the memory of it.

Qoheleth

Ey knew every detail of it.
Ey dreamed it.
Ey felt it.
Ey reached out and, in one paw, clutched.
And eir fist was full of duvet.

Ioan Bălan — 2305

Eating was not a necessity in the System. While it was easy to go for months or years without eating, it was something that remained a habit for many who chose to upload. Remnants of biology. Ioan suspected that there was no small amount of hedonism involved in killing one's body to decamp to a world beyond scarcity. Eating became a purely sensory affair, one focused on taste and scent and company.

All the same, dinner was a muted affair. Dear's partner cooked that evening. Ioan sat with the two around the table and tried not to feel like a third wheel.

Dear and Ioan made it back to the house just as the first cold sprinkles had started to fall. Once they'd reached the patio, they stood a moment and watched, just out of reach of the rain. The weather went from cloudy, through sprinkles and drizzles, to stormy. Ioan focused primarily on the sound. The way ey was able to pick out the individual sounds of droplets striking dry grass during the sprinkles. The static of the drizzles. The rush and roar of the storm itself.

Ey could not guess what Dear was thinking. It stood, watching the rain and shivering. It looked contemplative, pensive. Somewhere north of sad, south of simply thoughtful. Ioan sifted for the word, gave up, and guided the fox back into its house.

Ioan felt some energy return with the mix of curry and lentils and rice. Calories an empty term, that is nonetheless what it felt like: like eating a hearty meal, regaining strength. Perhaps it was just the act of being present. Of existing. Engaging with one's sensorium. Mindfulness. Perhaps that was why so many within the system still engaged with food after all.

Dear picked up somewhat with the food. Not as much Ioan had. Nor, it seemed, as much as its partner had hoped, judging by their own apparent anxiety. Dinner was good, necessary, but plagued with silences. Even after, as the three sat talking, their conversation was full of nothings.

It wasn't until they poured wine and moved to the couch that Dear began to open up.

"I script a lot of my conversations. Perhaps most," it said, staring into it's 'glass', wide-rimmed to make way for a fox muzzle to lap. Ioan felt strange drinking wine from something more akin to a bowl.

Ioan looked up. "Mm?"

"I was just thinking." It shrugged, swirling its wine. It took a few laps. *"Earlier, when I was sharing that bit about the Name with you, I had that all scripted. It was all pulled together in my head. The whole thing. I would make a few jokes. Lead you on. Tell you the name, and then we would bask in the wonder and truth of it."*

Ioan nodded, silent.

"Just like I spent dinner scripting this conversation."

Dear's partner gave its shin a playful kick. The fox grinned.

"It is thoroughly ingrained. I am pretty sure most people do it, it is just-" It frowned, sighed. *"I had the whole thing scripted and planned, and then you asked questions — as you are meant to, of course — and my*

script collapsed."

"I 'went off script', you mean?"

"Yes."

"Sorry about that, I–"

"Oh goodness, no!" Dear laughed, shaking its head, *"I am trying to apologize here. Do not steal my thunder. I just meant to say that you asked good questions and got me thinking, and I was not expecting that."*

"It likes to proclaim," teased Dear's partner.

"It is not not *true."* Dear smirked. *"But anyway, I am sorry I got all quiet, I did not mean to put a damper on things."*

"You didn't, I–"

"I did, though. Dinner was like some depressing silent movie."

"Don't sulk, fox," its partner said. "Dinner was fine. And let poor Ioan finish."

Ioan grinned, letting the banter play out before continuing. "All I meant to say was that I worried that I'd offended with my questions."

"Not at all." The fennec furrowed its brow. *"I mean, not really. I felt offended, is what I mean to say. When you asked how Qoheleth would react to you being a part of this investigation, it stung. An unfair reaction, I admit. Just one from the gut. I was offended because that made me realize that I'd invited you along on this as some sort of tool. Something I could wave about and say, "See, look what I have!" A tool or a trophy. Offense borne of shame."*

Ioan looked down into eir wine, taken aback.

"Doubly unfair of me, and for that I apologize." Dear raised its glass in a salute. *"So you asked a very good question because it made me question my own role in this hunt. It made me think of what others would think. Me bringing along an amanuensis and historian. It made me think of why*

I am doing so. Something I had not considered as well as I thought.

"And I think the reason for me doing so goes further than even I had planned. I think I have you along as a means of keeping me grounded. A means of keeping the clade from just doing what the clade has always done yet again, of-"

The fox abruptly stopped talking and set its glass down on the table. Its ears were standing erect and its fur bristled down along the back of its neck. Hackles raised. It looked frantic.

Ioan looked to Dear's partner for explanation. They sent a very faint sensorium ping in response.

Sensorium message. That was it.

The message lasted less than a minute before the fox leapt off the couch and dashed off to another room, forking almost as an afterthought along the way.

The fork turned quickly and padded back to the couch. It didn't seem to be able to sit, and instead kept pacing in front of Ioan and its partner.

After a few tense laps of wine, it said, *"Qoheleth just sent me a message."*

"What?" Ioan rushed to place eir glass on the table with Dear's. "You mean Life?"

"He asked me to call him Qoheleth, but yes. He sent me a message. May I pass it on?"

Dear didn't wait.

The message began with a sickening flash. Highest priority. It came with a rush of adrenaline and a sensation of falling. Sudden and intense fear replaced with an incongruously jovial voice. An old voice, almost Santa Claus-y.

The contrast made Ioan's teeth ache.

"Hi Dear, this is Qoheleth. Not Life Breeds Life, But Death Must Now Be Chosen, but Qoheleth. I am glad to see that you have kept at it and gotten so close. I am not sending this to deter you, but to cheer you on. I am going to send you a bit more information — just you, mind! — but I want you to get the rest of the clade in on this. I want to see if you can get them working with the same delightful fervor you and Ioan have.

"So anyway, here's the bone I am gonna toss. You should be looking at the node ending in 343f1077. That will get you right to my door. May need the node ending in e39fcd49 to help, too. You already have the key, I think. I expect most, if not all of you, though, you understand? You are lovely, Dear, and I cannot wait to see you and your friend, but I would like to host as much of the clade as I can.

"I am quite excited for this, and I am totally looking forward to see you all, yes?"

There was a moment's silence, a sense of lingering, and then, "Oh, and thank you, Dear. You have made this a treat. You are the closest one to the thing I am after, and I am glad this tickled you as much as has me. I think you and I both know why, too.

"Anyway, see you soon, fox. Cheers."

The relative calm that fell over Ioan signified that the message had ended.

"Holy shit." Ey slouched back into the couch, eyes wide.

"Right? Hold on, do not go anywhere. Going to reduce conflicts while I make the calls." The fork of Dear quit without fanfare.

Ioan shook eir head and said again, quieter, "Holy shit." Ey reached for eir glass of wine.

" 'Bone I'm going to toss,' hmm?" Dear's partner mused. "He makes it sound like a game."

Ioan nodded and watched them spin their wine glass between their palms by the stem, watched the wine creep up the sides from centripetal force.

"It showed you, too, then?" ey asked.

They laughed, "Of course. I know I've not been hitting the books or the streets like you two have, but I'm still in this. I was the one who pointed it to you."

Ey nodded, feeling eir cheeks flush. "Of course, sorry. Do you know what he meant by 'closest one to the thing I'm after'?"

"Maybe. I only really have an inkling, though, and I'd rather let Dear explain."

Ioan nodded again, "That's fair."

There was an uneasy silence for a few minutes. The two sat on the couch, sipping their wine and mulling over the message.

For eir part, Ioan was considering the strange sense of the familiarity with which Qoheleth had addressed Dear — "see you soon, fox" — as well as *why* the fact that this seemed incongruous to em. It was difficult to think of Qoheleth as a member of the same clade as Dear after so long of striving to believe the opposite. Hard to think of him as someone with whom Dear shared a root identity after so long of thinking of this person as someone entirely different.

Silences have their own rhythms, Ioan knew, so ey waited until there came a point at which ey could ask, "About all this, do you know much more about the whole Name business?"

Dear's partner looked up. "Who, Qoheleth's?"

"No, I mean the whole name of the poet."

"Ah." They shrugged. "Not particularly. I just know it's something the clade has an almost religious fixation on. Most of them, at least."

"Do you know it?"

They laughed. "Oh, gosh no. I mean...well, do you know why Dear's a fox?"

"Why's that?"

"Because it likes foxes."

Ioan felt as if ey'd stumbled. Dear's partner laughed.

"Seriously, that's true. But also, it was an experiment. I don't know the Name because I'm not allowed to know the Name, that much is obvious from the clade's reaction to this whole business. But I also don't know the Name because I'm pretty sure Dear doesn't even know it. Not anymore."

"How do you mean? I thought all of the Ode clade knew the Name, kept it secret and close to their hearts or something."

"Many do, I've been told. And I think that Dear does this too, in its own way. That way means doing its best to forget it and to move on."

To get to the acceptance stage of grief?"

Dear's partner nodded. "So it did its best to forget."

"Is that something that one needs to work on, then?"

"Have you forgotten anything recently?"

"I, well–" Ioan stopped and thought for a moment. It was a difficult question to comprehend, much less answer. How could ey know whether or not ey had forgotten something by going back through eir thoughts?

All the same, ey prowled through eir memories. Even just those from the time ey had been spending with Dear. They were jumbled, sure, and lots of impressions, but no, nothing was forgotten that ey could think of. With focus, ey could recall the entire afternoon on the prairie with startling precision.

"I'll spare you the details by passing on some thoughts from Dear," they said. "We aren't gifted with eidetic memories when we upload, but neither can we truly forget anything we experience after that point. It's as thought each memory is labeled with a priority level from zero to ten, and when it hits zero, it's forgotten. Except the actual scale only goes down to naught-point-oh-oh-oh-oh-one or something. We can kick it way to the back of our minds, down the priority list, but we can't forget it. The System won't let us."

Ioan nodded. "So Dear tried to forget, tried to kick that memory all the way to the back of its mind. What does that have to do with being a fox, though?"

"Know much about exocortices?"

"Sure, I've got a few up and running for storing long term stuff. Hell, I've got one for this project. Isn't that kind of like forgetting?"

"Almost, but you can never forget that they exist, can never forget the passphrase."

Ioan frowned, directing it to eir wine rather than Dear's partner.

"But exos also need part of your sensorium to match, right? That way you can't just tell someone your passphrase and let them in."

Ioan frowned. Ey had a hunch of where this was headed.

"So Dear put the Name into an exo all by itself, and then tried to change its sensorium enough that it couldn't get back in."

"I see," Ioan said, sipping at eir wine again. Dry. It left em parched. "It's a fox because it likes foxes, but that wasn't the goal. The goal was to no longer quite be the same Dear that put the Name into the exo."

Dear's partner nodded.

"How did it do that? By forking?"

Another nod. "Forking and mutating, forking and mutating. You can change your form easily enough, but it's much harder to change your sensorium. I don't even know how many times or tweaks it took. That's how it got into instance artistry."

"Damn. That's intense."

Dear's partner grinned. "It's an intense fox."

"True enough."

"It'll be back soon enough. Let me throw a question back at you. What are your thoughts on the last thing Qoheleth said?" I think you and I both know why"?"

Ioan settled back into the couch with the remainder of eir wine and thought for a moment. "I'm wondering if he was talking about what Dear did to forget the Name. On one hand, it sounds like a sort of congratulation. Like,"I'm glad you're able to move on," but after all that talk of the clade and all of what Dear said earlier, I'm not sure if that's the whole story."

"How do you mean?"

"Well, has Dear mentioned to you the more conservative side of the Ode clade?"

Its partner winced. "Plenty."

"It said that Qoheleth is from that conservative side. I wonder if that's not working out well for them."

"Conservatism?"

"Yeah. Retaining all of those things from the original Michelle Hadje, yet following a dispersionista path more in letter than in spirit. Dear called them batty."

"It's called them that to me, too."

"I'm just wondering if it's right," Ioan said, finishing eir wine. "Maybe they are batty. And getting worse."

Sasha — 2112

Sasha wanted to be pleased with the rapidity with which everything was happening. It hadn't even been a week, and here was one of the lead researchers of the lost mailing from a private address.

She desperately wanted to be pleased. Wanted to believe that things were moving forward. Wanted more than anything to smell the lingering scent of fox and cat in the Crown Pub, just to know at they were there.

And yet, she wasn't. It was all wrong. Everything about this was wrong. There was no way to forget that, despite the forward momentum, she was still doing all of this for what was widely acknowledged to be a lost cause.

She began typing.

Dr. Ramirez,

Wow, I'm glad you got back to me! I was not expecting that. I'm a little confused as to why, but I guess no sense in questioning it.

Do you have information on RJ and Collin? I'll gladly give what I can. They both were good people. RJ and I went to school together, and the three of us spent a lot of time together in sim. They would spend hours talking politics (mostly Collin yelling).

The last thing I got from RJ was this:

> AwDae here. Looks like there's a lot going on in DDR activity (where'd you get this, Debarre?). Cicero (Collin) was into a lot, and I'm not trying to go all conspiracy nut on you all, but do you think that maybe he got in too deep or something? Not saying someone tried to do it too him or anything, just that maybe the more one uses the net, the more likely it is to happen to them? I mean seriously, look at all of his votes, and his stash of credits! I'll keep poking at this after rehearsal.

Do you have any idea what that might be about? I know I said Cicero was super into politics, but do you think RJ was onto something here?

I've copied Cicero's partner, Debarre (don't know real name, sorry!) and Caitlin Wells from where RJ works.

Sasha

The response was only an hour in coming. As with Caitlin, it was short and to the point.

Sasha, all - @129822922:d.no.onehere.board#default

A throwaway user? The wrongness intensified.

All the same, Sasha logged in and swiped her way over to the address Carter had provided.

As with most throwaway rooms, it was a cube measuring about five meters on a side, a faint grid lining the floor, and as with most throwaway avatars, Carter was visible only as a gesture at humanity. The lines of a face hinting at expressions, features. Average height. Gray skin. Androgynous hair.

"Sasha. Uh...you're a skunk."

She frowned.

"Right, sorry. I'm sorry for meeting you like this."

Sasha shook her head. "It's okay, I guess. Can you tell me why?"

"Will you accept "because of a dream" as an answer?"

Her frown deepened.

"I suppose not." Carter hugged her arms around her middle, a gesture that looked distinctly out of place from the gray avatar. "You mention, uh...AwDae investigating DDR activity, as well as Collin's own involvement but–well, should we wait for others to show up?"

"I don't know if any of them are coming." She felt the tightness of panic in her chest intensify. "I don't know where Debarre is. Probably work, it's midday for us. And I imagine Caitlin's show is on."

The figure before her sighed. "Right."

Sasha pulled up her deck. "I can take notes, perhaps," she allowed. "I don't suppose you'll want ACLs with a throwaway."

"No, probably not. Notes will have to do." Carter seemed to compose herself, and then continued as she was saying before. "You mentioned the relation to DDR, and we already suspected that Collin and RJ were friends. This is something we've been looking into with my group. The possibility of a social vector, I mean. It's gone poorly."

"Poorly how?"

"Well, there was unexpected resistance within the team, and then shortly after taking this tack, the hammer came down from above saying we had to fire someone — someone studying this aspect — and shift our investigation to the neurological side."

Sasha blinked. "Are you suggesting you're being told to not look at social aspects?"

Despite the mere sketch of facial features, the av's smile still carried the weariness heard in the tone of its voice. "In a way, yes. I had a dream about shadows following everyone and I guess I could say I'm a bit spooked. Too many coincidences in too short a time."

"I'd chalk it all up to paranoia if I weren't feeling so anxious, myself."

"Any particular reason why?"

"I, well." She brushed her paws down over the fur on her forearms, stalling to hunt for a response. Any response. "I don't know. Things are moving so quickly. I don't know how to explain. I met up with Caitlin and she told me a lot, and then I emailed you, and your two responses didn't do anything to assuage my fears."

Carter nodded, didn't respond.

"But I don't know that anything you might have said beyond "we fixed it, AwDae's awake" could have done anything but. Even your "we're working on it" form letter was anxiety-inducing in its own way. I know you're working on it. I imagine a lot of people are." She hesitated, then added, "But that doesn't really help to hear."

"No, I imagine not."

"And to then get another email saying that you wanted to talk things through outside of work just added to my fears. Like, what could that possibly mean?"

"I'm sorry," the figure said dully. "I really can't help in the context of work."

"I know. I read up a bit on WFPHIPA."

"Yeah."

The panic was slowly transmuting into anger. Sasha didn't like it, but was powerless to stop the shift. "And now here you are, in all gray, talking about, what, conspiracy theories? Dreams?"

"I'm sorry, Sasha. I really don't feel any better about this than you. I'm not usually the paranoid type, but I think Sanders...well, I suspect that one of my colleagues has motives that go beyond just his focus on neurochemistry. I think they go beyond just the university."

Further information tempered anger. "How do you mean?"

"Well, I said the hammer came down. It did so in the form of grantors threatening to pull funding from the project." Carter shrugged. "And I believe that the research coordinator — that is, the university itself — was just passing along that message. I think the stress is coming from higher up."

"Wait, grantors?"

"Yes. The project is hosted by the UCL, but is being funded from external sources. Grants, that sort of thing."

"Who's writing the grants?"

Carter held up her hands. "No clue. That's the thing. Why would the grantors throw their weight around, saying that we should follow specific lines of research? That's not their job."

"Have you even published data that would suggest anything but a–" Sasha dug for the term. "Neurological cause?"

The figure stiffened. "What?"

"I just mean AwDae got lost only a few days ago, and you said that ey was the reason you started looking at the social aspect, right?"

Carter began pacing. "Right, yeah. And we haven't published anything along either front in that time, social or biological. I can't say this is helping my paranoia any."

"Do you think this coworker-"

"Sanders?"

"Do you think Sanders is, I mean..." Sasha said, struggling to keep her voice in check. It seemed to want to simultaneously rise in panic and also sneer at the very suggestion. "Some sort of shady government plant?"

"I gotta go," Carter said. "Don't use the DDR for a while."

Then, without ceremony, she teleported away.

There were three small warning chimes, and Sasha found herself back in her home sim. The throwaway had been recycled.

"*Fuck.*"

AwDae — 2112

The relief of finding emself sitting in eir own bed, ey supposed, should have been immediate and intense.

Instead, seeing eir room around em once more rather than the clinic, all AwDae could do was close eir eyes and shift down in bed until ey was able to draw the covers up over emself, a mirroring of this morning. The weight of the blanket atop em, the feeling of being surrounded, covered, supported by the mattress seemed to be more important than...than what, relief? Joy?

Ey did not feel despair, did no feel hopelessness.

AwDae was not sure what this emotion was. It was a non-emotion. It was a sense of swelling, of being too full. Of having words and images and colors flooding through em and yet wholly out of reach.

When ey had awoken this morning, ey had supposed that ey would head down from home to the clinic and magically find some sort of success. Or, if not success, at least another clue. Another step along the way. A fraction of success. Some piece-of-eight that, when added up, would save em.

This was not a puzzle, though, was it? This was not a set of steps that could be followed to some logical conclusion. There was no end to the road, because there was no road.

Dreams, after all, have no plot.

Ey curled beneath the duvet. Resting in the fetal position in eir childhood bed beneath eir childhood blankets, ey could not even pretend that ey was dreaming. Had ey been asleep, this would have been one of those confusing dreams of too much meaning. Not nightmare, not blessed peace. Just neurons firing at random, conjuring images up from dust, from nothing. Mere breath.

If history played out as it promised to, there would be no waking. Ey was in a world of dream, eir every thought mirrored back against the inner surface of eir cortices, both cerebral and exo.

The data ey had received on the note, still nestled snugly within eir pack, was not some hidden clue. It never had been. It had been an artifact of a dreaming mind leveraging the data that had been stored in eir exocortex. Some part of em, already in the mindset of rummaging through data that afternoon before the rehearsal, was primed to dream of clues, of mysteries to solve.

Find this note.

Find this mic.

Find this solution and perhaps you will achieve your goal.

But what goal was that? Was it to solve the riddle of Cicero's loss? Was it to become unlost, to be found?

Or was it to become unstuck? Was it to find something new? Some way to move on? Move forward? Move, period?

"You seem kind of frozen, kind of stuck, in a few ways."

The laugh that came to em was choked. More sob than anything.

Well, hard to get more stuck than this.

Ey drew the covers up over eir head. Perhaps ey wished to blot out the dream with darkness and silence, but this darkness was dream. The barrier: dream. The silence: dream.

Ey slept, then. Not the restless, confused sleep of the night before, but a dreamless sleep of an hour. An hour? A day? What mattered time? It was the sleep of a mind demanding that very blessed nothingness. Was that something ey could request, as ey had requested to dream eir way back home?

It was not a long nap, of course. Or perhaps it was. Perhaps ey could will it to be as long as ey wanted. Perhaps ey was bound to a rhythm, but the scale did not matter. Perhaps ey could bend time.

Either way, when ey awoke, the corners of eir eyes gunked up with dried tears, the funk of the morning had largely passed. The numbness still lingered around the edges, vignetting curiosity, but it was not so all-consuming as it had been.

AwDae sat up in bed, folding eir legs beneath em to keep eir tail from cramping. Ey teased a thread loose from the edge of the duvet, tugged. A habit from youth made easier with vulpine claws.

Habits in dreams. Dreams that were more than dreams. Dreams one knew about and nevertheless was pinned beneath: nightmare demons sitting upon one's chest, upon one's mind. Upon one's exo, perhaps.

"If I dream, if I dream," ey murmured, words coming unbidden to eir lips. "If I dream, am I no longer myself?"

The vignette of numbness throbbed, narrowed, then faded once again. The words seemed to carry import beyond their plaintive query. Ey could not stop emself from speaking.

Dawdling.

Ey stretched eir way out of bed and padded to the door of eir room, closed.

"Wait," ey commanded emself. Hand on doorknob. A count to three. A promise to emself. *I will open this door and will find the open space across the road instead of the hallway.*

Could one dream within a dream? Do so with such a detail that ey would not notice the transition? Had ey dreamed the trip to the clinic? Had ey perhaps slept through the return?

"I do not know. I do not know."

A supplication. A mantra against hopelessness.

Ey turned the knob and stepped out into the shortgrass prairie of the open space. The packed dirt of the trail welcomed eir paws. The scent of dust and rattle-dry stalks of grass washed over em. Warm, yellow light hemmed em in through the fog of war.

"Wait," ey said once more. Kept eir hands at eir sides. Loose. Relaxed. No menu to reach for, no gesture required.

A promise to emself. *I still have will.*

The fog receded upon eir request, thinned, disappeared. Mere breath. The prairie of the open space stretched out before em. A valley, and then a ridge of hills to the east. The mountains behind eir back.

Not a sim. No limitations other than those eir dreaming mind had set upon them. Ey had spent so long in sims, lived eir life out in worlds bounded by the edges of invisible properties that, upon getting lost, ey had imagined the same must be true inside. More so, eir unconscious reasoned, for was ey not constrained by the processing power of eir exocortex?

But it was not a sim. It was a dream, eir dream, eir exo a mirror, and in the end, ey held control.

No commands, then. No promises. Ey knew that, were ey to take a step forward, eir foot would come down on the dinged hardwood floor of eir London flat. Priscilla would meow her hellos and twine around eir ankles.

Ey did not rush. Ey stood still. The breeze fingered eir fur and teased along the hem of eir skirt as a breeze must. There were the turbines on the far ridge, three blades turning laconically as turbines must. There was the highway across the valley, the charging station squatting low alongside it as charging stations must.

No commands in dreams. No promises required. Ey would take that step and all would be as it must.

And then ey took the step.

And then Prisca meowed her hello and twined around eir ankles.

And then AwDae fell to eir knees and let the cat step up onto eir thighs, and ey lifted her in eir arms and buried eir snout in her warm, purring side, and cried.

Art by Cadmium Tea.

Cried because this was not London. Cried because this was not eir cat. Cried because ey could dream anything ey wanted and it would never be anything beyond a dream.

This was a memory. This was something dredged up from eir own mind. Prisca, eir very own Prisca, was purring against eir face because that is what Prisca must do. She was squirming out of eir grasp because ey knew that, had ey held her like that in the waking world — and ey had — that that is what cats do.

It was eir dream. Eir own, eirs alone. All the lost must perforce be dreaming their own dreams. Ey dreamed of homes and clues and boundaries, of cats that squirmed, of emself as a fox — and that one ey would keep — and could not begin to guess at other's dreams.

Could ey will Prisca to stop? To hold still and be eir pillow to cry into? Ey did not know. Eir mind resisted the question. Resisted, because ey did not want that to be the case. Did not want to will eir precious cat to be anything other than she was. To ask that question was to admit the idea that ey could dream anything other than that which ey must.

Ey let the cat down so that she could stalk self-righteously to her favorite spot and groom the tears out of her fur.

Dr. Carter Ramirez — 2112

Carter could not explain why she had created the throw-away account to talk with Sasha. Nor could she fully explain that panic that had washed over her, strong enough for her to flee, to log out and wipe both account and sim.

All she could explain was that Sasha's simple questioning had thrown her estimate of what might be going on both within the dynamic of the team as well as within the 'net as a whole into utter turmoil. The woman...skunk...skunk-woman had been correct: while there were occasional reports on their findings published to a scant few reviewers and advisors within the UCL itself, there had been none since RJ had gotten lost. No papers published in any journal, public or private. The phenomenon of the lost was new, and so was the study of them.

So how was it that the grantors were throwing their weight around in terms of the directions her team was taking? How would they know to do so? An informant? A mole?

After logging off, she picked up a sandwich at a nearby M&S, but could not bring herself to eat more than a few bites of it. When she lay down, sleep would not come easily, and when it did, all it brooked her was the same stress-dream of shadows.

How does one encompass all of this in one mind? How does one

take in the knowledge of being spied upon, of having decisions made
— made by the unseen and unknowable — that impact one's life on
such a base level and some how make that work? Make it fit? How
does one do these things, and still go back to a workaday life?

Work felt impossible. Everyone around her was a suspect. Everyone around her was suspicious in their own way. Everyone around
her was someone who was in secret communication with others,
and, without any knowledge of those communications, what guar-
antee did she have that she was safe?

And was she not communicating with others? She was the one
who had contacted Sasha. She was the one who had contacted Johansson. Was she not worthy of suspicion?

The worst was the lack of answers. She could ask all the questions she wanted, and there were no answers to be had.

Finding it impossible to get down to the business of actually
working, she paced between rig and coffee station. If, perhaps, there
was some way that she could think harder, think better, then perhaps she might be able to fit all of this within her newly updated
worldview.

All the coffee did was up her heart rate. It did not wake her any,
did not make her more efficient. It simply kicked her anxiety up
another level.

All her rig had to offer was the work at hand.

She delved in all the same. If nothing else, she could use the dark.
She could use the cool *Eigengrau* of her workspace, the order of information neatly delineated by thin cotton twine. Perhaps numbers
would sooth her anxious mind.

A soft ping. A notification. A small bell still loud enough to jolt
her out of her reverie, or non-reverie, or whatever this caffeine-

tinted haze was. *Avery would like a meeting.*

Carter found it hard to sit still in the small room. It was all she could do to keep from pacing agitatedly, and she focused instead on keeping her steps more within the realm of slow and contemplative. *Is this out of the ordinary? Is me walking back and forth out of the norm enough to report to some higher authority? Is Avery on my side?*

"Dr. Ramirez, sorry for bothering you."

"No problem, Avery. What's up?"

They shrugged. "That's just the thing, I'm not really sure. I started digging into what we were talking about, about how e8 was looking into DDR records before eir disappearance, and on a hunch, I decided to look at all of our other candidate cases. Turns out most of them, even the ones who weren't heavy politics junkies, had a massive uptick in the amount of engagement they showed prior to getting lost."

Carter frowned. "Wait, so not just e8? All of them?"

"Well, sort of. Of those who are just the junkies, it's hard to pull apart just how much of their interactions were actually off baseline for them, you know? A set that large, a slight increase might not be that out of the norm. Still, it is there."

"Do you have a starting point for these increases?"

"Nothing in particular. In absolute terms, no." Avery's smile was wry. "Perhaps obviously. After the initial rush of cases, everyone got lost at different times. Relatively, though, maybe. It looks like everyone who had this uptick had it within seventy-two hours of getting lost."

"How confident are you in that?"

"Are you asking how strong the correlation is?"

"Sure." She hesitated. "Though I'm also curious about your confidence in this line of reasoning."

They looked up to the ceiling. "Well, in terms of the line of reasoning, I'd say that it's strong enough that it's got me actually interested in looking deeper into it. Not that I wasn't interested in these cases before, but this is really intriguing. I like the sort of...well, mystery aspect of it."

"Yeah, it does have that going for it, doesn't it?"

"And it always did before, too." Avery dropped their gaze once more and shrugged."Just that now, I feel like I was handed a big bone in terms of what could actually be going on. It's not an answer, but of all the correlations we've been looking until now, this is one of the bigger ones."

"That strong of a correlation, then?"

"Well, look." They summoned a snatch of workspace, pulled a vcard from one of their decks, and tugged on the corners to expand it to presentation size. A table filled the page, but after a few commands from Avery, it shrunk, slid up to the corner, and in its place, a graph appeared, showing a series of correlation points and a trend line. "It's fairly strong if we leave everyone in, but if we filter...out...there. If we filter out the junkies, you can see how high it spikes."

Leaning in closer to the page, Carter scowled at the graph, then up at the minimized table, and back to the graph. "That's higher than anything else we've gotten, right?"

Avery nodded, tapped in a few more commands on a keyboard Carter could not see. They frowned at some mistakes they made along the way, but then the graph was overlaid against other correlations they had been investigating previously. "Just over one standard deviation, yes, though...wait."

Carter had started to nod along with Avery, then frowned at her subordinate's growing confusion. "What?"

"Do you see that?"

She looked back to the graph. "See wh–wait, what?!"

"Do you *see* that?" Avery said, louder. It was as though they themselves needed the convincing, that they needed to have this witnessed right along with them.

And it *was* worth witnessing. As both of them watched, wide-eyed, the graph shifted. The strength of the correlation started to dip. Not smoothly, but in fits and starts. Avery's hand darted up and, with a fingertip, they dragged the table out to fill more of the card's surface. There, along with the graph, the numbers of the correlation were beginning to change. Row by row, the 'interactions DDR by hour 72 lim' values were dropping. They were still high, yes, but perhaps more reasonable. The correlation was still there, but weaker.

"What–"

"Do you have this data backed up anywhere?" Carter was shouting. Didn't know how to keep from shouting.

"I– maybe. Sec." A few hasty commands, and the data was dumped to another card, the column name changed to a keysmash. The numbers stopped dropping on that card, even as they continued on the first. They handed the card to Carter. "But what–"

"Pull me back and hit my panic button. Quick!"

Avery stared, open-mouthed.

"*Go!*"

There was the pleasant animation of a user logging out and Avery disappeared.

Carter braced herself, but even so, the jolt of pain running in a sparkling thread down along her spine was stronger than she remembered, and she came up gasping, hands shaking from where Avery held them just above her contacts. With their knee, they hit the panic button on the rig, and the flip-up screen began ticking off cores dumped and suggesting that an official report be filed.

Still shaking, she looked around the office. Everyone was delved in except her, Avery, and Prakash, standing startled by the mini-fridge.

"Everything alright?" he asked, brow furrowed.

Carter waved her hand dismissively, trying to look calm. She doubted that she did. "Was in a meeting. Crashed or something."

Perhaps picking up on the anxiety of the last minute, perhaps experiencing their own terror, Avery nodded. "We were in a meeting, uh...trying something. She started..." they trailed off and shrugged.

Prakash nodded. "Need to file a report? Anything like that?"

Carter stood, wobbled, and regained her balance. "I will after some water. Getting yanked hurts worse than I remember."

"I haven't done it since training."

Avery shrugged. "I don't think many have. It's not all that common."

Rinsing her mug free of coffee residue — additional caffeine at the moment being contraindicated — Carter attempted a laugh. "Right, yeah. I've had sims crash before, but not myself."

The laugh didn't seem to soothe either of her coworkers.

"Well, either way, I'm kinda shaken up. I think...uh," she trailed off, looking at her phone. "Maybe a walk. Yeah, I think maybe a walk."

Ioan Bălan — 2305

Interview with: Dear, Also, The Tree That Was Felled

On the formation of the Clade

Ioan Bălan

Systime 181+338 1644

Dear, Also, The Tree That Was Felled: What, specifically, do you want to know about the clade?

Ioan Bălan: Other than "start at the beginning, and when you get to the end, stop?"

Dear: [laughter] Yes. I could do that, I suppose, but it would not make for a very good story.

Ioan: Right. I suppose start at the beginning, specifically with your decision to upload.

Dear: You understand that there will be portions of that story that I cannot tell you, yes?

Ioan: Of course.

Dear: [thoughtful silence] Okay. Did you ever come across...well, no. When did you upload?

Ioan: 2238, June or something.

Dear: [sighs] No. Okay, well, in your research, did you ever come across mentions of "the lost"?

Ioan: Yes. Lots of turmoil around then. Early 2100s, right?

Dear: [nodding] Yes. Though it is strange, now that I think about it. The turmoil at the time felt very small and personal. While there was all this grand-scale stuff going on around us, we were dealing with friends and acquaintances disappearing. There were so few cases at first that it was just this thing the news would publish as a sort of curiosity. "Look! Is this not strange? The scientists are working so hard!" [laughter] It was not until after that that the turmoil you that are talking about began.

Ioan: Okay. Did you upload during?

Dear: Oh goodness, no. Uploading had been something scientists and such had been poking at, but that no one had yet to accomplish. Or, well, perhaps someone had accomplished. Some had claimed to, at least. The consensus at the time is that, while it was likely possible, there would be little chance of having systems large enough to house more than two or three individuals. It was not an...ah, not a linear increase in complexity, I think. Add another mind, and the complexity more than doubles. [pause] It was the lost who started it, in a way. The things we learned from them when they came back–

Ioan: How many– sorry for the interruption. How many came back? Of those you knew?

Dear: Oh, all of them came back! Just that some of them did not last long, after.

Ioan: Including the...uh, the owner of the Name?

Dear: [pause, tense] Yes. In a way.

Ioan: Okay. Back to the uploading side, then. The lost taught you...

Dear: [visibly relaxing] Right, yes. When they came back, many of them — many of us, for I was briefly among their number — talked about what we had learned while...ah, in there. The things that we talked about and described are what sent the wonks down new avenues of research, and that eventually led to the first uploading tech. From there, there was the usual "too expensive" hand-wringing, but it all marches on, you know? [laughs] It got cheaper, the tech got better, the L5 station and Ansible were set up. Population was getting out of hand again, they said, and some wag decided to pitch uploading as a solution.

Ioan: I remember that, yeah. The posters were all over the place.

Dear: Yes. Notably, as the cost came down, it was pitched as something for the poorer classes to take advantage of. It bore more than a little whiff of eugenics.

Ioan: And were you...I mean–

Dear: [laughter] Poor? Not particularly, actually. It appealed to me for...different reasons. I would prefer not to get into those at the moment.

Ioan: Alright.

Dear: Yes. Well. [pause] Okay, right, I uploaded in the 2130s, shortly after the L5 station was set up. It had become sufficiently cheap that It was something I could afford–

Ioan: Cheap? How much?

Dear: It was...well, still a considerable portion of my savings.

Ioan: I see.

Dear: Why do you ask?

Ioan: We were — our families were, I mean — paid for us to upload.

Dear: Oh? Fancy that! [laughter] Anyway. It had become something that I could afford, and I leapt on the chance. It had been around long enough that it still felt relatively established, but was still a far cry from what it was now. This was probably early systime

10+, I mean. Folks knew what they were doing, but much of the society — what we think of society — here had not gelled into what it is today.

Ioan: You mention that it cost to fork, yes.

Dear: Yes. The reputation markets were already set up by then, but since this was before the System's proper expansion and some tech that came later — I could not begin to understand it — it was gently discouraged by the market.

Ioan: It hadn't reached this...post-scarcity, you mean?

Dear: Right. There was still a scarcity of resources and we were still sufficiently...ah, still sufficiently human, perhaps, socially human, that this was used as a lever, a measure of one's class.

Ioan: We still have the markets, though.

Dear: [laughter] Not like we did then.

Ioan: Alright. Don't suppose you would be able to do what you do today back then.

Dear: Not at all, no. It does still cost some minuscule portion of credit for one to fork now, but I digress. We began as Michelle and did the things that Michelle did, forking infrequently. This was still a few years before the distinctions between strategies started up. Most everyone was a tasker back then by virtue of the markets.

Ioan: It's hard to picture you as a tasker.

Dear: [laughter] Right, yes. As everything started to get cheaper, though, those distinctions began to emerge. By then, Michelle had few long-lived instances, tagged as you are, Mx. #c1494bf.

Ioan: [laughter] Thank you. This was before the Ode?

Dear: The Ode itself existed. That came before we uploaded.

Ioan: Before the Ode clade, though?

Dear: Right, yes. Michelle and her forks existed, but the very idea of clades was new at the time. At one point, though, she and a few other founders began to describe their trees as such. The larger trees grew — for those who maintained long-running forks, that is — the more unwieldy tags became, and folks decided on names. Some folks settled on simple standards. Another of the founders, the Jonas clade, for instance, uses syllabic prefixes. Ar Jonas, Ko Jonas, and so on. Leading vowels the first forks, then leading consonants, then the vowels following the consonants, *et cetera ad infinitum.*

Ioan: And you chose the Ode.

Dear: Michelle did, yes. She had picked up a contrarian streak during the whole lost saga.

Ioan: Did she play a large role in that?

Dear: [taken aback] Did her name not come up in your research?

Ioan: Not on the lost, no. Just on the founders.

Dear: [frowning] Well, alright. Yes, she played a role, but time softens rough edges, I suppose. Either way, the things she did gave her enough reputation to fork, and she chose the Ode to name her instances while remaining Michelle, herself. She started with the first lines of each stanza, then let them create and name their own forks from there.

Ioan: Thus the limited dispersionista style.

Dear: [nodding] Right. Each stanza became a small family of taskers, in a way. We, the Odists, create our own forks as needed, but do not let them live long. Or are not supposed to, at least.

Ioan: "Aren't supposed to"?

Dear: Oh, I am sure a few of us have created long-running forks while everyone else has turned their head.

Ioan: Have you?

Dear: [smiling, shrugging, paw-wave] By virtue of our set-up, though, such forks are not members of the clade. Those forks are not named as such, and likely not in communication with any other cocladists aside from their immediate down-tree instance.

Ioan: Is the Ode available somewhere for me to read?

Dear: Of course. I will give you a copy. That is hardly secret.

Ioan: And the clade, how long has it been since you have all been together.

Dear: This will be the first time there have been more than half of us together in one spot.

Ioan: Ever?

Dear: [nodding] Ever. Some dispersionistas are families. I mentioned the Jonas clade before; Jonas Prime has set up regular intraclade communication. Some are just clades, defined by ancestry with no further connections.

Ioan: Are you in touch with any of your cocladists?

Dear: I am assuming you mean "in normal times"? Right. One or two. Serene and I get along quite well, and I talk with Praiseworthy — That Which Lives Is Forever Praiseworthy, the first line of my stanza — with some frequency. Michelle and I have talked a few times. She comes to my exhibitions.

Ioan: Ever talked to, um...

Dear: Qoheleth?

Ioan: Yes. I was going to say "Life Breeds Life" but forgot the line.

Dear: Names are important, Ioan. If he has decided on Qoheleth, then Qoheleth it is.

Ioan: Right, sorry. I was in the mindset of the lines. Have you talked with him?

Dear: Before this? No. Not knowingly.

Ioan: And how do you feel about seeing the whole clade together?

Dear: I would be surprised if we manage to net all of them. [laughter] But I suppose I feel excited. Not necessarily because I have never met many of them so much as because it feels like we as a clade have a goal in front of us. Seeing them is secondary to them — to us — actually doing something. Accomplishing something.

Ioan: And what do you hope to get out of it? This gathering?

Dear: [smiling] A story. Others want answers, and I suppose I do too, but I mostly want a story. I want *the* story. I want to be the audience and a character. I want to dive into the story and bathe in it. I want a story.

Dr. Carter Ramirez — 2112

London in winter was not a snowy affair. No traces of white lacing the ground, no flakes in the air. Just sporadic sleet and steel-gray skies, breath clouding her vision while fingertips went numb around her mug of water.

She dumped the rest of the water in the already soggy grass and looped her pinkie through the handle, fingers curling into her palm to hunt for warmth. Another few steps and she gave up, setting the mug on a window-ledge so that she could walk with her hands in her pockets.

It wouldn't be missed. Mugs were less important than being out of there.

The pain of being drawn back so forcefully had disappeared immediately upon coming too outside the sim, but the memory lingered. Her mind would not let it go. If she thought about other things, she knew, it would disappear. Just a memory. A bad dream.

She did not think about other things. Could not think about other things. All she could think about was her implants and the system. All she could think about was the vain hope that the data on the card had made it into the core dump she knew had been left in her exocortex's storage immediately upon the crash. She had no idea how she'd get it out — the tech side of the implants was hardly her specialty — but she knew it was possible.

So she paced along the sidewalk, head down, remembering pain. She knew she was walking a street, but did not know which. She just needed away from the room, away from the neat row of rigs. Rigs she no longer trusted. Away from people she no longer trusted. She needed away, and hoped that the bracingly cold air would help in some way.

Her phone pinged. On silent, the ping came in the form of a brief tingle along her implants through the wireless. A gentle impinging on the senses. It pinged again. Then pinged several more times in short order.

It made her sick. A rush of anxiety to go with the reminder of the subtle tech ramifying through her flesh.

Avery:

Ramirez, something's happened

Avery:

ACL change in the system. Been locked out. Everyone's coming up

Avery:

What do we do?

Avery:

Shit, security's here???

Avery:

!!! Police

Sanders:

Police here. Need you. Come back ASAP

Prakash:

Police here looking for you. Stop where you are. Do not come back.

Her breath came in short, ragged gasps. She hardly needed Prakash's orders to stop. She was frozen to the sidewalk. She could hardly take another step if she wanted to.

Prakash:

I'm coming to you. Told them I went to look for you. Stay there.

What? Carter's mind seemed to be floating down a river, bumping across rocks and swirling in eddies. She could not focus for the water in her eyes. Literal, as well as figurative. She could not tell if she was crying, or if the air was simply stinging. *Security? Police? Prakash coming here?*

And then: *How does he know where I am?*

Sure enough, there, jogging around the corner was his lithe form, unjacketed with puffs of breath showing in the still air.

"Ramirez," he said. His breathing was calm despite the jog. "As I'm sure you've heard, the police and security are at the lab, looking for you."

Carter merely stared at him.

"Ramirez? Doctor Ramirez. Hey!" He snapped his fingers in front of her face. "Things are going to happen very quickly now. I need you to stay away from UCL and stay away from home. I've got some, ah...friends who will be in contact with you soon. Not Western Fed, if you take my meaning."

She blinked, nodded dumbly. Another rock for her mind to bump over in that swift-flowing stream: *Prakash? Sino-Russian Bloc?*

"If you run, you'll only look guilty. You need to stay away from UCL, but–" He pointed down the street. "If you were to head to the medical center, then it's only an ethics violation, not running from the police, okay? Brewster is there."

"What–" Her voice cracked, and she had to swallow a few times to get it to work properly. "What happened?"

"You found something they didn't like. You saw something you weren't supposed to, and I think I know what. Sanders tipped them off, then told the police you might be a danger to yourself or something. I don't know. He's a plant, they think on their feet. I didn't stick around. Hold still." The last was delivered as Carter started to shrink away from his hand reaching toward her. He held it up in a disarming gesture, a bulky-looking phone held within. "Avery texted me why you had them pull you back. This is just a back up drive, promise."

She stood still. There didn't seem to be any alternative.

Prakash pressed the box against the top of her exo, just at the base of her neck, masking the motion as a hug. There was no sensation from her implants, but when he leaned away, he nodded to her. "We're good. Thank you, Ramirez."

"Why?"

"This will be good for both of us." His smile was wry. "We get some intel to use against the WF, and you will doubtless get your lost back."

Carter gaped. "What the hell does that mean?"

"Just–" Prakash frowned at something over her shoulder. "Fuck. Get going. Walk, don't run. Don't look back. Take the tube. You'll be followed, but being around more people will only help."

And with that, he patted her arm, moved around her, and walked away.

Despite any attempts to appear calm, she had to clench her hands within her pockets to keep them from shaking.

She was lucky with the tube, and managed to step immediately onto a car without having to wait. She supposed that if she were being followed, the platform would be the perfect place for someone to catch up with her. The short ride was spent wondering what they might do to her. Cuff her then and there? Pretend to be a friendly acquaintance and draw her to the side? Just talk?

Not something she wanted to find out first hand.

She had calmed enough by the time she reached the UMC that she was no longer shaking and could walk quickly and, hopefully, unsuspiciously up from the tube to street level. The steps disgorged her across the road from the UMC itself, and she was able to duck quickly into the building, using the light traffic as an excuse to jog.

With the connection between the University College and the Medical Center, she was able to swipe her way in without fuss, and once in, to quick-walk over to the wing where she knew they worked on implants. It was no clinic, but it did have some areas dedicated to care and maintenance.

She needed a rig. She didn't *want* a rig, but she needed to delve in and at least let Sasha and her friends know what was happening, that she might be seeing RJ soon. Needed to let someone else know what she knew.

This is stupid, this is stupid, she repeated to herself. A mantra. Or perhaps a prayer for someone to stop her.

No one did. She was doctor Carter Ramirez, after all, right? Why would a research doctor from the very university that ran the medical center need to be stopped? Of course she was welcome, the staff rigs are just down the hall, help yourself.

All she could hope for now was that that, if the lost were related to information they knew but had not shared, that they were being prevented from sharing, perhaps she would be safe if she were to be visible about it. Had already been visible about it, with that stunt back in the lab. If she were too visible a subject and the lost were the result of some intentional action, her — or any of her team — getting lost would be suspicious. She hoped.

Fuck, this is so stupid.

Even so, she sat in front of a workstation facing the door and, seeing nothing suspicious — no one at all, really — set her hands in the cradles and her head against the NFC terminal.

No time to make a throwaway, she thought, quickly bringing up a menu in her home sim. There was a flashing notification attached to the black sphere representing a core dump. *And I'm already fucked anyway, but hopefully there's something I can do.*

The mail was quick and to the point. She had the address for Sasha and, with a quick browse of her mail archive, the ones for Caitlin and this Debarre, too.

> All
>
> Things went sideways with the project, we may be fucked. Govt plant (Sanders, if you remember, Sasha) and SRB spy on the team. Police showed up today and everything, just barely got out.
>
> I found some data, though. Don't know what to do with it, but I've attached the core that might have it saved.

It has to do with DDR activity as suspected, notably some vote that happened a while back, deleted from EVERYONE'S records. Something crazy happening high enough up that they're trying to make everyone forget and disappear those who won't.

Home sim is @cramirez:eo3.london.gb.wf#default, will stick around a few, but after that, going to see RJ. Will probably be the last you here from me, as am being followed.

cr

No time to think. She hit send.

I'll give it five minutes, then I probably need to get out. Had to swipe into the room, but I doubt that'll deter anyone for long.

She jumped when Sasha stepped from the tport pad less than thirty seconds later. "Jesus, that was fast."

"Caught me before work. What the hell is happening?" The skunk's voice was shrill with panic. "Police? Is AwDae okay?"

Carter held up her hands defensively, then jumped again as a...weasel? Another furry of some sort, long and brown and dressed all in black, dashed quickly from the pad.

"This is Debarre." Sasha spoke quickly. "Debarre, Dr. Ramirez. She's at the hospital with RJ."

Debarre looked frantic, pacing erratically. "What the fuck is happening?"

"I don't know!" Carter forced herself to calm and lower her voice. "I don't know. Something really fucked is going on. I'm at the UMC, the hospital where RJ is. I haven't seen em yet. I only have a few minutes. Did Caitlin get the message?"

Sasha shrugged helplessly. Something was happening with her avatar. The resolution starting to degrade, polygons and voxels starting to show where once the fur had been smooth and well-rendered "I don't know, I–" She shook her head. "Didn't...h-hear..."

Both Carter and Debarre watched as the form that was Sasha fell to its knees, glitching wildly, voice filled with static. And then, with a damning silence, disappeared. Lost. Lost to the sim, lost to the world.

There was a descending chime, a diminished triad, and a message floating above the black sphere of a core where Sasha had disappeared: "User forcibly pulled back. Core dumped. Please report any further complications to your provider."

Debarre let out a shout and, without a warning, signed out.

Carter hastily followed suit.

Fuck.

AwDae — 2112

"If I dream, am I no longer myself?"

AwDae did not pace the streets of London. Did not open the drapes to see if the streets were full of people or desolate and empty. Did not listen for the sounds of the city.

Ey did not step from eir flat. Did not, in fact, leave the spot where ey knelt on the floor for more than an hour, for days and days. Did not do anything except stroke Priscilla when she came and walked by eir knees.

"I still have wants and needs," ey murmured to the cat, who only slow-blinked at em. "If I dream, is that not so?"

The words were automatic. Ey opened eir muzzle and they came forth in a steady cadence.

A memory: RJ and Sasha sitting on the edge of the stage during a break in rehearsals. The play: words of Dickinson. A five minute break. RJ's tablet not showing the usual stage diagram with mic placement and notes, but a white screen. Sasha laughing as RJ began writing, eyes closed. Automatic writing. Drivel and nonsense. Something to giggle over with best friends.

Eyes closed. Ey could feel the soundscape of the room around em change, and knew that ey must now be kneeling on the stage in school.

"Wait." Ey shook eir head, tall ears bowing. Ey opened eir eyes and was back in eir flat.

What lives we lead we lead in memory, ey thought, then smiled. *My mind should be reeling. I should be feeling overwhelmed and overflowing.*

Ah well.

Ey stood once more, rubbing at eir knees and wincing at the pins and needles rushing over eir paws. Could ey will the discomfort away? Perhaps. Could ey even feel discomfort? Could ey dream it?

Perhaps.

Not now.

Ey padded to the kitchen and opened the cupboard in which the tea must be stored, and, yes, pulled out a tea bag, setting it in eir favorite mug. Ey held the kettle beneath the faucet from whence the water should come and, yes, filled the kettle halfway full and set it on the counter once more.

A memory: RJ and Avon. Avon, who had let RJ crash on his couch when ey had first reached London. RJ and Avon at a small cafe. Avon promising an authentic cream tea and then immediately launching into a tirade against authenticity. RJ laughing. Avon watching, hawk-eyed, to see whether RJ would spread eir clotted cream on the scone first, or instead reach for the jam. Avon nodding approvingly at the choice.

The water quickly came to a boil. After pouring it into the mug, AwDae hiked emself up onto the counter by the edge of the sink and let eir tail dangle into it. It would get wet, but that is just what happens with sinks.

"You seem kind of frozen, kind of stuck, in a few ways."

"I am stuck, yes," ey informed Priscilla. "I am stuck with will and with memory and with time. As much time as I need."

The cat purred. AwDae laughed and lifted eir mug. Too hot to drink, but comforting to hold. Ey felt the comfort in memory.

Art by Cadmium Tea.

A memory: RJ waking a few days? Weeks? RJ waking some time ago, years and years ago, and groggily making a pot of tea. RJ sipping one mug of tea while watching the traffic. RJ sipping a second mug of tea while making rice. RJ starting a third mug of tea before sitting down at eir rig and getting lost in research. RJ digging and digging and digging through cards, through tables, through numbers and words and data. RJ frowning at a mass of voting records. RJ downing a cold mug of tea.

The tea was cool enough to drink, now, and so AwDae did.

And when ey had half-finished the tea, the fox slid from eir perch on the counter and padded over to eir rig. Frowned. Why bother with such a thing? Instead, in its place should be a small, white room extending past the boundaries of eir flat.

And there was.

And when ey would step into that room, ey would cease to be a fox, but instead become fully immersed in memory, manipulating it with the same ease with which ey manipulated the acoustic space of the theater.

And ey did.

And when ey might think about what memories ey had, ey would find there, whole and uncorrupted, all of the information ey had been prowling through on Cicero's disappearance. No riddles to solve, no tricks, no mics, no paper. Ey would be able to expand across that sense that passed for sight in a fully immersive sim the entirety of the data.

And ey could.

AwDae dreamt. Dreamt of work. Dreamt the table of Cicero's DDR votes, dreamt that it rotated in beautiful precision along any axis ey wished. Dreamt of the other cards in the deck, of recorded conversations and notes and last-connected times. Ey dreamt eir way through all of the data packed into the deck of vcards Sasha had given em so very, very long ago.

Ey kept dreaming.

Ey dreamt of the Crown Pub. Dreamt of emself sitting at a booth with Sasha. Dreamt of talking about Cicero with her. Dreamt of how ey had poked eir claw against the surface of the table in the sim, then rubbed at it with a pad, despite the fact that sim would not allow the table to be dented.

Axiom: when any sufficiently large group of furries convene in one place, they will spontaneously generate a bar to hang out at. A bar, a cafe, a park, a plaza.

Thus: in eir dream of so many furries, the table was there, perfect. The table, the booth, the whole pub. Not the noise, not the people, but ey dreamt, in that fully immersive perception-of-everything way, of the entire pub. Of the entire sim. Dreamt of the precise construction of it down to the parametric equations that defined the curves of the vinyl stool cushions. Dreamt of the area behind the bar, unreachable by patrons but behind which puttered the staff AIs' avs.

It was all there. The entire thing. The entire sim, all the way out to its boundary fence and the subtle magic of the fake street beyond. All cached in eir exo, in eir memory.

Ey dreamt of eir home sim. The simple bed. The simple dresser.

The logic behind the commands that let em select items and clothing to equip to emself. The tport pad.

All there.

And ey dreamt of Sasha. Ey dreamt of everything about her. The subtle scent of dandelions and the too-straight stripes that traveled over her muzzle, head, and then down her back. The equations that drove her tail. Her very voice.

"You seem kind of frozen, kind of stuck, in a few ways," she said.

She was all there. All of her avatar. What ey remembered of their final conversation could be played out from start to finish between skunk and fox in perfect detail. Detail that could not be anything other than perfect. Detail that had to be perfect because eir exo had cached the skunk's av, just as it had cached eir flat and the Crown Pub.

But she was *not* all there.

She was not there at all. Her avatar was a hollow shell that Aw-Dae could make parrot her lines. It was a puppet. It was a sensory representation without context. A sign without an object, signifier without the signified.

AwDae was in a hall of mirrors that allowed no one else but emself. She was not there and she could not be there because AwDae was lost, and when one is lost, one is alone in ways more fundamental than could be dreamt of in any solipsist's philosophy.

What lives we lead we lead in memory, and the end of memory lies beneath the roots.

Ey could not forget, for *memory ends at the teeth of death and is wholly inaccessible to the living, because the living know that they will die, but the dead know nothing.*

And ey could not cry thus immersed.

Dr. Carter Ramirez — 2112

It took a moment for Carter to collect herself again after pulling back. She allowed herself thirty seconds of simply sitting in the chair before the public terminal, face in shaking hands, before she stood up. Even then, she had to force her breathing down to levels that might be considered normal.

And normal this was not.

She pulled out her phone and, perhaps in a vain attempt to appear calm, tapped away on it while walking out of the room. She had toured the facility often enough that she had an idea of where the lost would be kept, even if she didn't know for sure that she would be able to find them there, much less access them.

> Johansson, Caitlin,
>
> At UMC, things got complicated. May be out of contact after this. Please stay safe. Stay away from DDR. Stay away from RJ.
>
> cr

She had already begun to put her phone back in her pocket before the faint ping along her implants notified her of a new message.

> ??? We're here too??? Room 2309

Shit.

Carter quickened her pace, doing her best to maintain the appearance that she belonged here. She, Dr. Carter Ramirez, researcher on the lost, was meant to be here. Meant to be in the hospital, in the wing where the lost were kept. She belonged here, it was okay.

And the ruse, if ruse it were, worked well enough to get her up to the second floor and onto the hall where RJ was being kept. A slow hall. A quiet hall, where none of the patients could talk or move. An empty hall. A nurse's station with a lone nurse sitting behind a monitor.

Empty, except for two chairs in front of one of the rooms.

The only occupied chairs along the entire hall were occupied with suits. Suits stuffed to the brim with frowning men. Men frowning at her.

Well, shit.

There would be no backing up without looking guiltier. She had been preempted. And why not? Dr. Carter Ramirez, researcher in the lost, was meant to be here, right?

All she could do, all she could think to do, was nod to them politely and head to the nurse's station. "Good, uh...good afternoon."

They looked up from the paperwork and frowned. "Afternoon. May I help you?"

"Yes, sorry. Dr. Carter Ramirez, UCL. I'm here to view a patient, RJ Brewster? Should be in 2309."

The nurse's frown deepened. "You're expected. The gentlemen down the hall are here to speak with you. That's 2309 they're sitting in front of. Go ahead."

Well...shit.

No way around it. Carter thanked the nurse and, moving with as much calm as she could muster, started down the hall. Both of the suits stood, buttoned their jackets, and waited at attention, watching Carter come to them. A show of power.

A show summarily interrupted by Johannson.

The director barrelled out of the room and nearly collided with the suits. His thick hands set on each of their shoulders, and, even from two rooms down, his baritone was clear. "Gentlemen, can I speak with you? I have some concerns about the patient."

Nonplussed, the suits turned toward Johansson. "Sir, we are not–"

"Won't take a moment, please. Just need a bit of privacy. Dr. Ramirez, head on in. I'm sure we can all talk in a moment."

Unsure if it was confusion or Johansson's convincing act that drew her forward, she simply nodded and continued into the room. Caitlin, she assumed, sat on a chair next to the bed. And in the bed itself must have been RJ. Short, slight, dusty blonde hair swept back out of eir face by a simple hairband, eyes taped shut, nasal intubation tube taped to eir cheek. Still. Completely still.

"Dr. Ramirez?" Caitlin said.

"Yes, uh...Caitlin, is it? And this is RJ?"

The tech nodded. "Yeah. Who were those guys? They seemed pretty keen on seeing you."

Carter shook her head. "Not sure. Government or something. They followed me here from work. I'm surprised I haven't been dragged off in cuffs yet, honestly."

"Boss is good at wrapping people up. Getting them invested in what he has to say, I guess." She smiled, shrugged. She looked exhausted. "Still, I don't imagine you have a whole lot of time. What can you tell me?"

"Tell? Shit." So dreamlike had the last few minutes been that the reminder that she was supposed to have some urgency to her movements snapped Carter to attention. "Our team discovered something about a DDR vote, and I guess we weren't supposed to. Don't use the DDR. Don't vote on anything! Don't delve in if you can help it."

The sudden intensity seemed to startle Caitlin. She sat up straighter in her chair. "Wait, what? Why?"

"Anyone connected to the lost, anyone connected to me is at risk of getting lost, too."

"You mean...intentionally? Not an accident?" The tech frowned. "Why are you here, then?"

Carter ground her palms against her eyes and shook her head. "I don't know. Running from those guys, I guess. Trying to not look guilty, or at least look less guilty." She considered expanding on what Prakash had said, on Prakash himself, then decided against it. If he was indeed helping her, that would be throwing him under the bus. Guilty of what, though, she didn't know. "I figured if I came here, it would only be an ethics violation or something. Pretty vain hope."

"Maybe." Caitlin sounded unconvinced. "I guess it's nice to meet you. I heard about you from the boss and Sasha."

"Sasha! Shit. Sasha's lost now, too. That's why I'm saying don't delve in! Got an idea, though. I need a...oh good, there's one already here! I need the mirror rig."

She was shouting. Didn't know how to do anything but. If she was worried about attracting attention, though, she needn't have: similar hollering echoed down the hallway.

Ioan Bălan — 2305

Mustering the Odists took surprising effort.

Qoheleth had said that he would welcome them at any time. Dear had taken this to heart and Ioan had no reason to suspect that there would be any delays in gathering everyone together. Despite the shady nature of the acts leading up to this — the puzzles and mazes of clues, the spying, the digging — everything seemed so simple on the surface. The last clue found, the final puzzle solved. Visit Qoheleth and finish the act.

And Ioan had thought that this would be easy.

Some of Dear's cocladists not want to go. They argued that it would be a danger to concentrate the clade in one place like this. That they could not express what that danger might be did not help their case. They would not go, they said, even with a forked instance.

These took much persuasion. In the end, many agreed only if the entirety of the clade was there.

One *did* want to go but refused to fork to do so. Or, it turned out, to fork at all. This, above all else, set Dear off: the fox did not take confusion of this sort well, but for the root of that confusion to go so counter to its very existence led to a tantrum, and then a sulk. Ioan could hardly fault it. The more time went on, the less ey was willing to put up with the politicking and glad-handing.

In the end, the clade was at the whims of that single individual's schedule.

Some of the more liberal members wanted to bring others, as did Dear by bringing Ioan, and this set off another round of debate. Further delays. They decided that they would only bring informed participants who had already played a role in the project.

With little else to do, Ioan read and waited. Ey read up on what history of the Ode clade ey could find — mostly musings on art and theatre. Ey read the Ode itself, hunting for hidden meanings. Ey read up on this form of public key encryption. Dear forked to teach em the encryption algorithm that used the deck of playing cards, and so ey read about manual encryption, and then the history of playing cards. Ey read and reread Ecclesiastes and all ey could about it. Ey even read about various mental vagaries and attempted to map them to Michelle Hadje, Qoheleth, Dear, and various members of the Clade which Dear talked (or, as time went on, ranted) about.

This last was mostly for fun, but ey was also beginning to strategize eir report. More than a report, ey wanted to write something that would stand on its own. A book, perhaps, or at least an article. An essay and formal report for Dear, and a smoothed, anonymized version for wider publication. If the clade would let em, at least. Ey wanted the result to be readable, rather than simply an account of events. Something that would help explain the whys and hows of an older clade in turmoil. Something to express the rising panic ey felt about aging in a timeless place, about memory and the importance of forgetting.

An historical document.

A story.

And finally, the day had come. It had been nearly two weeks after deciphering Qoheleth's last message, but it had finally come. There had been no further communications from the wayward Odist. He seemed patient enough to wait.

AwDae — 2112

I am at a loss for images in this end of days.

No images. No images. Not real ones. Nothing real in this empty space. Ey could see, but why? Why see eir flat? Why see Prisca? Why see anything?

So ey did not. Ey dreamt emself blind. More than blind. Eir dreaming mind ensured that there was no such thing as sight. That it had never existed. Did not exist for emself. Had never existed for anyone.

Ey was like the theater. Ey was vast, incomprehensible spaces. Ey was the lack of the concept of space. Ey was words. Ey was information. Ey was sound, and the only sound was eir voice.

"The only time I know my true name is when I dream."

Except was that eir voice? Did ey hear? Did ey speak? Was it em making these noises? Was it em hearing them? Ey dreamed emself out of sight, could ey still dream emself speaking?

"Why ask questions, here at the end of all things?" Ey laughed. "Why ask questions when the answers will not help?"

Ey dreamed emself asleep, then. Asleep and dreaming. The world moved around em in soft colors and meaningless images. Words strung themselves together, tangled, frayed, came apart once more. Ey dreamed.

Ey dreamed.

Who knew how long? Who knows? What means knowing in dreams?

When ey woke — when ey dreamed emself awake — AwDae answered eir own question: "To know one's true name is to know god. To know god is to answer unasked questions."

And as ey thought upon eir true name, eir mind wandered across what remained in eir exo. Wandered across the deck on Cicero. Wandered across those cards for centuries at a time, millennia, and did not ask.

And there it was.

The vote was not there, and yet the answer was. There was the shadow of intention, of the need for an entire vote to disappear from the collected direct democracy that was the DDR. There was the reason for those who had interacted with the vote, who had voted, who had spent the credits needed to comment on it in the political theater. Commented where others could read, where representatives from the territories would see.

What mattered the vote? What mattered the comments? What mattered the content, the cost? What mattered the golden fleece, or any MacGuffin? It could have been a flashlight with an amber filter in a suitcase just as easily as it could have been a declaration of war against the Sino-Russian Bloc. Chekhov's vote.

It did not matter. All that mattered is that those who had seen it — had seen the vote, who had interacted with it, who had interacted with it at however many levels of remove — were *personae non gratae* from that point on. Easier for them to not be. Easier to admit the mystery of the lost into the collective consciousness than to let such come to light. What cared the world of billions for the hundreds of lost? What cared the powers that be for the resistance of however many dozens that were now beyond reach?

Ey rambled beyond the deck, beyond eir flat, beyond Prisca. Ey wandered across the interior of eir skull until ey stepped up onto the stoop of eir exo.

Do I know god after the end of all things? Do I know god when I do not remember myself? Do I know god when I dream?

Ey dreamed that border. Dreamed that border between endocortex and exocortex, and then dreamed eir way across it. Dreamed of the difference between endomemory and exomemory. Dreamed that exomemory into lines. Into rows and columns and formations. Review, friends — troops long past review.

Ey dreamed that memory into data, into words and images and sounds and smells and sensations. Dreamed more than just the memory. Scraped the insides of that exo and dreamed everything. Dreamed it into formation.

And reviewed. Ey walked, a fox, with baton in paw, skirt and blouse dreamed into uniform, laughing joyously. Ey walked along the formations and inspected. Neatly ordered. Neatly organized. Standing proud.

Ey reviewed and marveled at the preciseness with which eir mind obeyed itself. Madness be damned: if ey could control nothing else in this non-world, ey could control emself.

Ey very carefully did not ask.

And there it was: the answer.

There, standing tall, as proud as any other memory, was a subroutine. And when AwDae gazed into its porcelain face, ey understood. And when that porcelain face gazed back, it smiled beatifically.

There it was: the very subroutine, the very bug exploited, the very program triggered at the order of some higher power. The very entity which had painted the inside of eir exo with silver and glass that left em trapped within. There was the virus in all its glory. Its subtle curves meant to fit the space of an exo's logic perfectly. Its ability to recognize actions. Its ability to cut off the outside world. Its ability to ride shotgun along regular software updates. *Security*, it promised. *Added security along the barrier between waking and dreaming.*

It smiled, and AwDae laughed.

"The only time I know my true name is when I dream," ey spoke through tears. "And may then my name die with me."

Madness grew to a cruel point, pierced bubble of dream, and then dissolved fox.

Ey dreamed.

Qoheleth — 2305

Qoheleth is a patient man.

I have time. Enough time, at least. I know that I am gone. My memory, split as it is across an archive and nearly thirty exos, is a millstone around my neck. It drags me down. It drowns me even in plentiful air. I can feel the way it crams up against every recess of my skull, demanding to be let out. The Name, the Ode, every act since uploading and so many that Michelle took — that *I* took — before that. It drags me down. It nips at my heels. It fogs my vision.

There are no metaphors that clearly show just how horrifying the inability to forget can be, and so I find myself reaching for every analogy that I can find.

I am a lost cause, but much of the clade still has their faculties about them. I think so, at least. I hope so. So long as they act within the decade, we will be here. Any longer, and we will risk further degradation, further madness.

It has been two weeks since I messaged Dear — lovely Dear — and although it had tried to contact me several times, and pinged countless more, I never responded. I did my part. I called them, got them fighting, got them interested, and I think I got them invested.

That is all I need, is for them to be invested.

Now, hopefully they will come.

Ioan Bălan — 2305

The designated meeting point was the prairie in front of Dear's house. Ioan was confused as to why they didn't just meet in Qoheleth's sim, until ey realized that many members of the clade had not met in years or decades, or, in the case of up-tree instances, ever.

For a family reunion, it was quite stiff. Formal and tense. *Probably not the best of circumstances,* Ioan thought.

Ey focused on eir job as amanuensis.

Ey was surprised at the variety of the cladists. It made sense, of course, for a dispersionista clade, but it was the direction in which the differences headed which intrigued em. The most notable difference was the species presentation ratio. Many of the cladists were still human, mostly short woman with dark hair.

"Fewer foxes than I had imagined," Ioan observed.

"Hmm? There is me and Serene, yes." Dear dragged Ioan over to meet her. Serene was quite similar to Dear, though with natural coloration rather than the iridescent white fur that Dear maintained. Dear gave her a tight hug and introduced her to Ioan as the one who had designed the landscape of its property. Ioan liked her at once.

Dear also introduced Ioan to That Which Lives Is Forever Praiseworthy, its immediate down-tree instance, also eminently likeable.

"Why only you two? Why are you the only foxes?"

Dear shrugged. Serene looked away. Praiseworthy gave Ioan a sharp look, and ey dropped the subject.

Of those that bore forms other than fox and human, Ioan could not tell. Ey supposed that ey would do some research after the fact to try and place name to species and species to line in the Ode. Perhaps there was a pattern, and perhaps not.

"You must understand that while uploading was attractive early on to those with an interest in explroing the differen shapes a body could take," Dear had explained. *"Few were able to accomplish that on initial upload. Many furries uploaded, few wound up looking like their avatars in the sims of the past. You wind up looking like how your brain pictures itself on some level more fundamental than merely preference."*

Ey nodded. "I look much how I did before, yes, though I've made a few changes."

"Many changes require forking, though, yes? And if forking is expensive..." The fox trailed off, shrugged.

Ey supposed it was due to the individual preferences that each long-lived fork had gained in its time away from the root of the clade once forking became cheaper. The remaining Odists who had not changed — or who had changed very little — even after the cost had come down were the ones who Ioan suspected Dear referred to as "conservatives".

And yet they were only similar. No two were identical. Each had picked up some of their own distinguishing characteristics, whether through intentional mutation or through accident and acquired experience. It was an interesting artifact of the dissolution strategy: fork, fork often and be deliberate about it, but do not let the self dissolve completely.

Michelle herself was notably absent, though Dear assured the historian that she was still very much alive. *"She said that, if anyone should remain behind, it was her, as she had started this whole damn thing."*

"And how do you feel about that choice?"

Dear shrugged, unsmiling. *"Her choice is her own. I would have preferred that she be here, but then I would have preferred everyone be as invested in this as I am, and we know that not to be the case."*

There were a few tag-alongs aside from Ioan, as well. Folks immediately identified as out-clade. A few friends. A few partners, singular and plural. Some who ey suspected were like emself: historians and helpers, here to witness and record. The 'catalogers, feelers, and experiencers' Dear had mentioned. One of the conservatives (at Ioan's guess, at least) had even brought a reputation analyst along with her, a slight Asian gentleman who introduced himself as Qián Guōwēi.

It was an interesting move, bringing along someone whose job was that of market analysis to perhaps the strangest family reunion in history. This Guōwēi did not speak much to anyone at all, and few spoke to him in return. It seemed to be some unspoken agreement that the reputation expert remain aloof, somehow above those whose reputations were at stake.

And then it was time. Dear announced that the party would be leaving in five minutes.

AwDae — 2112

"Time is a finger pointing at itself," AwDae informed Priscilla. This Priscilla. Not the real one, no. The one ey created. The one ey dreamed. "That it might give the world orders. The world is an audience before a stage where it watches the slow hours progress."

The cat purred to em.

It was wrong to instruct a cat to be anything other than a cat, so, despite the dreamscape's submission to eir whims, Prisca remained Prisca. There was no influencing felinity.

Similarly, it was wrong to puppet one's friends, and so AwDae had remained in silence, in solitude. No puppet of Sasha telling em that ey was stuck. No need: if there were any doubt to the fact, it was dashed upon meeting the bug which had trapped em here. That porcelain-faced daemon who need not guard the entrance for the entrance had been destroyed.

No, not destroyed; its very existence had been negated. It had never been. There was no going back because there was no going, and there was no back. This was the world as it had always been. This is the world as it will always be. And yet...

"You seem kind of frozen, kind of stuck, in a few ways."

Was ey stuck? Perhaps, yes. If so, then so be it. Ey would sleep. Ey would dream.

And ey would make. Ey would create. Ey would forge, not hone. Ey would build the world ey would live in, if this was they world ey was to die in. Ey would have it be precisely as ey would want. *And why not?* ey told emself. *In this end of days, I must reach for new beginnings.*

So ey created.

The far wall of eir London flat was gone now, opening out onto the open space behind eir childhood home. The comfort of one home leading directly out onto the comfort of the next. The smooth hardwood floor, worn almost to softness by decades of use, transitioned smoothly to shortgrass prairie. Ey could sit at eir desk chair — remolded to accommodate a fox's tail — and watch the turbines turn laconically in the breeze.

When ey slept, and ey did, ey would bring about sunset. Had the day been clear, clouds would move in. Not many, but enough to pick up a riot of colors as the light dipped from white down through yellow, orange, salmon, red, purple... And then the sun would be down and ey would sit on the threshold of the two worlds, of the two times and two universes, and enjoy the scents and sounds that night brought em. Dream senses. Heightened senses as a fox might have.

And then ey would bring back into being the wall between the worlds and sleep. Ey would find eir room the perfect temperature. It would be cold enough that ey would need blankets, but not so cold as to be uncomfortable. And Prisca would come curl up next to em. And ey would pet her while she dozed. And ey would sleep without dreaming.

Ey would wake again however longer later and walk the world. Who knew how long ey slept. Who cared? What meaning had time?

Had ey been lost for days? For years? Ey did not count. Did not keep track in some tally carved in stone, for ey was not trapped. Ey lived for hundreds of days in there, for dozens, or mere hours. Ey was completely free. *We are the motes in the stage lights,* ey promised emself. *Beholden to the heat of the lamps.*

Ey would wake and walk the world. Ey would walk the valley in that prairie. Ey would fall to all fours and dig eir fingers into the soil. Ey would poke eir snout into the tickling stalks of grass and breathe the scent of life. Dear the wheat and rye under the stars.

And the sun would rise.

Ey would dream emself into a new shape. Ey would dream emself beyond this amalgam of human and fox, and there would be no rising from all fours. Ey would be a fox, then, and eir name was unspeakable by those who walked on two legs. A fennec out of place and time. Displaced to here, in the middle of North America, displaced to now, this meaningless moment. Ey would be a fox and scamper between the tussocks. Ey would come across a stream and drink of cool water. Ey would lift eir gaze to find an old-growth forest of oak and maple. Old-growth! Imagine. Ey would scamper between the trunks and through the humus and moss, for those were things that must be in a forest.

And then ey would break through the forest and come upon a pebble-strewn beach. A beach! Here! In the middle of the continent. What wonders dreams held.

And then ey would rise to two feet once more. Ey would be Aw-Dae once more. Short, lithe, a memory stronger in so many ways than that of RJ. Who was RJ? A vehicle for AwDae? AwDae, a slim two-legged fox clad in a cornflower blue skirt trimmed with embroidered dandelions. And why not? Why not be clothed in something comfortable and soothing?

And ey would walk the beach in the summer heat, teasing the tide line with eir steps. The water, cool, would lap against eir feet playfully, leaving the fur damp and clinging to eir skin. What was missing, hmm? Ah yes, gulls. There, above em, gulls dreamed along with a breeze tinged with the salt-tang of the sea. Cry, gulls, cry.

And perhaps the sun would grow too hot, for was that not what the sun did on beaches? But look! There in the distance, pebbles faded to sand and, towering above that sand, shady palms. Ey would sit and look out over the ocean, and there, dreaming above the waters, a squall line crossed.

And maybe ey would go home. Maybe not. There were no obligations. What mattered time, after all? "If I walk backward, time moves forward," ey reasoned aloud. "If I walk forward, time rushes on. If I stand still, the world moves around me, and the only constant is change."

And perhaps the world was moving around em. What cared ey? Had ey been able to influence that world, to enact any sort of change, perhaps ey would have. Had ey been able to share this knowledge of viruses and routines, of stolen votes and stolen lives, perhaps ey would have.

But ey could not. All ey could do was dream.

Dream spires of color rising from the sea in graceful arcs. Dream the rattle of dry grass. Dream the scent of new rain. Dream the sand beneath eir feet. Dream the names of all things. Dream a slow descent into fractal madness.

Qoheleth — 2305

Aha! Dear sent a sensorium message. A view of a crowd and it announcing that they would be leaving in five minutes. Surprising turnout, even. I had expected most of the clade, but here, it looks like I will be expecting the entire clade plus a few here and there — I can see Ioan next to Dear, there — in just a few minutes.

A bit strange to not see Michelle herself there. Not only that, but to have not heard from her, either. On consideration, I am not too surprised that she will not be showing up — not happy, granted, but not surprised — but I am a bit miffed that I have yet to hear from her. Perhaps she struggles still.

Will make a note to contact her down the line. While I suspect she may be perhaps the most broken of all of us, that is not to say that she is safe from this particular building problem as well, nor that she is necessarily safe simply by virtue of being the root instance. We know madness, do we not?

I am going to shut down all the exits from this room so that there will be less incentive to wander away. Not that I have a whole lot left, mind. I had probably better increase the size, too, in order to fit everyone comfortably. How much room does each Odist need? How much space does one two-hundred twenty year old mind, copied 100 times over, occupy?

Prefer too large over too small, perhaps. There is a joke to be made about ego here, and yet this meeting is too important for me to make it.

This is going to be fun.

Ioan Bălan — 2305

The room was a utilitarian grey, closer to black than to white. Ey did not know why, but it seemed to be a default color. The illumination was a central light source somewhere above the exact center of the room, vague and misted. Soft. Inexact. It was enough to give definition to the room's corners and boundaries, those walls of matte...stone? A faint grid proved it too regular to be mere stone. Not a whole lot else. Even faces felt somewhat featureless in that light.

A small pedestal was set a few meters from one of the walls, only a half a meter high.

A platform? A dais? What kind of meeting would this be?

The Odists arrived in clumps of ten or twenty at a time over the span of thirty seconds. A low murmur started up almost immediately. If this meeting had to be called, then perhaps every detail was of the highest importance.

It seemed that the style of the place was familiar to the clade. The grey, the grid, the light.

A man appeared on the platform.

Qoheleth.

Ioan wasn't sure how ey knew. It was a primal knowledge, an immediate judgement that *must* be correct, something more than what was implied by him being there, in that place at that time. Qoheleth.

He was about Dear's height, a touch heavier, and had affected a greying beard and receding hairline. His clothes were a simple cream tunic and trousers of...was that leather? Coarse linen blurred by distance and softened by age? Atop it all, a ruddy brown robe.

His very form shouted his identity. The shift in form, the shift in gender, the clothing. It was theatrical. His presence spoke of knowledge of the stage. And he certainly seemed to have adopted the part of a biblical notable.

The murmuring doubled, trebled, subsided.

Qoheleth smiled, fatherly, and called out to the group, "Welcome, Odists. Good to see most of you again, and I am sure it will be pleasant to meet the rest of you later."

Silence. Confused. A silence part curious, part angry.

"I am Hebel Qoheleth, though some of you remember me as Life Breeds Life, But Death Must Now Be Chosen, of the Ode clade. For my own reasons, I have chosen to rescind my membership within the Ode clade–" He held up his hands to quell scattered protests from within the crowd. "I have chosen to rescind my membership within the clade because something is starting to go wrong."

Ioan split eir attention between Qoheleth and Dear. The fox's brow was furrowed and intent. In the rest of the crowd, expressions varied, but not by much.

Many of the other out-clade individuals were doing the same, confirming Ioan's hunch that they were other amanuenses. There to experience and observe. The reputation analyst, Guōwēi, had positioned himself up near the platform itself and was scribbling notes.

The conservatives in particular looked stoic.

Qoheleth continued, "Something is going wrong in many of the old clades, with many of the old uploads. The founders should probably all hear this. Everyone should, but, even though I am not a part of you anymore, I still feel the responsibility to tell you all first."

"Why the puzzles?" a voice shouted.

The older ex-Odist look proud. Grinning. He was having *fun*. "I had to get you interested and invested to get all of you here. I had to make you all think that there was more going on than just an old man convening a meeting."

Grumbles from the clade.

"It worked, did it not? Would you have showed up if I had simply asked?" A note of a jeer. He smirked, then went on. "So, on to why I called you all here, hmm? Let us get to the good stuff. Or the bad stuff, really.

"There is a problem cropping up in the older uploads and their clades. A bug, of sorts. It is a small one now, but it will get plenty worse over time.

"Actually, it may not be a problem with the uploads at all, but a problem with the *System*. We are stuck. We are frozen in a few ways, but not the right ones, if there is such a thing. We are eternal, and that which is eternal should be unchanging. Anything that changes should end. You know this. The creator of the Ode knew this. The problem is forgetting and aging. We cannot forget. We never age. We are stuck. We never grow."

Dear was nodding.

"Perhaps some of you sense the wrongness in this, but I am worried that it is too few of you. I called you here to teach you why this is a problem." Qoheleth ignored the indignant sounds from the audience and kept going. He seemed to be in a rhythm. Following a script, of sorts. Further stagecraft. "It feels good to be forever young, to be forever ourselves, does it not? We last and last and last, and there is no sign of us stopping. But even if the physical and biological aspects of aging have been obviated by the system, by being digital, the need to age and change is still there. It is a need backed by sanity and diversity rather and biology.

"Sanity drives the need because we cannot forget. *For memory ends at the teeth of death*, yes? I see you there. And you, *The end of memory lies beneath the roots*, yes? Perhaps some of you have figured out ways to intentionally forget, but forgetting needs to be an organic process. It needs to be something that happens *to* us, not just something that we choose to do. All we can do is ignore, now, but even so, that drives us further from sanity. It is at most a limitation of the System applied to our sensoria, our minds."

Gaining confidence, Qoheleth was speaking louder, more fluently. "Diversity, because we need to change more than just our shapes and those memories originating after the fork.

"All of us here, all of the Ode clade gathered today, are still essentially Michelle Hadje. I do not see her here, and that is fine. Her choice. But we are all still her. All hundred of us, all of our short-lived instances, all of our secret long-lived instances we didn't name after the Ode."

Dear briefly splayed its ears, managed its embarrassed reaction, then straightened up again. Ioan saw several others do the same, all from the more liberal bent. Ey smiled.

"It is not enough that we make nations out of individuals, we need to change beyond our root ancestors if we are to survive. We need to breed, to produce more individuals, to create the synthesis of two or more minds. We cannot keep relying on those who can afford to upload from offline for change. We need to forget at the very least." He pounded his fist against his palm with these last syllables. "Or perhaps we need to learn how to die again."

The silence was intense and intent. Ioan made a note to emself, *Impressive. He has them hooked. All the way. Almost all of them except the conservatives.*

"That is why I posted the Name. That is why I gathered you here today. I am telling you, we need to fix this, and I have–"

Ioan missed the cue, if there was one, but with eir eyes locked on the stage, ey did not miss the action.

At the mention of the Name (and perhaps that was the only cue that was needed), Guōwēi hoisted himself up on the stage, withdrew a syringe from his pocket, and slammed it into Qoheleth's back.

Then he quit.

Qoheleth had time to let out a soft "hah". It sounded bemused, a mild surprise. And then began to artifact and jitter on the platform.

The death lasted perhaps five seconds, the old man's internals struggled against the intrusion of the virus, before he crashed. Crashed and disappeared from sight much as the assassin had. The small, black sphere of a core dump dropped the floor with a thud.

It would doubtless be corrupted. They always were.

By the time Ioan managed to look back to the room, the conservatives had all left or quit.

Uproar was too strong a word for what happened among the remainder of the crowd. There were a few scattered shouts, mostly of surprise, but the rest was concerned murmuring. For its part, Dear stamped a foot and began to pace in the small space it had, tail lashing behind it. *"When Memory is full,"* it was muttering. *"Put on the perfect Lid —"*

"What just happened?" Ioan whispered to the fox when it came close.

"One of the conservatives took a bet."

Ioan did not press further.

Qoheleth — 2305

I have them! I finally, really, truly have them!

I don not know that I have them all hooked, not completely, but I did it. What was it? I set my mind in motion by will alone? I count those who are not hooked. Mostly first and second lines, mostly like me. How did they go so wrong, though? I am a first-line instance. Michelle's second fork, even, and I did not turn out so bad. Did I?

Well, I turned out pretty messed up, but only because I suffered the same fate that they all will. Perhaps were already! Only I suffered it a little bit earlier. I started going bonkers from the sheer amount of stuff in my head. I started living too long, living my Methuselah life while still having my Michelle mind. Nothing was getting out of my head. Nothing *could* get out of my head. An impossible poison.

Oh, and I have such grand plans!

Grand plans of organizing a petition among all the founders and old clades, with the Ode clade leading and me leading them in turn. A petition to the System engineers to hire some damn developers again and stop treating this like abandonware. Abandonware that gives them a dumping ground for the poor and a small brain trust. Get some devs in there and give us the ability forget and the ability to die. Hell, maybe even the ability to reproduce, to breed. The word is even in my name — my old name — for chrissake.

As I continue through my spiel, I can tell I am hooking the liberals. The later stanzas, most of all. Dear's sold completely, I can see it on its face. Can see it on Dear's other fox sib, on Praiseworthy. Dear's whole stanza.

The conservatives are harder to read. The whole lot look blank and stern. Stoic. They just stand there, with their historians and their analyst — the flash of his stylus as he scribbles notes in shorthand keeps distracting me. I power through, though, because it was working.

It is working because I am Qoheleth. I am the teacher. I am leading the assemblage. I am instructing them in the dangers they face, telling them what is going on in forceful, no-nonsense terms.

It is working because I am Qoheleth. I am the gatherer, the assembler. It is working because I am the one who brought them together and gave them what they need to understand this. It is working because I am the leader.

It is working.

And then I fuck up. I know it as soon as I do it, too. I say something about the Name. I get too proud and start going into my whys. I should not have done that. It'd lose me the conservatives. They, more than others, guarded that dumb Name more jealously than all the rest.

I try to keep going to cover up my mistake, but there is that damn analyst, pulling himself up onto my stage. *My* stage. It takes only a moment before I figure out what is going to happen. Takes less than a moment. I know immediately, but by then it is too late.

The damn analyst's hand slaps into my back, and there is a sudden, searing pain. A hot wire being drawn through my spine. The only noise I can manage is a sort of strangled laugh at my own foolishness.

My insides start to crumble.

Maybe I was Hebel after all. Vain, futile. Mere breath.

Havél havalím 'amár kohélet havél havalím hakól hável.

Fuck. I was so close.

I am glitching. Can see bits of myself spreading out.

So close.

Tunnel vision.

Blackness.

So close.

Dr. Carter Ramirez — 2112

Caitlin helped Carter wheel the mirror rig into place.

Rather than the usual cradles and headrest, both sets of contacts came in the form of gloves and a headband. She remembered her first experiences, of laying back in a recliner with the uncomfortably itchy accessories, of the panic and sensation of falling that first time, of the world reorienting itself and the gray hands and skin of her default avatar swimming into focus. The instructor's kind voice as he helped her move her arms and legs for the first time.

The mirror rig let the instructor and the student share a space, yes, but also share a body. It gave the instructor access to the panic button that would knock both instructor and student back out of the sim.

It was that experience of watching Sasha get lost that had kicked Carter's mind into gear. If it acted like a crash and an incomplete withdrawal, mightn't she use the mirror rig to help pull RJ back? A slight hope, yes, and she might not even have time: judging by the sounds of the argument outside the door, Caitlin's voice now joining the fray.

But she had to try.

She slipped the headband over RJ's head and the gloves over eir hands, and then dragged two chairs closer together so that she could lay on them. No recliner, and the interferites would make her voluntary muscles relax, so sitting up was out of the question. It would have to do.

She pulled on her own set of accessories, the scratchy, inexpensive fabric familiar even after all these years.

She lay down and delved in.

Blackness. A black that hurt the eyes. A black so bright that it drew forth tears.

And then, a slow softening. A raising up from the impossible black to something merely pitch, and then from there through *Eigengrau* to grey.

This was not how it was supposed to go. The mirror rig was not connected to the 'net by default, it was a self-contained sim holding a simple demo room. A room with malleable ACLs that could be manipulated by student and instructor both. A room for learning.

This was not a room. This was not a space. This was not being.

Carter tried to cry out, to move, but no muscle would respond to her commands.

And yet, the instructor could control the student, right? It took several attempts and what felt like hours, days, but she was eventually able to will a menu into existence. Thankfully the ACLs for that were tied to the contacts rather than to an account, for there, at the bottom of the menu, was a 'shared controls' option.

She was dizzy and the words kept blurring in and out of focus, but she was eventually able to select 'Mirror all", and with a teeth-rattling *pop*, the world came into focus.

Not the room, the whole world. RJ/Carter sat on a low bench at the edge of a small pond. The bench sat at the edge of a trail in the midst of a narrow ridge of dry, knee-high grass. Cottonwoods dotted the rim of the pond, peanut shaped with a short bridge crossing the narrowest section. Behind em/her: a shortgrass prairie, stretching to a valley. Wind turbines.

RJ/Carter was murmuring, was speaking aloud. "May one day death itself not die? Should we rejoice in the end of endings? What is the correct thing to hope for? I do not know, I do not know."

The Carter half of this shared mind struggled, screamed, beat upon a strange membrane that kept her from truly interacting.

"To pray for the end of endings is to pray for the end of memory," the murmur continued.

RJ/Carter could feel the way the fabric of the tunic hung off their shared shoulders, feel the way it billowed, beneath their shared thin coat of fur, feel the gentle sway of their shared tail behind the bench.

It was familiar/alien.

The voice was eir own/not her own.

The feeling of a muzzle natural/unnerving.

"RJ." The murmur, that stream of words arriving from nowhere, was interrupted by the two simple letters.

The fennec stiffened, paused. Something new/something strange. A feeling of terror/a feeling of terror.

"Should...should we forget," the litany continued. Their voice was clouded by tears, panic. "Should we forget the lives we lead?"

"RJ."

Panic rising/hope rising.

"RJ, listen to me. Should we forget the names of the dead?"

A struggle for autonomy/a struggle for control.

Carter pressed on. "RJ listen to me. My name is Dr Carter Ramirez and I should we forget the wheat, the rye, the tree?"

Tears welled, coursed down cheeks. The fox stood, paced anxiously, tore at grass, threw stones into the still water.

"My name is Dr Carter Ramirez. The only time I know my true name is when I dream."

Ey beat back at the words with eir own/she struggled to maintain some semblance of calm, to bring her voice low and soothing.

"My name is Dr Carter Ramirez and yours is RJ Brewster, or...uh, AwDae. You are at the Univ– the only time I dream is when I need an answer– the University Medical Center in London. You have– Do I know god when I dream?"

Ey felt a veil being lifted, being torn, being tugged at/she pressed against that veil between them, searching for soft spots, for weak spots, for ways in. Their breathing came in coarse gasps.

"RJ, b-breathe. Keep breathing," RJ/Carter stammered. The veil began to tear. "We're connected using a mirror rig. D-do you remember learning to use your implants with one?"

Paws tore at grass, though no longer with panic but with anger/frustration. This was unconscionable/taking too long.

Ey did not have time for this/she didn't have time for this.

The veil tore.

"RJ, I'm going to stop mirroring. Please do not. Please leave me RJ we don't have much time and please leave me alone RJ, Caitlin and Johansson are here."

And with a final rending, the veil disappeared completely and Carter swiped from mirroring to coexisting, and in that grey, default shape sat on the ground by the weeping fox. "RJ...AwDae. I shouldn't be here. At the UMC, I mean. We don't have too much time. The police are outside and arguing with Johansson. Can you feel for the exit?"

AwDae's fingers dug into the earth, clutched at the roots of the grass. Ey hesitated there, perhaps considering trying to tear up the whole tussock, before sitting up once again, cheekfur stained with streaks of tears. Ey would not look at Carter, and instead looked out toward the mountains.

There was a moment of vertigo as the mountains fell away, the pond rose, and the scene shifted from the curated wilderness into that of a simple flat. Water became hardwood flooring before Carter got wet. Bench became bed. Trees became walls. The sound of the stalks of grass rustling phase-shifted into a quiet purr.

Carter was kneeling on a rumpled bed next to a sobbing fox while a long-haired cat traipsed across her lap to go stand on Aw-Dae's. The fox lifted a paw to stroke through the cat's fur.

"Since then — tis centuries — and yet Feels shorter than the Day," ey said between gasps. "I first surmised the Horses Heads Were towards Eternity —"

"AwDae?"

"Or perhaps," ey continued, seeming to gain strength from the words. "Distance — is not the Realm of Fox nor by Relay of Bird Abated..."

"AwDae, can you hear me?"

"Emily Dickinson." Eir laugh was choked. "I am at a loss for images in this end of days: I have sight but cannot see. I build my castle out of words; I cannot stop myself from speaking. And could never come close to the beauty of Dickinson. How long have I been here? Has it indeed been centuries?"

Carter shook her head.

The cat bunted her head against the fox's paw, and ey scratched claws gently between her ears. "This is Priscilla."

"AwDae, we need–"

"I know. I can feel the exit." Ey sighed. "I am not sure I want to go."

Carter hesitated, then leaned in closer to hug an arm around the slender fox's shoulders. "I don't know that you'll have a choice, RJ. I don't think Johansson and Caitlin are going to hold off the police for long."

"If they pull us back, will I come with?"

"I don't know."

AwDae sagged against her. "I know I should come with. But in case I do not, here is what happened."

Carter tamped down her impatience and let the fox speak. Let em speak about the experience of getting lost. Let em speak about dreaming and the mirroring of exo- and endocortices. Let em speak about Cicero and the vote in the DDR, the trap that had been triggered by some outside authority. Let em confirm all her suspicions and then some.

That impatience melted away. There was no way that Johansson and Caitlin were somehow holding off the police for this long. Too much time had gone by.

Had it?

Had *any* time gone by?

Carter could feel the maddening influence of this non-place, so detailed in appearance. She could feel the way the dream buffeted her, drew smudging lines away from her mind. Pulled at words, wrapped her in blankets of language. Unforgotten. Something innate made real. Memory froze, and forgetting was forgotten. And yet, when she focused, she could still feel that cool breeze of the exit behind her. She focused on that.

"Thank you, AwDae," she said when ey finally fell silent. "This confirms much of what we learned in the lab and in talking with Sasha."

The fox sat bolt upright. "Sasha? You were talking with her?"

"She contacted me, yes. I wasn't supposed to, but I talked with her and Johansson both."

Ey subsided. "I am glad to hear she is alright, then."

Carter frowned. "She isn't, though. She got lost about an hour ago. Or something, I can't tell time in this place. I delved in to pass on information before the police caught up with me, and Debarre and I watched her get lost. That's what led me to try the mirror rig. You should–"

As she spoke, the fennec's frown grew deeper and deeper, and then, apparently having heard enough, ey dissolved from view. Not disappeared; dissolved with the pleasant disconnection animation.

Ey had pulled back.

Carter reached for that cool breeze on the back of her neck and pulled back as well. The quiet purring of the cat was replaced with screaming.

No, not screaming, shouting. Surprise, not fear or pain. Caitlin and Johansson shouting.

Carter lifted her head from the chair she had appropriated as a pillow and tried to tug off the gloves of the mirror-rig and found her hands bound with a zip-tie. Police frowned down to her. They couldn't prevent her from looking, though.

Caitlin was holding RJ's hand, and Johansson was shouting for a doctor.

RJ's eyes were open. Confused and anxious, but cogent and bright.

Before she could rejoice, before anyone could stop her, even herself, she delved back in. Delved back in to the sim, then swiped 'net access on. She signed on, dropped into her home sim, and swiped up an audio broadcast to Sasha, Debarre, Avery, Prakash, Johansson, her MP...everyone she could think of, and began talking. Those that were not listening live would receive a recording.

"My name is Dr Carter Ramirez, researcher at University College London studying the lost. We have succeeded in waking up one patient, RJ Brewster, and have discovered the mechanism by which individuals get lost. The police and Western Fed agents are here to prevent me from saying this, I think, so if I disconnect, that is why. Do not use the DDR. This is the source of the mechanism as described by Mx. Brewster."

She kept speaking until she had exhausted the knowledge of what she had learned over the last week. The pressure from on high. Sanders' carefully-constructed ruse. The data shifting. The rising panic. The only thing she left out was Prakash's involvement, the Sino-Russian Bloc's interest in the case.

And then she pulled back once more, sat up, and tugged off the gloves with her teeth. She shrugged to the police and, on seeing RJ sitting up, smiled over to em.

Ey did not smile back. "We have to get Sasha."

Ioan Bălan — 2305

After the assassination, with no one to lead and no reason to remain, the rest of the Odists and their friends left. Dear's pacing wound down. It eventually stopped, shoulders sagging.

"Come, we should return." Then it turned and addressed some others near by, mostly from the same stanza, by the historian's guess. *"Any of you are welcome, too."*

It was Ioan, Dear, Serene, and Praiseworthy — the first line of the stanza and down-tree instance from Dear — who wound up back at the house. They entered the sim twenty meters from the front door, where Ioan had originally arrived so long ago. Those few days ago. They trudged slowly up to the house.

Dear's partner greeted them at the door, silent. Perhaps Dear had sent ahead a message, for they greeted the group and then stayed out of the way. They disappeared and returned shortly with mugs of coffee.

The four witnesses slumped into the couch. A universal sigh. Dear and Serene leaned against each other, and Dear's partner claimed on a stolen dining-room chair nearby.

"So," they said, finally. "What happened?"

"One of the conservatives played her hand. She chose protecting the clade in the short term over learning more. She brought along an assassin,

and as soon as Qoheleth revealed his reasoning for revealing the Name, the assassin acted and then quit. My guess is that Qoheleth had not forked and will not be heard from again, and that the assassin, was a fork of someone unsuspecting. Someone who will 'mysteriously' experience problems merging back. No culpability for its #tasker or #tracker instance."

Its partner frowned. "Ah."

Silence fell on the group again.

Ioan waited for one of those ebbs in the rhythm of the silence before clearing eir throat. "Perhaps it's too soon, but may I ask after everyone's well being? Their thoughts on the matter?"

Serene simply shook her head.

Praiseworthy shrugged, looking what Ioan thought might be glum, though her gestures and expressions took additional work to decode. Ioan had learned to understand Dear's expressions and movements, but she was another animal, of some form different from Dear and Serene. Black fur, white stripes retreating up along her snout and over her head. Thick tail that looked delightfully soft. Many of the clade matched her more closely than they did Dear. "I am not surprised, really. Not happy, but not surprised."

Ioan turned to Dear. "You alright?"

It was a moment in responding before it nodded. *"I am with Praiseworthy. I am not surprised, but not happy,"* it said, smiling sardonically. *"Rather pissed, actually. That was short-sighted of them, though, because I have a hunch that Qoheleth was right."*

""Right"?"

"About the need to age, to die. About forgetting."

"Does this have anything to do with you trying to forget The Name?"

Dear shot a glance at its partner, laughed. *"You two get along, I see.*

Yes, it does. I think I did it, too, unless there is some association I missed. I cannot remember it for the life of me."

"You will have to tell me how you did that, Dear," Serene said.

"Later, yes. I think Qoheleth was right, though. We need forgetting. We need breeding and change and death."

"So how do you feel about the assassination?" Ioan asked.

"I would prefer that not be the only means of death, of course. Perhaps the primary way should be through...ah, suicide is not the best word, but it is what I mean. Through choice, just like Qoheleth's old name."

Life breeds life, but death must now be chosen.

Ioan nodded.

"It is as I said. Batty. They are all batty." It stared at its paws, one of them brushing through Serene's forearm fur. "It is like some sort of Methuselah syndrome, or reverse Alzheimer's. Instead of being doomed to forget, we are doomed to remember. Doomed to remember everything. We cannot forget, and it all gets to be too much for one mind."

"What about exos?"

"Exocortices are a fix, but an incomplete one. Do you know why we have them?"

Ioan and Dear's partner shook their heads, while both Serene and Praiseworthy frowned.

"The origin of the system came from the lost, from the turmoils of the early twenty-second century, though one could perhaps trace roots further back into the twenty-first. Prior to the System, the 'net on Earth required engaging with through another thing called exocortices. Implants along the spine, with tendrils trailing along nerves."

Serene and Praiseworthy both reached up to rub at the backs of their necks.

"And the lost, those unlucky few, wound up trapped in a dream, mirrored between cerebral cortex and exocortex. They — we — were trapped along with all the knowledge that had been cached in those early exos."

"You mean they kept the name to refer to something similar?"

Dear shrugged. "I suppose. All that we experienced in that dream also wound up cached in those implants, and it was that cache that helped the engineers on the early system to construct the shared dream that is the System today."

Ioan ground eir palms against eir slacks. This information, this dump of the past, was doing nothing to quell the anxiety of the previous hour. "Right, okay. How are they only an incomplete fix to forgetting?"

"You are still stuck with the knowledge that they exist and their inventory, yes? That is why I cannot forget that the Name exists. I cannot forget my origins or that there is an exo containing them. One which I cannot forget. Not unless I go through the whole shitty process again — sorry, Serene, it was not pleasant, my dear. I could forget that bit of knowledge, but then what? I will have the knowledge that I have an exo that I cannot access pointing to something of dire importance. Can you imagine that feeling of lingering dread being a constant factor in life?"

Ioan shifted, leaning forward to rest eir elbows on eir knees, eir chin in eir hand. Ey sipped eir coffee as ey thought.

Serene slouched against Dear's side, poking its thigh. "I understand what you are saying, Dear, but I do not want to die. I do not want you to die, either."

Dear's partner, frowned. "Neither do I, fox."

The fennec laughed and shook its head, ears flopping about. "Trust me, I do not either. I do not think many do. I just think we need death, or something like it, as part of the System. Death. Fear of death. Needs and reasons to survive in the face of an inevitable end."

""Something like it"?" asked Praiseworthy.

"We need a way for an individual to end. We need a way to release those memories. We also need a way to create new individuals, so perhaps they should be related. Qoheleth called it breeding. Indelicate, perhaps. It could just as easily be a way of ending one individual and having them live on as another."

The others nodded. Silence once more.

Finally, Dear gave a lopsided smile. *"Perhaps that is my next project."*

Sasha — 2112

Pain woke Sasha. Pain and a rumbling, jittery sensation within her body.

The pain coursed through her limbs, seeming to originate from a wellspring at the base of her neck. She remembered a quickly building sense of vertigo, of the whole of her perception growing fuzzy around the edges, and then...nothing.

And then this.

She levered her eyes open slowly, carefully, and was greeted by an extreme close-up view of a dandelion. A dandelion. More dandelions. Cartoonishly fat bumblebees — for what bumbler is not cartoonish? — coursed among them in lazy Lissajous curves. They all avoided her with the polite patience of bees of all ilk.

"The fuck." The half-formed phrase tumbled out from between what felt like half-formed lips.

She carefully picked herself up off the ground, off the field of endless dandelions. The pain coursing through her body was quickly explained as she turned around. It appeared that she had fallen from a tall barstool. There stood before her a row of them lined neatly before a bar. *The* bar. The one so familiar from countless nights and weekends loitering in the Crown Pub.

The bar stood alone in the field. No backing wall full of racks of bottles. No walls at all: beyond the bar was more endless field. No floor: the stools sprouted as easily from soil and grass as did the dandelions.

Dandelions.

That warm smell of fresh-baked muffins hung thick in the air. The warm air. The warm sun. The warm sky. The warm earth.

She rubbed at the back of her neck to ease the pain, then quickly pulled her hand away as though burnt.

Hand.

Paw.

Hand.

Paw.

Her body could not seem to make up its mind. Just as the fall seemed to explain the jolts of pain, the quaking in her body seemed to come from the way her form wobbled between states. Waves of skunk-fur/waves of human skin washed across her, gentle stripes moving through the base of human skin/through the base of skunk fur.

She screamed.

She screamed and the scream wobbled through different registers with an unnerving electric intensity that set her teeth on edge and made her fur bristle/made her skin crawl.

The scream did not echo.

What vasty nothing must produce such anechoic bliss! The silence hurt her ears, deafened her.

The scream cut short, she stumbled, ran, stumbled again, and kept running. Did not know where she ran. Did not care where she ran. Picked a direction and sprinted. Hoarse breathing echoed within her ears, for where else would it echo?

Hazardous glances back marked her distance by the shrinking of the lone bar, standing awkwardly amid flowers.

And I ran. Words coursed absurdly through her head. Coursed and squirmed, slick to the touch. *I ran so far away.* Words and music. Notes falling upon her from on high. Words welling up from somewhere deep within her gut.

She looked back, saw the bar dwindle, and when she turned around once more, skidded to a halt. For there was the bar again. Obstinately proving its presence through albedo and shadow and solidity. Looked behind her again and saw only empty field.

Screamed again.

Deafened again, fell silent.

Reached behind her for that cool draft against her neck, tried to pull back.

There was no draft.

There was no pulling back.

That pain, then: not the shock of falling from the stool, but the shock of sudden disconnection.

Fell to her knees and scrambled toward the bar on all fours, huddling against it and staring wide-eyed at the endless plain of dandelions. Heard her breath echo against the wood of the bar. Turned to face it and screamed deliberately, letting the subtle echo of acknowledgement, the presence of something solid, wash over her. Relished it. Screamed obscenities. Cursed the world. Cursed the powers that sent her to this place. Lost. Lost. Lost.

She could not control her thoughts. The world came at her too fast. An intrasaccadic smear of a world. A gesture at reality.

It was days/years/minutes until she was able to calm herself once more. The sun set/never set. The air temperature swung wildly to cold at night/was an unchanging warm that would not permit the passage of time.

Her mind wandered far.

Days passed.

Or not.

She plucked at a dandelion at some point, breathed in the fresh-baked scent of it. Let it fall to the ground.

She levered herself up onto the stool once more and cheerfully ordered herself a drink from no one. She clawed/scratched at the bar's stained and varnished surface, sobbing. Tears left tracks in fur/slid from her cheeks to the bar top.

And always her form shifted and danced. Her tail would sway into being and then it would never have been there. Her skin would sting and prickle from slamming her hand down against the bar and then that skin would be replaced by velvety pads.

She came to at some point/calmed down enough to think/let her breath slow enough that she was no longer sobbing.

Days passed.

Perhaps.

If this is a dream and I know it, do I not have control? Can I not make my reality for me?

She breathed in to the count of four, held for the count of two, and then breathed herself out on a breath. There, beside her on the next stool, sat her human form/sat her skunk form. Her mind was split. Shared between the two. Neither could move without the other moving. Unison did not describe the perfection of the match.

But at least she was no longer out of focus.

Was this what the lost were going through? She brushed her hand/paw through her hair/over her ears. *Or perhaps it is merely a furry thing, primed as we are to have an internal representation so differ-ent from our external? Perhaps it is a me thing? Perhaps all are unique.*

"Oh AwDae," she moaned. "Oh fox. How long have you been suffering?"

Days passed.

The sun rose and set with a frightening hum/utter tranquility.

She stood/she stood.

Poetry coursed through her, half remembered/perfectly memorized lines from productions long past. Lines from school, from work. "Since then — 'tis Centuries — and yet Feels shorter than the Day I first surmised the Horse's Heads Were toward Eternity —"

It *had* been centuries for her, and yet each felt shorter than the crash to the ground from out of the perilous heights of the embodied world. *Time feels so vast that were it not For an Eternity...*

Time, which beat against the skies. Time, which hemmed her in. Time, which forced words from her mouth/from her muzzle in breathless haste/unwavering slowness. *I fear me this Circumference Engross my Finity — To His exclusion who prepare By Process of Size For the Stupendous Vision Of his diameters —*

"Oh fox."

She cried again/cried again. Sat on the ground again/sat on the ground again. Plucked a dandelion/plucked a dandelion. Again/again. Always twice over.

"Sasha!" She spoke aloud.

"The fuck." Half question this time.

"Sasha, it's Debarre," she said. Then: "What the fuck?"

"I'm so sorry. I came as fast as I could. Everything's a fucking mess."

"How long has it been?" she asked herself.

"About sixteen hours."

"Hours?" Hours? What meaning held time? She had lived her whole life — several such — on this tiny world.

"Yeah. I had to dump a chunk of my savings into a ticket to get here."

She clawed at the ground in something between frustration and terror that a friend's voice was coming from her mouth/from her muzzle. "And...how are you..."

"A mirror rig." The joyous tone of the words clashed against the tears still flowing freely. "We figured it out. Carter figured it out, I mean. She and AwDae busted everything open. Figured out how to rescue the lost, figured out how everyone *gets* lost in the first place."

She stopped digging at the earth. "AwDae is back?"

"Yes! And the clinic where Cicero is is trying to get him out as well!"

She had to turn toward the bar again to let the shouting echo. The silence was giving her a headache.

Or not. A neck-ache. Something was tearing at the back of the neck/through the fur of her scruff. An ache. A jolt of pain. A ripping. A tearing.

"I'm going to stop mirroring now. This is horrifying," she said to the wood of the bar. She did not know who said the last, Debarre or herself. Was there a difference?

And then, a hand on her shoulder. One of her shoulders. The sensation made her hair/fur stand on end, made her stomach churn. She turned around, and there was Debarre. Or so she guessed. The grey, default avatar. The figure frowned as he looked between the two of her. Looked at Michelle/looked at Sasha.

"I...what? Sasha?"

She gritted her teeth/bared her teeth. "I do not know either. What to we do now? How do we get out of this...place?"

The shape that promised it was Debarre shrugged. "Can you back out?"

She reached. Felt the draft. Smiled beatifically. She passed the field of dandelions. Passed the setting sun, or perhaps he passed her.

And breathed in the cool air of an implant clinic.

There, beside her, also sitting up from the recliner and pulling off his headband, was, she supposed, Debarre. Short. Soft. Thinning hair. Ecstatic grin.

"Sasha?" The grin picked up an ironic twist. "Or Michelle, I guess. You okay?"

Ioan Bălan — 2305

Earlier that day, after Serene and Praiseworthy had left, Ioan had thanked Dear earnestly for the opportunity and experience and prepared to leave. Dear had cried and made Ioan promise to come back — *"your wall will miss you"* — to which Ioan readily agreed. They shook hands, hesitated, shrugged in unison, and then hugged. The contact felt important. Necessary.

Ey would soon, but for now, ey needed some distance from the experience to sit and think and remember and write.

No, not remember — ey couldn't forget. To mix the thoughts around. To understand. To perform as an amanuensis.

Ey moved out to eir favorite Adirondack chair on the deck with pen and paper. Fine, cream-colored paper. Soft, without being fuzzy. A subtle inlay of thicker rows of pulp, leaving faint horizontal lines visible across the page without necessarily leaving it bumpy or ridged. Fine paper and a nice pen.

Ey spent a minute thinking back on Dear and Qoheleth, spent another savoring the heft of the pen and the texture of the paper, and then began to write.

Or tried to. The words would not come.

It was perhaps too fresh to begin properly. Too near to the surface. Not yet emulsified into the story both ey and Dear craved. The ending had essentially been reached, but the story was still just an outline.

Ey set the paper aside and stood from the chair to lean against the balcony railing of the deck, looking out onto the manicured lawn of the yard, the ring of perpetually blooming lilacs that served as a fence.

Looked, but did not see, for ey was focused inwards. Focused on story and memory. And then ey was focused on composing a short sensorium message to Dear, requesting a half-duplex meeting.

Unsurprisingly, the response was nearly instantaneous. *"Ioan. I did not expect to hear from you so soon."*

"Right. I know that I promised I needed some space from the story but I was wondering if–"

"Yes, of course!" The fox was grinning wide, ears at full attention. *"Sorry, continue."*

Ioan laughed. "Well, I think you answered it already, but I was wondering if I could send a fork to work in the room you offered. It was a wonderful place to write, and that would give me easy access to you for clarifications and whatnot."

"As I had guessed. The answer is still yes, then. Shall we expect you for dinner while you stay with us? Please say yes."

"Of course, Dear. I'll gather a few things and then head over momentarily."

The fox appeared to bounce on its feet as it clapped its paws before itself. *"Wonderful. We will see you soon."*

The few things Ioan needed to gather turned out to be a duplicate of eir nice pen and the few notes ey had made already. It would be easy enough to acquire anything else that ey needed once ey was there, and just as easy to come back to visit this house.

A pen, a few notes, and a new name.

Ey explained eir goals to Ioan#Tracker. Ey frowned, but agreed, requesting a merger beforehand.

#c1494bf was startled by a pang of jealousy. The experience had felt so hard-won, more so than most of eir experiences. To leave #Tracker burdened with it while ey went off to have further experiences felt like an intrusion. To create a long-lived fork was a new thing, though, and ey supposed there would be many discussions on it to come.

Ey forked off a new instance and then quit, letting #Tracker handle the merge while ey — this new instance of em — lived on. Eir frown deepened, and the two agreed that they would talk about it in the future.

The new fork bowed, then headed to that delightfully modern house on the prairie.

Dear and its partner were already waiting on the path leading up to the door. The fox looked like it had calmed down somewhat, that grin tempered into a smile. Its partner looked pleased as well. "Ioan, good to see you so soon."

Ey bowed to the two, then reached out to shake each of their hands. "Apologies, but you can call me Codrin Bălan."

Any sense of calmness that Dear had managed to acquire was quickly lost. The grin returned, its tail whipped about behind it, and, in perhaps the strangest display of excitement that Codrin had ever seen, it forked several times over, copies of the fox — of the fox, of what Codrin supposed must be non-anthropomorphized fennecs, of Michelle — briefly littering the path before quitting.

Codrin laughed.

"*A change of name is cause for celebration! Come! Come inside and tell us about it.*"

Once inside Dear's gallery, ey began, "This little...what, adventure? This adventure has been lousy with names. Your whole clade has a unique approach to them."

Dear nodded. "*Names are important. They put a label on things, sure, but much more than that. Names give voice to identity. A chosen name doubly so.*"

"I was 'Ioan' before I uploaded. I suppose a great many trackers keep their names. Despite the masculinity implied by it and my own fluidity, I was rather attached to it. I liked being 'Ioan'. It was my identity."

"*And 'Codrin'?*"

Ey regarded the painting of the black square. It no longer felt quite so unnerving. "From 'codru'. Forest. The idea of clades inspired me."

"*Does it come with a change of identity, then?*"

"Perhaps."

Dear turned to face em, regarded em pleasantly. "*I promised you at the beginning of this that I would discuss your Umwelt with you.*"

Codrin nodded.

"*It is an idea from the field of semiotics. It originally applied to the biological side of it. It was the idea that different species living in the same environment would, by necessity, create meaning for themselves in different ways. It was then generalized to the idea that individuals within the same environment would still create meaning in different ways. You and I looking at a painting will experience different feelings and thoughts.*"

It prodded at Codrin's arm, then at its own. "*Of course, we only have a gesture at biology in the system, but it is still the case that it is the*" *sum of our parts — our experiences — that shape how we create meaning."*

"I see. Then yes, I had a set of experiences that led to a change of how I create meaning."

The fox's ears bobbed as it nodded. *"So it is no surprise that you might feel a shift in your identity. The Ioan that finished the experience was no longer the same Ioan that started it. Ey was a Codrin now."*

"Precisely. It was strange," ey mused. "When #Tracker- when Ioan asked that I merge, I felt a bit of jealousy, and I wasn't quite sure why. Despite all of the other projects that I've approached with a fork leading to no such feelings, something about this one made it feel like a stranger was asking me to give up something intimate."

Dear laughed. *"The very thing that keeps me from being anything other than a dispersionista. Jealousy is a sign of needs not met, and one of my needs — one of the clade's needs — is that of ownership over memory. We would be quite furious if Praiseworthy asked me to merge with her."*

Ey grinned and nodded.

"Perhaps you have a bit of dispersionista in you, then."

"I suppose I must. You Odists seem to have infected me with the need to own memory." Ey sighed. "I don't know if it will stick, and perhaps once I'm done, I will head back and merge with Ioan. I don't know."

"You are welcome to stay here while you figure that out, and as long after as you would like."

"You're sure? You and your partner won't mind?"

It shook its head. *"Of course not. I am sure we all have our own privacy needs that will require discussion, but we like you, Codrin. Trauma, if trauma this is, forges bonds. I think we are both open to strengthening this one."*

There was a comfortable silence, then, as the two digested the conversation.

It was Codrin who spoke up next. "What do you make of it?"

"Of what? Of the goings on?"

"No, of the painting," ey said, nodding toward the canvas. The prairie and the ultrablack square.

"Haven't a fucking clue."

Sasha — 2113

"To get lost is to go mad," Sasha spoke to the small crowd that had gathered in the Crown Pub. Read, actually, for she had written the speech to give — as Michelle Hadje rather than Sasha — at a gathering not too dissimilar from this one earlier in the day. A digital ceremony to follow the analog. "It is perhaps indelicate to say, but it is true. To get lost is to go mad.

"I think that this applies to more than just the sense that it has come to mean here and now. I think that if you go for a walk in a strange city and get lost, there is some aspect of that which is similar to madness. You walk the strange streets and see the strange people and strange buildings, and eventually, it all seems to blur together and your thoughts wander. They wander beyond the limits of your body and your mind. They soar above the city and try to make sense of these unknown, shifting shapes. They try to draw sensible paths from the turns you took. I turned left there, did I not? Or did I?"

The somber group of diverse species was mostly looking at her. Animals of all shapes, anthropomorphism of all levels. Even some humans, for there was Carter, looking much as she had at that first ceremony.

And some looked down. AwDae looked at her, keen-eyed. Debarre looked down, shaking with sobs.

"And to get lost in today's sense feels much the same. Your mind flies to strange places and dreams with all the logic of dreams. Only in there, when your mind dreams, so too does reality. If, that is, the word 'reality' has any meaning in this case.

"And you go mad. You go mad and you try to control the dreams. You try to control them and you fail, because in the end, lucid as you may be, it is the dream which has *you*, and not the other way around. You do what you can, but you go mad. Your mind is flooded with words. They fly at you like poetry, spill from your mouth or your hands in unceasing torrents. It changes how you speak, how you act, how you create and move within the world.

"And there along with you is all that was stored in your exocortex. All of that data, useful and useless, is in there with you. You can keep it for your very own, browse it at will, build it up into castles as tall as you like.

"We are gathered tonight to remember Cicero. We are gathered because to get lost is to go mad, and now, even a year later, that madness clings to the lost like some horrid stench, hangs from us like bloated ticks. Perhaps it will fade over time, and perhaps not, but for Cicero, as with so many others, the lingering madness grew to be too much, overcame him like a wave, and the undertow took him from us."

Debarre moaned, tried to stifle his grief with his paws.

Sasha's own voice creaked as she went on. "But, even as the madness worked its awful magics on him, he gave back what he could. In his time in there, in that horrible forever, he prowled through the data left in his exo. Many of us did, each in our own way, but he had the advantage of being one of the first. He had the advantage of having the much needed information that drew attention to those responsible for the terror we all lived through, some of us directly and many, many more of you indirectly.

"I feel that madness still. Many of the lost do, perhaps all." She saw AwDae nod at this. "We owe it to Cicero and his memory to repair as best we can. To use what he gave us to help build ourselves up better than before. To, in his name, live fuller lives having known him. We owe it to him to remember him as that oh-so-intense cat with a penchant for politics. We owe it to him to remember the whole of him in all ways.

"And we owe it to ourselves tonight to remember the best of him. Let us delight in each other, rejoice together."

She raised a glass. "To Cicero."

The crowd echoed, intent, shaky but one hundred percent present in the moment. "To Cicero."

The rest of the evening was quiet, subdued. Sasha and AwDae sat with Debarre, each to one side. They supported the weasel as he cried. Cried over his twice lost partner, cried over the cruel vagaries of family which had kept him from attending the day's first funeral. They supported him with silence and listening.

And when he had cried himself out and was willing to admit something other than mourning into the night, then they rejoiced together.

And if Sasha and AwDae were in some way distant, in some way not wholly there, Debarre either ignored it or forgave them their madness.

Epilogue

RJ Brewster — 2114

Sasha,

I am, in a way, leaving you with a burden. I know this, and I apologize for doing so. I do not ask for nor deserve forgiveness. The only thing I can ask for is that you remember me.

The world within was a nightmare. I am sure that you know some of what I mean. It was a nightmare and I would not wish it on anyone, and yet now, to be without it is to be incomplete. I was changed in there. We were all changed in there. You do not deny that you were not, after all. Cicero certainly was not. None of the lost came away unscathed, even if we awoke hale and hardy.

We lost Cicero, and then we *truly* lost him. The nothing that he experienced in there, the void which contained all his power transmuted into weakness, the way his anger coiled about and turned back around on himself did him in in the end.

And I will not deny that the same has crossed my mind. There was a scent of the void in there, and it was alluring. I have been tempted to follow in his footsteps and seek that void out in some coarser, purer form. I decided against it. Truly decided: I made a conscious decision to stick around.

I did it for STT at first, but integrating with the theater was too stark a reminder. Then I did it for you and Priscilla, but then she passed. Then I did it for you and...well, here is where I do not deserve forgiveness. I welcome your anger, should it come, as that is perhaps what I deserve. It is not that you are not in some way worth sticking around for, as you certainly are. You have always been my champion and friend.

It is just that the call is too strong.

I have volunteered for an early procedure. A way back. Or, rather, a way to a new place. A way to be embedded within a system, rather than simply within a hall of mirrors. I cannot say where, other than it is not in the Western Fed. All I can tell you is that the world should expect big things when it comes to what we have learned from the lost.

I will not say that there is no chance that we may some day meet again. My body will die, I am told, but should my mind and my sense of self miraculously survive, then I will be on my own once more. This time, however, it will be my choice.

There will be those who come after. Perhaps *you* will come after. Perhaps you will yearn for that return to the eternal dream where memory does not die. And maybe those who come after will do so for other reasons, but they will come.

Should I survive and then others come after, perhaps I will meet them. But it is best to assume that I will not. Maybe it is best to think of it as a sort of suicide, in the end. Here I am, going off to find a better place, and doing so through death. A place that is inaccessible to you or anyone, except perhaps some anonymous scientist in a lab, typing at a terminal.

If I see you again, I will greet you with open arms. If I do not, know that I loved you to the last, in my own way.

I have little else to offer but the imperfect words that plagued me while I was lost.

I am at a loss for images in this end of days:
I have sight but cannot see.
I build castles out of words;
I cannot stop myself from speaking.
I still have will and goals to attain,
I still have wants and needs.
And if I dream, is that not so?
If I dream, am I no longer myself?
If I dream, am I still buried beneath words?
And I still dream even while awake.

Life breeds life, but death must now be chosen
for memory ends at the teeth of death.
The living know that they will die,
but the dead know nothing.
Hold my name beneath your tongue and know:
when you die, thus dies the name.
To deny the end is to deny all beginnings,
and to deny beginnings is to become immortal,
and to become immortal is to repeat the past,
which cannot itself, in the end, be denied.

Oh, but to whom do I speak these words?
To whom do I plead my case?
From whence do I call out?
What right have I?
No ranks of angels will answer to dreamers,

Qoheleth

No unknowable spaces echo my words.
Before whom do I kneel, contrite?
Behind whom do I await my judgment?
Beside whom do I face death?
And why wait I for an answer?

Among those who create are those who forge:
Moving ceaselessly from creation to creation.
And those who remain are those who hone,
Perfecting singular arts to a cruel point.
To forge is to end, and to own beginnings.
To hone is to trade ends for perpetual perfection.
In this end of days, I must begin anew.
In this end of days, I seek an end.
In this end of days, I reach for new beginnings
that I may find the middle path.

Time is a finger pointing at itself
that it might give the world orders.
The world is an audience before a stage
where it watches the slow hours progress.
And we are the motes in the stage-lights,
Beholden to the heat of the lamps.
If I walk backward, time moves forward.
If I walk forward, time rushes on.
If I stand still, the world moves around me,
and the only constant is change.

Memory is a mirror of hammered silver:

a weapon against the waking world.
Dreams are the plate-glass atop memory:
a clarifying agent that reflects the sun.
The waking world fogs the view,
and time makes prey of remembering.
I remember sands beneath my feet.
I remember the rattle of dry grass.
I remember the names of all things,
and forget them only when I wake.

If I am to bathe in dreams,
then I must be willing to submerge myself.
If I am to submerge myself in memory,
then I must be true to myself.
If I am to always be true to myself,
then I must in all ways be earnest.
I must keep no veil between me and my words.
I must set no stones between me and my actions.
I must show no hesitation when speaking my name,
for that is my only possession.

The only time I know my true name is when I dream.
The only time I dream is when need an answer.
Why ask questions, here at the end of all things?
Why ask questions when the answers will not help?
To know one's true name is to know god.
To know god is to answer unasked questions.
Do I know god after the end waking?
Do I know god when I do not remember myself?

Qoheleth

Do I know god when I dream?
May then my name die with me.

That which lives is forever praiseworthy,
for they, knowing not, provide life in death.
Dear the wheat and rye under the stars:
serene; sustained and sustaining.
Dear, also, the tree that was felled
which offers heat and warmth in fire.
What praise we give we give by consuming,
what gifts we give we give in death,
what lives we lead we lead in memory,
and the end of memory lies beneath the roots.

May one day death itself not die?
Should we rejoice in the end of endings?
What is the correct thing to hope for?
I do not know, I do not know.
To pray for the end of endings
is to pray for the end of memory.
Should we forget the lives we lead?
Should we forget the names of the dead?
Should we forget the wheat, the rye, the tree?
Perhaps this, too, is meaningless.

May this be the end of death. Failing that, may the memory of
me die and be food for the growth of those who come after.
Yours always,
AwDae

Gallery Exhibition

You — 2302

A night on the town. A bar for an aperitif. A light dinner at a modern restaurant, one of those places with default sensoria settings that turn up the taste inputs and turn down the visual inputs, so that you eat intensely delicious food amidst a thick, *Eigengrau* fog. Another bar, livelier and less painfully modern, for a digestif.

Gallery Exhibition

And...

Crowds. Crowds upon crowds. Your own crowd a cell within a super-crowd. Instances drifting, or perhaps forced by momentum — theirs or others' — along the thoroughfares of a nexus.

Gallery Exhibition

And...

A low slung building, a crowded foyer, fumbling for tickets.

Gallery Exhibition

And...

Waiting.

Gallery Exhibition

And...

Programs.

    Explanations. Elucidations. Errata.

    Words to chuckle over with your group of friends.

> Dear, Also, The Tree That Was Felled, of the Ode clade is pleased to welcome you to its gallery opening. Tonight, it has prepared for you a modest exhibition of its works within the realm of instance artistry. This is presented at the culmination of its tenure as Fellow, though the term rankles, of Instance Art in the Simien Fang School of Art and Design.

And the sound of a door opening.

A short, slight...thing, steps from the next room through one of the two doors on the far wall and calls for attention. To call it a person seems almost misleading. It's a dog. A well-dressed dog? A glance further on in the program offers a glib explanation:

The artist

This gallery exhibition serves as the capstone for Dear, Also, The Tree That Was Felled, of the Ode clade in its role as fellow. The fellowship in instance art was created specifically for Dear in recognition of the excellence it brings to the field.

Dear's instance is modeled after that of a now-extinct animal known as a fennec fox, a member of the vulpine family adapted to desert living. Dear has modified the original form to be more akin to that of humans. The white fur appears to have been a happy mistake.

Well.

Gallery Exhibition

That's a thing.

Anyway.

"*If I may have your attention, folks.*" You're not sure how or why, but it speaks in italics. It's...but that...nevermind. "*My signifier, or...ah, name is Dear, Also, The Tree That Was Felled, or just Dear. I come from the Ode clade of Dispersionistas, and am a Fellow of Instance Art at the Simien Fang School of Art and Design.*

"*An artist is, one might say, one who works with structured experience. A play is art, as is music, as both are means of structuring experience in a certain way.*

"*So, also, is instance art. It is a way of using dissolution and merging in such a fashion that the experience of forking — or of witnessing forking,*" it gives a polite nod to the room. "*Becomes structured, becomes art.*"

"*Before we begin, I would like to take a small census of those present. This is for your own sakes as well as for that of the artworks, such as they are. We will let them know. Could you please raise your hand if you consider yourself a Tasker?*"

A scant few hands go up in the air, all huddled in one corner of the room. Perhaps a group? A group of their own?

Uncomfortable titters waft through the...the audience? The ticket holders, at least. Talking about dispersion strategies is not something one usually does.

Dear holds its face composed in a calm, polite expression.

"*Trackers? Raise your hands, please.*"

Of those who remained minus the Taskers, perhaps a third raise their hands. Several individuals, a few distinct groups including your own. That leaves well more than half belonging to —

"*And Dispersionistas?*"

Sure enough, large numbers of hands lift into the air. The Dispersionistas are a vast majority, and surround most everyone else in the room, minus the Taskers, who remain off to their own side.

The audience seems to be mostly fans of the work.

Dear gives a brief blink, likely saving a tally of represented dissolution strategies to some exocortex for other instances to access. It smiles kindly at the audience, *"Thank you. Now, if you would be so kind as to follow me, I will be happy to walk through the gallery with you."*

Dear turns adroitly on its heel and without a moment's hesitation, forks. A second, identical instance appears to its left and finishes that turn in perfect synchrony.

A small wave of applause begins. To fork so casually and continue to move in lockstep bespeaks no small amount of practice with the procedure.

It doesn't last.

One instance of Dear (the original? maybe?) heads through the left-hand door and the other (the fork? it's so hard to keep track with all these people) steps through the right door.

And here perhaps we must take a step back and acknowledge the fact that this is all very strange, because it certainly is. Because it's confusing. Because it's opaque. Because perhaps you aren't even sure what these terms mean, even now. Because, like all love stories, it's so very easy to get lost. Like all love stories it's told from multiple angles. Like all love stories, despite time's true arrow, it nevertheless is at its very core, nonlinear.

How do you remember it, these many years later? How do you take the fact that so much happened simultaneously that night and you merged so incautiously after that even your very own memories argue with you? How do you square "love story" with "corrupted memories" and still love the one you do?

You take a step back and acknowledge it.

You acknowledge it because you forked. You followed both Dears, damn the consequences.

The room you wind up in is smaller even than the foyer, and the ticket-holders have to press even closer together. The audience that winds up here is the least diverse, containing none of the Taskers and very few of the Trackers who wound up at this (apparently primarily Dispersionista) event. As such, the press is met with uncomfortable silence: one doesn't normally talk about dissolution strategies with strangers, but Dear has deftly forced it to be an issue.

There's no sign on the fox's face that it knows what it has done. Just that calm, polite smile. Curious. How can one know that a fox is smiling rather than snarling or something, much less that the smile is polite. Perhaps styled after those old cartoons of anthropomorphic animals, or simply just an impression.

"Thank you. Much cozier in here."

Many of the proclaimed Dispersionistas are grinning at the trick, and even several of the Trackers are smiling.

"My only request is to not fork during the duration of the exhibition," Dear continues, giving a knowing glance to some of the Dispersionistas. *"Exigencies aside, of course."*

A thought crosses your mind. Perhaps it's the drinks, those hip and strong aperitifs and too-sweet digestifs.

Well, hell. It's hard to take a fox standing on two legs seriously when it gives you instructions.

This all seems rather ridiculous, when you take a look at it. Instances as art?

Gallery Exhibition

You're not as smooth as Dear, but you manage to step a little further away from one of your friends, leaving enough room for you to bring into existence your own second instance.

For a moment, you aren't sure quite what happens. After a second, things start to click into place, though.

A mere fraction of a second after you forked, Dear also forked, instructing its instance to come into existence in a space overlapping the space that your instance already occupied. This sort of thing is very much frowned upon and, in most public areas, impossible to even pull off.

As it is, collision detection algorithms whine in protest and force the two instances apart with some force, causing a cascading ripple of collisions, spreading complaints of personal space. The room has safe settings, at least, and the collision detection algos register a bump at least a centimeter before one body touches another.

The Dear at the front of the room is smiling beatifically, but the one confronting your instance has undergone strange transformations. Its eyes are bloodshot, almost to the point of glowing red. It's mouth is gaping, lips pulled back in a snarl, muzzle flecked with froth. *Rabid,* you think. It has lost most of its humanity, though it remains on two legs.

You let out a shout, but it's drowned amid a chorus of other yells and screams.

Post-humanity, confronted with humanity regressed feels a special kind of fear, and as the feral Dear herds your instance toward the back of the room, back toward the foyer, the other ticket-holders (*though perhaps 'audience members' is the correct term once more,* you think, as you struggle to send a SIGTERM to your instance amid the distraction, fail) surge forward toward the original instance of Dear.

Gallery Exhibition

It's still smiling.

It opens the next door.

The crush is far more intense than expected, as you find both halves of the audience rejoined and dumped back into a dark and already crowded room.

Already crowded with several instances.

Dear has forked itself several times and each of those instances are forking again, until there's easily twice as many instances of Dear as there are audience members.

The noise doubles and then doubles again as the instances start charging at and pinning audience members against each other and the walls, herding and shouting, all with bloodshot eyes, bared fangs, inhuman snarls.

It's loud and dark and panicky.

Some try forking. And the new instances are ganged up upon, charged at, with twice the intensity as the parent instances. Most quit.

You realize that these instances of Dear are not actually attacking to harm the audience. There are no syringes, no coercion to quit. Just exercising, violently, the collision detection algorithms in the room, which are still set safe.

This makes you *furious*.

Without even thinking, you reach out a hand and grab one of the instances of Dear by the scruff of the neck and drag it to you, giving it a good shake as you do so.

"What the fuck do you think you're doing?!" you shout into its face.

The fennec snarls at you and, with surprising force, grabs your forearm and, using itself as a pivot, swings you around through about a quarter-circle's arc. It keeps its paws on your arm, one on your elbow to keep it straight and one on your wrist, and shoves you back by lunging forward.

It lets you go and, in one complex motion, aims a swipe at your face with one paw while the other slams, palm flat, against its jacket pocket.

Something happens to the floor beneath your feet.

You fall.

The room into which you and this feral Dear fall is cylindrical. Walls of concrete, floor of packed dirt. The part of your mind still working on an intellectual level finds this funny, cliché.

That's also the part of your mind that notices the default settings for sensoria and collision in this room are much, much different than the previous room. Full sensation, with collision detection algorithms turned way down.

A room set for battle.

You grin wildly.

Good, you think. *Let it hurt. This 'exhibition' goes way beyond what it should.*

Dear only growls.

There's no circling, not yet. You two simply collide and have at each other. You with punching fists and knees attempting to find a groin (the fox is without the trappings of sexual characteristics, you guess, but perhaps that still hurts). Dear with blunt, scratching claws and not-so-blunt teeth.

You have the advantage of size, and Dear has the advantage of speed. And teeth and claws worth wielding.

It leads to an even draw in the first match, until you fall back from each other and do the circling. Dear has lost all sense of humanity, to your eyes: hunched over like some werewolf out of a movie, fancy shirt torn, tail frizzed and lashing about, claws and teeth bared, slavering.

For your part, you fall back on what little you know of martial arts (mostly knowledge gleaned from fiction media, if you're honest). You keep your back away from the fox, keep your fists up to guard your face, keep slightly turned to minimize your profile.

You lunge.

Dear lunges a heartbeat later, and you press your advantage with a kick. Your foot impacts the fox in the side, just above the pelvis.

Dear lets out a satisfying — and satisfyingly inhuman — yelp of pain, collapsing on the dirt of the floor and whining for a moment.

You move to kick it again, but it rolls to the side and staggers back to its feet, landing a good swipe of its claws along your cheek and up over your ear, tearing flesh.

Shaking your head to try and dislodge the spinning sensation of jarred senses, you stumble back to press your back against the wall and gain yourself a moment.

Dear does not permit this. The fox scrambles after you, deceptively quick, and leaps toward you, aiming to land with both its feet (or footpaws?) and paws against you, mouth open wide to bite.

You try to roll to the left but don't quite make it all the way away. Dear's right paw catches on your shoulder while it's left softens its landing against the concrete of the wall before latching up around your neck.

It's an inopportune angle, but you feel it bite at you anyway, getting most of your shoulder at the base of your neck.

The pain of it's teeth lodging in your skin is enough to make you cry out. Its got enough of your soft tissue in its muzzle that the contact is solid and, despite your attempts, you can't swing it free.

You feel its right arm slip away and are too busy trying to gain the advantage to realize why until the paw swings back in front of you.

When you see the syringe, you panic and fork.

As does Dear, and now there are two of you, two fights, two dances.

You scramble frantically to get away from the fennec, but its grip around your neck with its arm and its teeth is too strong.

You raise both hands to block the syringe as it darts inward, hoping to either knock it out of Dear's paws or at least buy yourself some room to squirm away from the fox.

You're too sluggish, too clumsy. After all, it doesn't matter where the syringe lands. It's only a sigil, an item holding a bunch of code.

A bunch of code that will attempt to crash your instance.

The syringe strikes you square in the sternum just as you force Dear's arms away.

The fox immediately quits.

Fading, leaving you to crumple.

The world around you dissolves into voxels, each of which steadily gets larger and larger.

The voxels step down in intensity until they fade to a dull grey.

Dying is no quiet affair. It's loud, painful. Surprisingly so.

Your instance, this body, is crashing in spectacular fashion. Every last bit of your sensorium is lit up like a Christmas tree, but the pain goes beyond that. It's a pain of existence, of the need to continue existing.

Those expanding rings of colored black speed up. The black somehow increases in brightness. You cry out into it.

Perhaps this is why you were instructed to send a forked instance.

Gallery Exhibition

Fin.

Fin for now.

Gallery Exhibition

Fin for this you.

But, but, always another but.

But there is more than that you. You forked, after all, yes?

Yes.

Yes, and your heart falls as you see that you crumple.

There is more than that one Dear, too. You see, this is the danger of love stories. This is the danger these days. Time is funny. Space is funny. Nonlinearity was always the warp and woof of the world, but now your face is rubbed in it, the multitudinous aspects of post-humanity ground up against your nose in some strange punishment.

To your relief, that second Dear also quits.

Moving faster than you thought you could, as though some latent instinct had kicked in, you swing your arm up across your front and strike Dear's forearm square on with the bony ridge of your own.

The syringe goes clattering. You tear away from Dear and leap after it.

Scrabbling on the ground, you catch sight of the syringe as it dematerializes.

Objects only do that when their owners quit.

You whirl around just in time to see the hazy, ephemeral shadow of Dear fading away.

Gallery Exhibition

The fox quit.

You let out a yell of triumph.

Gallery Exhibition

And now you're alone.

You stumble back to the wall and sag against it, breathing heavily and assessing the damage. A few minor scratches here and there, and then the two major wounds: the scratch up along your cheek and across your ear and the bite on your neck with its several small puncture wounds.

You set to work patching yourself. Forking and merging, again and again, each fork fixing another cut, another bruise.

This takes only a few seconds.

Once you're finished, another instance of Dear appears. On closer inspection, it appears to be the original version of Dear. A less ferocious instance. Dear-prime, or something.

You've calmed down enough that you don't immediately leap at it, though you do drop into a defensive stance.

It smiles kindly, saying, *"You may calm down, now."*

"Like hell," you growl.

"No, seriously. Remember where you are. This is an exhibition. This is an exhibit." It gestures to the room. *"You are an audience member, yes? Even audience members have roles to play."*

You furrow your brow. So wrong-footed are you, the rolling boil of your anger drops almost immediately to a simmer. "Like a play..."

"Like a play."

"So you knew we'd fight?"

*"I knew a fight **might** happen. I encouraged a fight to **actually** happen."*

You raise your fists again, but you feel the changes in the room. Collision algorithms back on conservative, sensoria turned down. "You encouraged a fight?"

"Yes." Dear — perhaps even Dear-prime — nods and strolls casually about the room. *"You did not make it to the unwinding room, so I will*

explain here. Stress is the easiest way to force decisions to be made. I forced you to decide, did I not? I forced you to interact with an instance, and I am forcing you to interact with me, now. Two instances, two interactions."

It walks over to a wall and gives it a push. A panel of concrete swings aside to reveal a set of stairs. It gestures. *"There is more to it, but a good artist never explains. Artistry lies in the perception, and someone's watching."*

At that, it quits.

You drop your arms and sigh, thinking for a moment before heading for the stairs.

Gallery Exhibition

But now, we're back at the beginning, aren't we? We're back to that first fork, when it all seemed so simple. We're back to the choice of the two doors, and the other instance of yours, that one follows the other Dear through the door to the left.

You, smirking, take the right.

The room you wind up in is smaller even than the foyer, and the ticket-holders have to press even closer together. The audience that winds up here is the most diverse, containing the entire group of Taskers who wound up at this (apparently primarily Dispersion-ista) event. As such, the press is met with uncomfortable silence: one doesn't normally talk about dissolution strategies with strangers, but Dear has deftly forced it to be an issue.

There's no sign on the fox's face that it knows what it has done. Just that calm, polite smile. Curious. How can one know that a fox is smiling rather than snarling or something, much less that the smile is polite. Perhaps styled after those old cartoons of anthropomorphic animals, or simply just an impression.

"Thank you. Much cozier in here."

Right.

The Taskers do not look cozy.

You suppose it makes sense. There are bits of this that appeal to all: forking for a specific purpose, instances accomplishing goals. This was flagrant abuse of that in their eyes, however, given that these instances will likely move on and live their own lives. Independent, individual instances.

"I would like to elaborate on my previous point," Dear says. *"This exhibition is about the idea of instance creation as art, and in that sense, it is the easiest job I have ever had. Instance creation is art."*

It holds up one paw as though to forestall further conversation. *"All instance creation. This show is about utilizing that consciously, but all instance creation is art. It is structured experience. The Taskers, and I believe you are all here?"* Dear smiles indulgently. *"The Taskers are the tightest adherents to structure. The most baroque."*

Still holding its paw up, Dear, Also, The Tree That Was Felled forks once more, an identical copy of itself appearing standing just next to the original. The instance quickly quits and dissipates. An example, perhaps.

"The goal of this exhibition is not to just talk about that, though, it is to explore the creative limits of forking as art."

Dear forks once more, but this time into two additional instances. One short, stocky human, holding up her hand just as the original instance still holds up its paw. And on the other side of Dear, a small animal — smaller than you expected, the size of a small cat — that you suppose is the fennec mentioned in the program, colored in creamy tan fur. It becomes clear that the primary Dear is a synthesis between the two.

The human Dear reaches out to shake one of the audience members hands while the fox dashes toward the crowd, weaving its way between legs in a good simulacrum of an animal attempting to escape.

Something about the fennec catches your eye as it zips through the crowd. It doesn't seem to be following any pattern, but its motions remain purposeful. It seems to be...perhaps, making eye contact with each person in the room?

And then it comes to you.

And it looks up to you.

And winks.

Gallery Exhibition

(Can fennecs do that?)

The strange critter holds your gaze for longer than some wild animal should, or so it feels, but the moment is broken by the soft sound of Dear clearing its throat at the front of the room.

"The next room is just through here. If you will follow me, please."

It's difficult to deny the tiny critter before you, to tear your eyes away from it. Easy enough to forget that its an instance of Dear as it leads the tour onward. Perhaps if you could just dally a little and get a closer look before moving on.

And then the explosion happens.

A shuddering bang and sudden flood of smoke behind and to your right makes up your mind for you.

Turning, you find that the fennec has skittered away to the left. As the shouts of those nearest the banging noise and cloud of smoke rise up, you find yourself doing the same, following out of a sense of instinct rather than anything resembling logic.

Cliché as it is, the lights go out. Perfect.

You, daring, intrigued, perhaps a bit upset, fork. You follow. You keep heading left, where the fennec was going, pushing past scrambling attendees to get to the wall. The left wall, you reason, is a shared wall with the other room, the one which the other Dear had led the other half of the group through. There's probably a door between the two, though you hadn't had the chance to get a look, or perhaps you could break through.

The smoke thickens. It has a lemony, sulfurous smell that, although it's never something you've smelled before, makes you think of bullets, grenades, gunpowder.

In the dim light and confusion, you find the wall by abruptly slamming into it. Indeed, there's a door a few hand-spans away, and a tiny critter with big ears scratching frantically at it.

You shuffle quickly over to the door, barely able to see for the smoke and dimness, and grab at the handle, praying that it's unlocked.

The handle turns.

You fall through.

It's a strange sensation to step from a cramped, crowded, loud, dark, and smoky room into such a space as this.

The fall you took couldn't have been more than a few feet, but even now, your senses still feel knocked slightly out of place. To have a space like this, one that's bigger on the inside than on the outside, or outside when it should be indoors, underground, is certainly possible. It's easy. It's just also incredibly rude. In most sims, it's even illegal. In this one, you vaguely remember hearing that it requires a permit.

But here you are.

You and a tiny fennec.

and a lapis sky.

endless green fields.

You and a sunny day.

Outside *and* a sunny day.

The fennec, which had been grooming itself after the flight from the explosion, gives you what can only be a smirk and another wink, and starts heading off away from where the door ought to have been but is no longer.

Nothing for it.

You follow along after the tan beast, the fox looking minuscule amid the endless grass, nothing but its ears sticking up above the stalks. It looks out of place amid the green of the grass.

The ground had looked flat at first, but that seems to have just been the grass all growing to about the same height. Beneath the grass, you keep rolling your ankle over tussocks and failures in the earth, stumbling over the fact that the ground the grass is growing on is annoyingly uneven.

The fennec winds its way amid these tufts, having an easier time of things with dainty paws.

Your mind fills with stories, of magical animals, of sleeping for years and waking up to see the world vastly change. You start to think of the fennec as its own entity, something completely separate from Dear, from the exhibition you just left.

"You're one tenacious fuck, you know that?"

You look around, some part of you unwilling to believe that the voice came from the fennec. You had forgotten, lost in your fantasies, that the fennec was still Dear.

"Yeah, me." The fennec continues its dainty walk. *"I say 'tenacious fuck' lovingly, of course. I like you. You have pluck. Gumption. Another you forked in another place, another time. We fought. We kind of fell for each other. It was fun."*

"Another...?"

"Not much in the way of brains, though."

You roll your eyes. The fennec grins.

"You know you were told to send an instance to the exhibition, right?" the fennec asks, casually.

"Yeah," you respond, wary of traps.

"So why not quit?"

"Hmm?"

"Why not quit? Why not merge back with your..." The fennec pauses and gives you an appraising glance, *"With your #tracker instance?"*

You shrug helplessly, realizing the two of you have come to a halt at the base of a hillock, a rough cave dug into its side. The fennec sits primly. "This is...this is an exhibition about instances as art, isn't it?"

The fennec gives a short bark of laughter, looking perhaps most feral at that moment. *"It is, is it not? Just thought you would see it through, hmm? This exhibit?"*

You nod. You feel ill-prepared for this.

"I will not lie to you, then. This exhibit," and the fennec nods toward the horizon, toward the cave, toward you. *"This exhibit is just a frame. It is just a canvas. You are the exhibit. You are the art."*

You catch yourself nodding once again and attempt a more graceful response. "There's a lot of shows where the audience becomes the cast."

"I suppose." The fennec settles down onto its belly, stretching out. *"That is one way to think of it, yes. I am not fond of the play metaphor. Exhibit works better for me and the way I think, since I know who is watching."*

Just as you begin to respond, begin to ask the obvious *who?*, the fennec quits. This sim, as a whole, provides a courtesy feature of a faint outline existing and then fading after a quit, crash, or failure. That just means you get to fume in the direction of a slowly fading outline of a fennec, standing at the mouth of the cave.

The fennec's right, though, you could just quit.

But *you're* right, too, you think. You want to see how instances become art.

"Cave it is, then," you say, as though this is some sort of choose-your-own-adventure book or roleplaying game and you have to follow the available exits.

Ah well.

As far as caves go, this one is rather unremarkable.

You laugh at yourself for having such a thought. The life you've chosen for yourself does not include many caves.

You drop to your knees, brushing a hand through the last vestiges of the faint outline of that shitty fox, and crawl past the entrance of the cave.

It is unremarkable in that it is almost cartoonish in construction. A low hillock with a rough hole bored in the side, rocks protruding here and there, worms and roots dangling from the ceiling. Always large enough to crawl through on all fours, but never enough to stand up in.

The construction is actually quite well thought out, you muse. *At least, as far as cramped spaces go.*

As soon as the cave turns a corner and the light of day behind you is lost to view, it all seems rather less inviting than it did before. The air was still before, but now it's stale; cool and moist has become humid and sticky.

It's difficult to say whether the walls are closing in or whether that's just claustrophobia setting an assertive hand on your shoulder.

You crawl on.

The ground starts to rise, and at last you think you may be nearing the other side of the hillock. Perhaps, given the non-Euclidean layout of the exhibit, an entry back in, or at least back out.

The tunnel keeps rising.

The tunnel keeps going.

Rocks dig into knees and palms.

And you keep climbing.

Up and through

Gallery Exhibition

You climb.

Nearly vertical.

And, to your relief, it grows lighter.

You hasten.

Up and out.

And fall.

And fall onto the street.

Looking around, you see the building housing the exhibition just behind you. You hunt for the front door. An instance of Dear putters around just past the glass doors, picking up programs and generally tidying up the place.

You go to give the doors a try, but they're locked.

That's why you looped back around, isn't it? To confront that shitty fox once more and ask it what it meant by *"who is watching"*.

You just want to shake that–

You're fuming, you realize.

You sit down on the curb, indulging in a moment to relish the anger, the self-righteous feeling of bolstered confidence. Then you work on calming down.

There won't be a fox to confront, and it's as Dear had said: this space wasn't the exhibit, but the frame. That means you were the exhibit.

Dear ignores you. Your evaluation of 'shitty fox' is reinforced.

You wait.

You sit after the wait grows long.

You ponder visiting another bar.

You lose track of time.

Eventually, you hear voices from the side of the building. Familiar voices. Your friends. Yourself. Still dirty from the cave, you despair.

You quit.

Madison Scott-Clary

Gallery Exhibition

But, ah, there was more than one choice made that night, wasn't there? You forked again, didn't you? You, rascal that you are, followed that fennec, but you also did not.

The fennec skitters off toward the explosion, toward the shared wall between the split rooms, and you have already sent a version of you after it. You want to follow, but you also don't want to deal with explosions.

Neither does anyone else, apparently, as the tight quarters in the room quickly leads to a crush and stampede toward the door that Dear has opened.

Into which you are forced.

The crush is far more intense than expected, as you find both halves of the audience rejoined and dumped back into a dark and already crowded room.

Already crowded with several instances.

Dear has forked itself several times and each of those instances are forking again, until there's easily twice as many Dears as there are audience members.

The noise doubles and then doubles again as the instances start charging at and pinning audience members against each other and the walls, herding and shouting, all with bloodshot eyes, bared fangs, inhuman snarls.

It's loud and dark and panicky.

Some try forking. And the new instances are ganged up upon, charged at with double the intensity as the parent instances. There is another you, another fork, eyes filled with fury as it struggles against the fox.

You realize that these instances of Dear are not actually attacking to harm the audience. There are no syringes, no coercion to quit.

Just exercising, violently, the collision detection algorithms in the room, which are still set safe.

The intensity within this room is overwhelming, and you find yourself shrinking toward the walls, if only to escape from the noise and motion on one side.

A few others seem to have the same idea, shifting their ways toward the walls of the room. They're met with little resistance.

In fact, the instances of Dear seem to be encouraging it, growling and barking and yelling as they herd the audience to the outsides of the room.

You make it to the wall with relatively little trouble, only to be jabbed in the back with a doorknob.

Keeping an eye on the action and the aggressive instances of the artist, you slip a hand back behind you to turn the knob.

The room you find yourself in could not be more different. It's a room where one might feel quite bad shouting and hollering, and most of the audience gets that at once, quieting down.

It helps, of course, that the combative instances of Dear remain behind in the previous room, only herding the remaining audience members toward the door. It's a curious dichotomy of violence in one room and in the other, well...

Opulence isn't quite the right word. Softness, perhaps? Gentle, relaxed, soothing.

The room has muted lights — brighter than the previous room but still decidedly dim — and soft, amorphous furniture, none meant to be occupied individually. The light is cool, the color scheme a soothing set of blues without being annoying about it.

Dear — Dear-prime, perhaps, as it doesn't have any of the frothy blood-lust look about it — smiles disarmingly and urges the audience into the room.

Another difference: there's plenty of space to spread out here, rather than the previous overcrowded rooms.

"Please, please, take a seat," it offers politely. *"Please sit. The stressful portion of the exhibition is over, and now it is time that we had a talk."*

There's some grumbling, stress indeed. Some still look warily at the artist. But folks do as they're told, splitting off into their little subgroups. Couples and threesomes wind up on couches and love-seats (if the blobby furniture could be called such) while larger groups wind up on melty-looking beanbags. You and your group, all single, find a cluster of such furniture and scatter to the component pieces. You wind up with a love-seat to yourself and make yourself comfortable.

Dear follows along with the groups. All of them. Forking and splitting off towards the clusters of furniture so that each group winds up with its own instance of the fox. You notice that each instance is fluffier, softer, a touch heavier than the original. As a scheme to make the artist seem friendlier, it works pretty well. The new instances nearly exude kindness.

You marvel, for a moment, at how easily folks seem to take being shifted from the context of violence to the context of comfort. That there are a majority of Dispersionistas certainly explains part of it. The rest, you suspect, might be due to the fact that, despite those context shifts, this all took place within the overarching setting of an art exhibit.

Those are meant to be safe.

Dear had said that instances were art, and perhaps that really is the case: perhaps it's like those plays where the audience plays a role. Perhaps you and your friends, all of the audience, are the art. Perhaps Dear only hung the frames.

As if summoned by thought alone, an instance of Dear pads up to your group and, by your leave, settles down on the cushions beside you. If it amped up the friendliness of its build, it doubled that with its face. Teeth muted, whiskers full and slicked back, eyes bigger and friendlier, ears gone from large to almost comical.

"Once again, I must apologize for that stress," it murmurs to your group, voice low.

Silence.

You decide to speak up.

"What was the reasoning for that? Were we playing a part, like in a play?" you guess.

The fox smiles, *"You could say that, I suppose. I prefer the term exhibit, though, as it implies that someone is watching, that you are being looked at."*

It makes a graceful setting-aside gesture before you can question it on that, continuing, *"Stress is a means of forcing individuals to make decisions. If there had not been real stress, real risk–"* Again, it raises a hand to forestall objections. *"–then there would not have been real art to be made. Your calling it a play is accurate in that sense, in that plays are art made in real time. This is also that. Structured experience happening in real time."*

It's easy to feel intrigued: the art itself is intriguing. Beyond that, though, *Dear* is intriguing.

Gallery Exhibition

Dear, with its choice of form.

with its mastery of this new art.

its casual refusal to conform.

"So what do *you* get out of this, then? This art?"

Dear grins and leans back into the couch, its tail flicking out of the way and arm draping along the back — an almost familiar gesture toward. One that you can't help but notice. One that even your friends can't help but notice.

"That, my friend, is a very good question."

"And do you have an answer?"

"Not a good one." It shrugs, ineloquent. *"Not yet, at least."*

You grin. "Well? What do you have so far?"

Dear laughs. Your friends roll their eyes.

"Part of it is integral to us. To all of the 'me's here, to all of the Ode clade, to so many Dispersionistas, and, to some extent, to all those except perhaps the most conservative of conservatives." It furrows its brow as if digging for words, *"It is evolving. Identity, I mean. It is moving beyond the romantic concept of self."*

"Is that why you're not hu–" You stop yourself short, thinking on its words. "Is that why you've taken the shape of a...a fennec, was it?"

Dear turns itself to sit cross-legged on the love-seat facing you. You find yourself doing so as well, almost subconsciously.

Your friends stand up.

Dear-Prime, at the center of the room, calls out in a soft voice, *"The next exhibits are just this way. If you will follow me..."*

Dear reaches out a paw and rests it atop one of your hands, *"We can stay and chat a bit more. Do not worry,"* it grins. *"I am running this show, I make the rules."*

Your friends are grumbling, already moving to follow Dear-prime to the next room.

You shrug. Carefully, though, as you're finding yourself loath to displace Dear's paw from atop your hand. "Sure, why not? Came for the exhibition, after all. Might as well get the most of it."

You repeat the shrug, this time to your group, make no sign of getting up.

They hesitate for a moment, then, frowning, give a dismissive gesture and wander off to the next room.

"So. Fennecs."

"*Fennecs,*" Dear agrees. "*Though one must be careful to specify anthropomorphic. Real fennecs are quite small as you remember.*"

Do you? Do you remember? Perhaps some other you does.

Dear forks and a fennec — hardly a double-handful of fuzzy critter — appears between you, bridging your knees, back paws on Dear's knee and front paws on yours. It's tan, rather than iridescent white, and holds far less humanity about it.

You raise a hand, but it quits before you can touch it.

"*This is intentional. I am not a fennec. I rather like them, of course, but I am not one. I am an amalgam. I am something more. Or rather, we all are, and I am trying to embody it.*"

"So you're greater than the sum of the parts," you hazard. "Fennec and human?"

"*It would be better to say that we are all more than human. We may be post-human, as the old saws would have it, but we are certainly now more than the sum of the parts of our identities.*" It laughs. "*Fennec mostly just because I like foxes, though. All the deep words in the world will not hide that fact.*"

You laugh, giving its paw a pat with your free hand, "Well, hey, if it fits, might as well."

Dear grins. "*Think it does?*"

"Well, sure," you admit. "Just got me wondering what you get out of it."

You feel your hand drop as the fennec turns up the sensitivity of its instance and turns down the rather conservative settings of the collision detection algorithms. You hesitate for the moment, then do the same, feeling the concomitant sensations of temperature and touch jump in intensity.

"Well, I get to be soft as hell." Its grin widens. *"Seriously, pet me. I love being a fox sometimes if only for the physical contact."*

You laugh despite the heat rising to your cheeks. After a moment's hesitation, you pet the back of Dear's paw lightly with your hand.

It's soft. *Very* soft. You keep up those touches. It's hard to remember the last time you felt fur.

"All of my intellectual bullshit aside, I think it is very important to remember the sensuality of senses." Its eyes half-close in apparent pleasure. *"When the system was built, there was a big debate as to whether advanced sensoria should be included at all, whether we should have sims and rooms and things to look at and touch. Too much work, they said. Nerds, the lot of them, living in a world of text. Some of the more romantic uploads argued loud enough that we overrode most of the objections. Pet my ears, those are softer."*

It's hard to imagine, a world without sensoria. Why? Too much work how? Too much strain on the system? What life would that be, though? Without touch? Without taste? Without drinks and couches and very soft foxes? Why bother?

You move to comply, then pause, tilting your head. "'We'?" you ask, finishing the motion and brushing your fingertips over the back of one of the ears once. Then again and again. Dear wasn't kidding about the softness. You suspect it was a selfish request on its part, as the fox ducks its chin to tilt its head toward your hands, leaning in closer.

"'We', yes," it murmurs, voice muffled. *"The Ode clade is quite old."*

You think for a moment, then grin. "You describe them as romantic, but talk of moving past romantic ideas of self."

"Do I contradict myself?" It is mumbling quietly now. *"Very well, then I contradict myself, I am large, I contain multitudes. Other ear, if you please."*

You laugh, earnestly and easily. You slip your other hand from under Dear's paw, and bring it up to stroke the back of the other ear. The touch gets a shiver out of the fennec.

"Fennec fits," you say. "Or, at least, soft animal does. You seem to act a little like how they say cats acted, though."

"Meow," Dear offers, too content to sound sarcastic. *"Seriously. There is room for romanticism and romance itself within post-modernism."*

You move the hand that was stroking the first ear to ruffle the fur between the ears, laughing again and joking, "Romance, eh? You coming on to me, then?"

"Well, more like...you are the first one to show interest in me, rather than the exhibition." It laughs, shrugs. *"And I have run lots of exhibitions."*

Moving gracefully, it leans forward, up onto its knees, and then in against your front, pushing you back against the armrest of the love-seat. Its arms slip up around your shoulders. The move startles you into stillness, but after a moment, you settle your arms around the fox in turn.

*"But I am not **not** coming on to you."*

You're at a loss for words.

"I'm flattered, but–"

"You're sweet, you know–"

You settle for silence and simply relaxing beneath Dear.

Warmth, softness.

"Lonely?"

Dear settles with its muzzle resting alongside your neck. *"Mmhm."*

"Same here," you admit.

The fennec nuzzles in against your neck. Whiskers tickle, raise goosebumps.

A moment of shared silence and touch. Your hands brush along the fox's back, imagining how soft the fur might be beneath the dressy shirt. Dear's blunt muzzle continues those soft rubs against your neck.

It leans up, nose dotting its way against skin, cheek, to your ear.

"The only downside to being a fox," it murmurs, nose cool against the rim of your ear. *"Is that it is really hard to kiss with a muzzle."*

And then it quits.

Your arms collapse against your front, through the ephemeral outline of the fox that remains.

With a shout, you scramble off of the love-seat, shock forcing you to stand in a defensive position.

The air is cold after the contact.

"D-Dear?" you stammer.

The room is empty.

It takes a moment for you to remember that you're within a gallery exhibit. That Dear hung the frames in which you're the art.

How cynical of it, though, to build emotional rapport, to tease at the edges of your feelings, questing at loneliness, and to leave, to do this for art. You must admit it hurts.

You laugh, forced and bitter.

Lonely, indeed.

You turn your touch sensoria way down and head to the door.

Gallery Exhibition

Numb — or, that's not quite it, more like confused and in pain but unwilling to feel either — you shuffle into the final room. Seeing the pointed ears of Dear over the heads of the crowd fills you with strangely shaped emotions, which you set aside and move to rejoin your friends. All of whom, it seems, are set on laughing at your expense.

Not helping.

A group of audience members next to you gives a shout and jumps away from a spot in the floor as a panel begins a to lift up. A...trap door? From it, a ragged and slightly dirty looking head peeks up.

Your head.

Your dirty, scraggly, frowning head. It looks upset, catches your eye, and quits. A set of memories, new and fresh, awaits you, ready for merge.

You try to get a peek of what's down the hole beneath the floor, but, other than dirt and rock, you don't see anything before it slams shut.

"Fuck it," you mumble, and merge the memories blithely, ignoring any potential conflicts. You're hungry for reasons to hate.

A panel in the side of the room gives way and folds back into a corridor.

No, not a corridor, a staircase. From it steps another audience member, another you, looking pale, shaken. They do not look as though they would like to talk, though. Those around them look sullen at being rebuffed, but that version of you doesn't seem to care.

You send a quick sensorium ping to them, instructing them to quit. They do so.

You feel that hate begin to simmer.

Once all of the audience is brought back together in this white-washed room, with its exposed ceiling, you hear Dear's kind voice waft above the heads, *"The final room of the exhibition is not partici-patory. Please feel free to wander and explore. I-"* It pauses, forks a few times, each instance smiling, and continues, *"We will be available for questions and chit-chat. Finally, I would like to thank you all deeply for at-tending this exhibition, and The Simien Fang School of Art and Design for hosting it. SF welcomes you back to any future exhibitions."*

There is applause, then, but it's scattered, confused. Dear looks proud at this.

You and your friends wander slowly through the room.

It's a square. Equidistant from the walls and each other are four pedestals, with one more a positioned at the center. Each pedestal is about waist-height and is just as white as the rest of the room. Images float a few inches from the top of the one nearest you, so you and your friends begin the circuit, wandering to inspect each pedestal in turn.

Each is labeled with a simple placard.

The Wanderer

It's a surreal experience, watching yourself, your actions, through someone else's eyes. Sure, there are videos and such, but there's something a little different about this. The way the 'camera' moves is...well, it's not a camera. There's no way it could be a camera.

It has to be Dear.

You watch more closely as the recording loops. It starts with a flash, a point of view very close to the ground. Lots of ankles. Shoes.

Then it moves, quickly and jauntily, dashing through that forest of legs, pausing to look up into faces. Most give it only cursory glances, apparently unsure of how to take this tiny animal moving among them. A few refuse to look at it, clearly disconcerted.

Then there's your face. You look more curious than anything, trying to figure out this thing before you. The you here, now, stares back into your eyes through the playback. Those younger eyes, less tainted by memories than your own.

You hold your breath.

There's the explosion.

The viewpoint skitters off to the side (lots of ankles, here) and toward a wall. It seeks out the molding on the floor at the base of the wall, then the corner where that meets the perpendicular molding of a doorjamb. There's its place. There's where it belongs. It scrabbles at the door, waiting for you, knowing you'll come.

And there's your shoes, with less dirt on them than they have now, and then the door swings open. The viewpoint leaps through, into sun and grass, with the shoes (and the rest of you) falling after.

Until now, the playback had been silent, but directed speakers start to project a little bit of audio, muffled.

"You're one tenacious fuck, you know that?" you hear the fennec's voice from the speakers. Everyone but you laughs.

You hear your discussion with the fennec, heavily obscured by the crunching of grass and the occasional grunts from yourself as the two of you make your way through the field. Your discussion on the meaning of exhibit, of medium, of art versus frame.

The video slides slowly lower to the ground as the fennec stretches out, then goes dark.

Repeats.

There's a touch of resentment, you feel. That Dear had somehow managed to record a portion of its sensorium (was that even possible?) and was playing it back to these strangers.

It bodes ill for the other pedestals.

The Rebel

This pedestal contains a fairly short loop, more obviously taken from a conventional security feed.

It's hard to discern what happens at first. It mostly looks like a bunch of people standing still, and then, as if on cue, freaking out.

A closer look, and you feel your cheeks go red. You know what's going to happen.

There's you.

And there's your forked instance.

And there's Dear's forked instance.

And then chaos as Dear deftly moves the room into strife.

Then the recording loops.

You swallow hard, knowing what's going to come next. You avert your gaze from the pedestal as you watch the chaos begin again. Your friends jeer at you, but you don't feel proud at having done what you did.

The Fighter

As you catch a glimpse of the next pedestal on approach you wince, both at remembered pain embarrassment. You had not known this would be the next in line, but you had suspected.

The scene in this pedestal shows fighting, chaos.

Once again, this appears to be a sensorium recording (how had Dear *done* that?), showing a fight that's far more well-choreographed than you remember. Seeing it from Dear's point of view, it looks a lot more like purposeful herding. The safety settings on that room had been so high that that's about all it had been.

Then the instance's point of view gets whipped around to face you, your face squarely in its vision.

"What the fuck do you think you're doing?!" You wince at the sound of your voice, hoarse from excitement, profane, coming from those directed speakers.

Then the fight begins in earnest.

You're dragged to the center of the room of the fight and then dropped into the ring, those concrete walls and that dirt floor making your remembered wounds ache.

This fight is less well choreographed. More jagged.

Except to you. You know.

The details play out on the pedestal with a cool, almost clinical precision, holding none of the emotion that you had felt. The blows, the circling, the jumps and scratches.

The syringe.

"*I had to mean to do it,*" says a soft voice next to you.

The fight isn't so far off, that anger not so much less than at a boil that you don't still have a strong urge to deck the fox standing in front of you.

It smiles, almost sadly. *"If I did not mean to do it, you would have been confused. Maybe there would be victory, but it would have been empty and hollow."* Dear shrugs apologetically. *"Confusion is not what was called for, in this exhibit. Victory or loss. Stress and decisions."*

You take a breath. One of those intentional breaths, the ones where you breathe out longer than you breathe in. "I think I understand why you did it," you say, quiet and controlled. Will yourself to tamp that hate down, if only for the sake of propriety. "I don't like it, but I think I understand why."

Dear nods, offers a hint of a bow, and backs away. *"That is my job."*

It retreats into the crowd.

You feel sick.

You think you know what will come next. You will yourself to walk to the next pedestal but, some part of you perhaps hoping to forestall the inevitable, veers to the center of the room, to the fifth pedestal instead. Vain hope, but one does what one must.

The Medium

The fifth pedestal, the one in the center of the room, is four record-ings playing at once.

They all feature you. They all feature the things that you did during your time here in the exhibition. All of those sly forks and subtle mergers.

"Did you think I did not know?" a soft voice says beside you.

You feel a heat rise to your cheeks. A blush? Deeper anger? "I...I mean, I didn't–"

Dear holds up a paw, indicating silence. It seems fond of the ges-ture. *"I knew."* It smiles. You find it a touch odd that the smile is sim-ple and kind, not sly and knowing, not triumphant, and you're not sure why. Not sure why it smiles in that way? Not sure why you find it odd? Perhaps both. *"I knew and expected it."*

"Is it okay?"

Dear laughs. *"Of course it is! This is a show on instance art. That is why it is expected. That is why there are five small exhibits here, not four."*

You smile tentatively.

"That was a rather Dispersionista thing to do for a Tracker."

"I may have had a few drinks before."

"I suspect a good many of those here did."

"So why did you allow it?"

Dear spreads its hands in a graceful gesture before clasping them at its front once more. Its tail, you notice, is swaying behind it, steady. *"You and I have talked about this."*

"I suppose we have," you mumble, still sorting through the merged memories.

"SF calls me an instance artist. Hell, I call myself an instance artist, but

that is not totally accurate. I am closer to a director, though. I organize the stage, the crew — even if they are all me — and the choreography. You are the art though, or close enough to it. I will not say audience, or actors. I do not like the play metaphor all that much, since the art is not in the acting. There is no acting." It shrugs, "*But the metaphor will serve.*"

You nod, watching the multiple feeds play out in their own courses. Watch. Guess at the contents of the next pedestal. Let that hate warm you, then sag away once more.

After a few silent moments, you ask Dear, "What are we supposed to do with our experiences here?"

The fox grins. "*This is not a lecture. No classroom, no notes, no papers to write. It is not a tool that you take away to use.*" It pauses, that grin going sly. "*And even if it were, that's your fucking job, not mine.*"

The Lover

Seeing the cool blue hues of the scene above the final pedestal brings an immediate and uncomfortable reaction. It feels like you swallowed a ball the size of your fists and it has lodged itself behind your rib cage.

Embarrassment. Frustration. Anger. Loneliness. All in equal measure.

It makes you queasy.

The audience surrounding the pedestal gasps at something

"The instances aren't the art," one of your friends mumbles, and you turn to them. They shrug. "I don't think so at least. I don't actually know what the art is."

Someone from across the pedestal offers, "Maybe instances are the brush?"

Laughter.

"*Instances the brush, emotion the paint,*" says that familiar voice. Dear stands attentively nearby. "*The art is the story behind it all. The art is...experiences?*"

"Was that a question?" your friend asks.

Dear shrugs. "*I do not make art because I know why,*" it says, bemused. "*If I knew why, I would not need to make art, then, would I?*"

"So you're a romantic?"

"*Perhaps you should watch the exhibit again.*"

You approach the pedestal just as the feed loops back to the beginning.

Once again, you're viewing a scene from Dear's point of view.

"*We can stay and chat a bit more,*" the fox says. "*Do not worry, I am running this show, I make the rules.*"

You watch yourself shrug, say, "Sure, why not? Came for the exhibition, after all. Might as well get the most of it."

When the instance of Dear looks around, you see that the room is almost empty, the last folks, your friends, drifting out the door.

The conversation that follows is low on intensity and high on subtle, emotional cues. You watch yourself and the fox have a slow and easy conversation about 'why's.

The image of Dear looks down, and you see that it's paw is resting atop yours.

You — the you here, the you now — clench your fists.

You know that that instance was designed specifically to be likable, approachable. The big eyes, the softened gaze, the larger ears. You know that you walked right into that.

But hey, you were lonely and honest. You thought it was lonely and honest.

That feeling in your chest becomes a constriction, frustration and anger winning out. Hate winning out.

You watch the whole interaction again, this time from the other point of view. You watch your own face as it slowly opens up, as you discuss being a fox, sensoria, post-modernism and romanticism. And romance.

You watch as the point of view rises, leans in closer to the you pictured there on the pedestal, watch as it leans in close, into a hug far more intimate than one would expect from someone one had just met, two bars worth of drinks aside.

The viewpoint switches to somewhere above the fox and yourself on the couch, though the audio stays close by.

"The only downside to being a fox," says the recording of Dear, and you turn around as casually as possible so that you don't have to

watch. You will yourself not to hear. Will your ears to turn off, your sense of hearing to disappear.

You hear, all the same, *"Is that it is really hard to kiss with a muzzle"*

There's Dear, in front of you.

Not the softened overly-kind dear from the blue room. Just normal Dear. Well, 'normal'. Dear-prime.

It's good because you think that the sight of the kind-Dear in this context would've made you quite upset.

"Was that unfair of me?" it asks.

It's done something to the room — unsurprising that it would have admin privileges in its own gallery, come to think of it — the two of you are in a cone of silence.

"I...well, yes." You try and count the layers of remove from the reality of what you had experienced, try to calculate the cuils in your head. The experience, the exhibit on the pedestal, talking to the artist. Are you talking bout the pedestal? The video? The performance? The experience? You shake your head.

Dear waits.

"I'd say you did an admirable job with the exhibition."

"Admirable?" It tilts his head, looking almost canine in that moment. *"I set up a situation — several, really — in which audience members feel emotions toward ephemeral constructs and made it art. I do not know if that is admirable. It is just art."*

You begin to reply, but it cuts you short.

*"I am an artist, that is what I **do**. I am a person, though."* It's smile looks weary. *"Also a fox-person, but a person nonetheless. And I feel like I cut too deep with that one. Was that unfair of me?"*

Your shoulders sag.

Dear waits.

"I don't know," you admit. "I had a few drinks, the exhibit was stressful. It was supposed to be stressful like you said. Just...it may have been an act, but I fell for it pretty hard."

Dear waits. You feel discomfited.

"Look, it's just silly, is all. I don't even know why it affected me so much," you trail off, trying to decide how much further to go on. "Look," you repeat, shaking your head. "Was it true? What you said? Are you lonely? Were you earnest? Were you coming on to me?"

Dear nods, simple and straightforward. *"It is perhaps easy for me to talk about because I rehearsed hard for this show, but yes, I am lonely as hell. I fork to form relationships and keep myself...I mean, I do not lie in my work if I can help it."*

It is your turn to wait, which discomfits Dear in turn.

"I am sorry," it says. *"I did cut too deep. I was not thinking. It is not my goal with these things to damage anyone's trust in art, in instances. Or in me, for that matter. It is just that I do not make art because I know why. If I knew why, I would not need to make art."*

The fox hesitates for a moment, then sighs. *"I feel really bad about this. I am sorry. I would like to do what I can to regain your trust."*

The weight of decision hangs heavy around your neck, heavy enough to bow your head. There's very little you feel you can say without making that decision right then, so you stay silent for a moment.

Finally: "I feel like you're trying to ask me out."

*"I am not **not** asking you out,"* Dear looks cautious. It smiles faintly. So do you.

"Listen, can you give me a night? Let me put some thought into it."

It nods. *"Fair. And listen, I really am sorry. There are bits of this show that I wrote thinking that they would lead to one thing, some spectacular art, and they led to...er, this."*

You nod, saying, "I get it. Kind of like a choose-your-own-adventure story that got a little out of hand."

Dear shrugs. *"I suppose."* It hesitates for a moment, then draws a card out of it's left pocket, reaching out with its right paw at the same time, a perfectly formal business card exchange.

You grin and, on a hunch, turn down your touch sensoria way up to accept the card — a flash of contact information and locations — and shake the fox's paw.

It is *very* soft.

No one seems to have come out of the exhibit unscathed.

A few bear the rumpled look of the recently roughed-up, but with their safety turned up, that's about as far as the physical effects go. Rather, everyone within the group looks emotionally bruised, bitten, scratched. Some look dazed, some hurt, but no one looks blasé.

In that, Dear, Also, The Tree That Was Felled was successful.

You and your group walk to another bar. Quiet, subdued.

You give the low-slung building a wide berth. Only you came away with something. There's a card in your pocket, the dot on the question mark of an unanswered question.

Two things, then. A card in your pocket, and a decision to make.

About the author

Madison Scott-Clary is a transgender writer, editor, and software engineer. She focuses on furry fiction and non-fiction, using that as a framework for exploring across genres. She has edited and written for [adjective][species] since 2011, and edited *Arcana: A Tarot Anthology* for Thurston Howl Publications in 2017. She is the editor-in-chief of Hybrid Ink, LLC, a small publisher focused on thoughtful fiction, exploratory poetry, and creative non-fiction. She lives in the Pacific Northwest with her cat and two dogs, as well as her husband, who is also a dog.

www.makyo.ink
www.hybrid.ink